M

“Cate,” he said
and trying to rem
encountered a wo
met him with
real warmth.

She was close enough now that he could see her features clearly. The color of her eyes was lost to the night, but they were wide in her face, her still lips parted slightly in surprise, or dismay . . . or something else. Tregaron could see a pulse beating above the deplorably high, cobwebby trim of her bodice. He imagined the bold lines of her collar-bones beneath, the soft hollows beneath those.

He had never questioned that there was something stirring, undeniably appealing to him about this woman. She was vibrant as sunlight, bright as summer. He had simply never considered that she might take on the properties of moonlight as well—soft, alluring, drawing a man like the sea. . . .

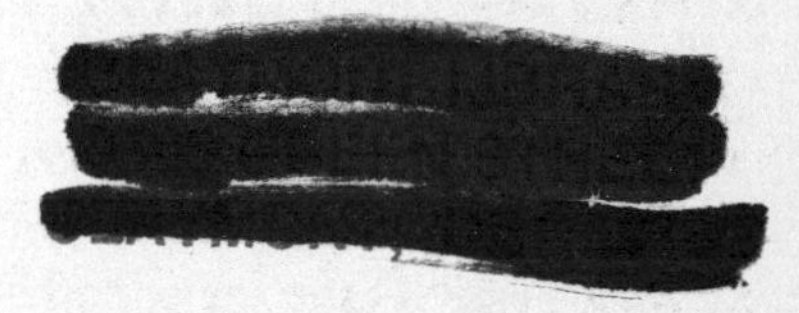

Coming next month

BELLE'S BEAU

by Gayle Buck

Miss Annabelle Weatherstone is making her first foray into the gaiety of the London Season–taking the place of her twin, Cassandra. Before long, Belle catches the eye of Lord Adam Ashdon–but her resemblance to her sister sparks a case of mistaken identity that may throw the lord for a loop!

"Of all the talents in the genre, none sparkle more brightly." —*Romantic Times*

❑ 0-451-20197-3 / $4.99

CAPTAIN CUPID CALLS THE SHOTS

by Elisabeth Fairchild

Captain Alexander Shelbourne was known as Cupid to his friends for his uncanny marksmanship in battle. But upon meeting Miss Penny Foster, he soon knew how it felt to be struck by his namesake's arrow....

"An outstanding talent." —*Romantic Times*

❑ 0-451-20198-1 / $4.99

To order call: 1-800-788-6262

A Grand Design

Emma Jensen

A SIGNET BOOK

SIGNET
Published by New American Library, a division of
Penguin Putnam Inc., 375 Hudson Street,
New York, New York 10014, U.S.A.
Penguin Books Ltd, 27 Wrights Lane,
London W8 5TZ, England
Penguin Books Australia Ltd, Ringwood,
Victoria, Australia
Penguin Books Canada Ltd, 10 Alcorn Avenue,
Toronto, Ontario, Canada M4V 3B2
Penguin Books (N.Z.) Ltd, 182–190 Wairau Road,
Auckland 10, New Zealand

Penguin Books Ltd, Registered Offices:
Harmondsworth, Middlesex, England

First published by Signet, an imprint of New American Library,
a division of Penguin Putnam Inc.

First Printing, November 2000
10 9 8 7 6 5 4 3 2 1

Printed in the United States of America

PUBLISHER'S NOTE
This is a work of fiction. Names, characters, places, and incidents either are the product of the author's imagination or are used fictitiously, and any resemblance to actual persons, living or dead, business establishments, events or locales is entirely coincidental.

For my Z, who was
with me through every minute
of this book

The hook was baited with a dragon's tale. . . .

—Sir William Davenant

Chapter 1

In White's Club on that Wednesday, several gentlemen scurried, shoved, and wriggled in their effort to be the first with the announcement, "Tregaron is back in Town!" All, as it happened, had been trumped by the man delivering the kippers for breakfast and by Lord Paxton's tiger, but the club's members could rarely be bothered to listen to those persons most likely to give reliable information.

In Bond Street, behind the gilt-painted windows of Schwarz and Noble, tailors par excellence, Mr. Noble murmured, "Tregaron is back!" into his partner's ear. Mr. Schwarz, in the process of draping an illustrious duke's undistinguished son in brown superfine, promptly handed the bolt over to their senior clerk and accompanied Mr. Noble in a search for the best black wool they had in stock and for a hushed conference weighing one man's custom against losing that of others among their clientele.

A number of Society matrons, still young, most lovely, but each with at least eight years of marriage behind her, gripped their morning chocolate in pale fingers and recalled that year, murmuring, "Tregaron has returned," to the long, empty expanse of dining table before them. Their male counterparts, in some cases their husbands, muttered the same words, several into the shell-like ears of their mistresses, others to their favorite hounds.

More than a mile away from Mayfair, in the rank shadows of a Clerkenwell hovel, a blowsy, red-faced woman slung an empty gin bottle across the room. "Tha' blighted, filthy rat is back!" she slurred. "Back, the devil take him!" Her husband continued snoring into his half-finished tripe, not so much as stirring when the aforementioned rodent scuttled right over his wrist and made off with half a loaf of coarse bread.

At that moment, the Marquess of Tregaron stood in the first-floor bow window of his Hanover Square town house, the bright London day spread before him, and the wreckage of nearly a decade in full evidence behind. He wasn't particularly interested in either one. Given his druthers, he would have remained in Wales, where the very air scourged land and man alike, the ale rolled over his tongue like an ancient ballad, and the women asked for nothing more than a bit of esteem and a coin or two.

Tregaron well knew, however, that content as he would have been to stay on his rough, beautiful Welsh estate forever, it was not to be. Duty called. He had ignored it long enough—eight years, to be precise. Ignored his parliamentary seat, his London house, his all-important, grit-one's-teeth-and-see-to-it responsibility of begetting the next Marquess of Tregaron on some good-blooded, eminently respectable, dull-as-two-short-planks Society chit.

"God spare me," he muttered through clenched teeth.

Turning, he gave the unlit drawing room a cursory glance. Eight years, he had discovered upon returning, was more than enough time to wreak havoc on a house—broken windows, broken parquet floors; dust and rot, mold and mildew. Tregaron knew now he could have taken more care in closing up the house, could have had the pipes and cisterns checked, ordered all the furniture well covered, hired a caretaker to look in every once in a while. He knew, but didn't care, any more than he had all those years earlier.

Money would set the house to rights, and he had plenty of money. He had, too, his plans for what it would buy. He'd considered simply purchasing a new house entirely, putting this one—lock, stock, and dismal memories—up for sale. But that had struck him as self-indulgently weak and wholly unnecessary. He owned a perfectly good house already. It simply needed a few repairs and some alteration.

He'd seen more than enough for now. In fact, if he could possibly arrange it, after the single meeting arranged for the following day, he would not set foot in the place again until the job was done.

The architects' preliminary designs had suited him well enough. Perhaps had he taken more time, he would have engaged a better-known name. Wyatville, perhaps, or one of the Reptons. Even nose-in-the-air Nash, Tregaron mused, would certainly have pitched in for the right fee. Notoriety, after all, was no match for obscene wealth. But the marquess had not wanted to bother with either the long wait or the necessary flatteries involved in engaging the famous. As far as he was concerned, Buchanan and Buchanan, virtually unknown now, whoever they might someday be, would serve his purposes just fine.

He whistled, then called, "Gryffydd!" The Welsh herding dog that was his only steady companion sprang from the shadows in a flurry of yellow fur and scrabbling claws, sending dust and bits of refuse scattering in his vigorous wake. "Shall we go?"

The animal was clearly more than ready to be shot of the place, loping solidly toward the stairs before the words were gone from the air. Tregaron didn't blame him. It was a dismal room in a dismal collection of rooms, suited best for detritus, vermin, and ghosts.

He paused in his own exit to glance at a portrait leaning against the landing wall. It had once hung above the mantel and was one of the few personal items that had not been disposed of years earlier. The marquess just hadn't been able to see it destroyed. The beauty of the subject was still undeniable; neither time nor neglect would dull that. "Don't think you can haunt this place any longer," Tregaron muttered. "Or me. It's over now."

As far as he was concerned, his relationship with the lady was indeed very much over. Unfortunately, he knew Society might have some different opinions on the subject. Fortunately, he knew, too, that his wealth and title would spare him from having to hear many of those opinions spoken to his face. As the Ninth Marquess of Tregaron, he would be spared a great deal. He could take the rest.

He followed his dog into the afternoon sunshine. It was Wednesday; it was May. It was London, full of elegant comforts and lofty entertainments. The Ninth Marquess of Tregaron was on his way to the first dark and dingy tavern he could find, where he planned to get comfortably, loftily drunk in as short a time as possible.

"It is Wednesday." Catherine Buchanan wearily removed her bonnet and handed it to her sister. "I find it excessively difficult to believe Uncle Angus went to church."

Lucy shrugged. "I am only repeating what he told me." She surveyed Catherine's simple straw bonnet and frowned. "Really, Cate, can you not even try to be fashionable? I would be heartily ashamed to be seen walking along Oxford Street with you in that hideous thing."

Cate suppressed a smile as she handed over her equally unfashionable brown spencer. "How fortunate then that we won't be walking in Oxford Street in the foreseeable future, then. I wouldn't want to watch you suffer."

Her sister rolled vividly blue eyes, set off to perfection by her azure muslin dress. "Sometimes I cannot believe we are related!"

"Yes, well, that makes two of us."

In all truth, most people were surprised to learn they were sisters. Lucy looked like a china doll, all pink cheeks, red-gold ringlets, and delicate limbs. Cate, on the other hand, was as tall as many of the men of her acquaintance, with lively, gingery hair that always seemed to be wresting loose its pins, and pale, freckle-dusted skin that pinkened only in moments of extreme mortification, of which she had relatively few. The only feature they shared was the Buchanan blue eyes, and while twenty-year-old Lucy had spent a great deal of time mastering the proper degree of lash fluttering, Cate preferred to look directly and clearly at life. At six-and-twenty, she felt no need to flutter her lashes at anything, least of all the young men for whom such twitches had been created.

Right now, she pinned her sister with the most direct of gazes. "So Uncle Angus is at church. What of Uncle Ambrose?"

"Some museum," Lucy said carelessly. "I really do wish you would come shopping with me, Cate. I cannot very well go out alone, and I really am in desperate need of a new morning dress."

"If I remember correctly, the one you are wearing is less than a month old."

"Oh, pooh. The ribbon is quite the wrong color for the season."

Cate surveyed the flimsy white trim. Then, choosing a bottle of ink from the multitude on the parlor table, she handed it to Lucy. "Here, paint it blue. I hear cerulean is all the rage at Almack's."

"Cate, really!"

"Really, Lucy. Why, the Princess Lieven whispered it to me when we met at the baker's this morning. Blue, she said, was quite the color for the season."

"You would not know the princess were she to tread upon your toes!"

Cate feigned confusion. "No? My goodness, perhaps it wasn't her at all! I thought I detected a hint of the wharves in the woman's voice."

Her sister was not amused. "For the last time, will you come shopping with me?"

"I will not. I've matters to see to here, and you've no money. Besides, I have no desire to change my dress, and you have already given your opinion of this one."

"Oh, Catey! I might just as well have stayed in Edinburgh. I'm naught but an ill-dressed captive here! Why will you not call upon Deirdre Macvail and Sibyl Cameron? I am certain they attend all the best entertainments and would introduce us—"

"Lucy." Cate carefully returned the ink bottle to the table. "Deirdre Macvail is now the Duchess of Conovar; Sibyl Cameron is the Countess of Hythe. Neither was my intimate in Tarbet, and I daresay neither would be overjoyed to suddenly have me turning up on their doorstep now. No"—she lifted a hand when her sister began to protest—"not another word on the matter. I'll not be imposing on mere acquaintances for social connections that will ultimately make no difference."

"No difference? How can you say so? Deirdre is a duchess—"

"And we are but minor gentry from an unimportant village in Scotland," Cate said firmly. "Dream as much as you like, Lucy love, but the fact remains that our branch of the Buchanan tree is too close to Trade for the *ton*. There will be no invitations to Almack's for us. None."

The tone brooked no argument. Lucy said not a word as she huffed from the room, ringlets bouncing, but nonetheless managed to leave volumes of pique in her wake. All in all, a familiar state of affairs.

Well, Cate thought wryly as she set aside her meager purchases, that was that. For the moment, at least. What she had said would be painful to rosy-dreamed Lucy, and for that Cate was sorry. But it was no more than the truth. There would be no entree into Society. There would be no foisting themselves on long-distant acquaintances from Scotland, nor draping themselves in extravagant fashions whose expense would be much better applied toward keeping food on the table. Lucy's new morning dress, and her dreams of being the toast of the *ton,* would not be coming to pass anytime soon.

Cate peered down at her own, serviceable yellow muslin. There was a large ink spot above her ankle. Indigo blue, if she was not mistaken. A replacement would have to wait, too. Her eyes drifted back to the table. Of course, she thought fancifully, should her uncles not receive the new commission, she could simply soak the whole dress in ink.

Sighing, Cate pushed several bottles aside and lifted a half-filled teacup from the papers below. Lord Tregaron would be expecting his final designs. They were, she thought with some excitement, rather good. The open plan and simple plasterwork would work beautifully in the solid Palladian structure, the new floors and ceilings bringing life into years of disuse. Yes, the marquess should be well pleased with the drawings.

If he ever saw them. Cate set the papers aside more gently than she was inclined. Splendid designs notwithstanding, Ambrose and Angus Buchanan would lose this commission, too, should they insist on not being where they were supposed to be.

They were supposed to be right there in the little rented house in Binney Street, preparing for their interview with Lord Tregaron the following morning. Instead, they were, respectively, at a church and a museum.

Cate knew perfectly well that they were snug in some pub. Church and museum were simply their ideas of enlightening places. The elder Buchanans were never quite so enlightened as when they were bright-eyed with ale. They would, no doubt, totter tipsily into their museum and church at some point to squint at whichever piece of statuary or fresco was their subject for the day. With luck, they would then totter home.

She loved her uncles with the same simple, complete acceptance that she gave her sister. Like Lucy, they were good creatures at heart. They certainly hadn't blinked twice at the concept of taking charge of their late brother's children nine years earlier, nor had they ever been in the least bit stingy with their affection. But, just like Lucy, they never seemed to quite have their heads turned to practical matters. Angus Buchanan was happiest when mucking about in his clay and plaster; Ambrose preferred to be covered in oil paint.

They were rather dismal architects. It was not that they didn't possess the talent, Cate conceded. On the contrary, both were artists of great skill. But they loathed the arithmetic and necessary attention to physics that came with the task of designing a building or merely altering one. Had they had their druthers, the brothers would have happily remained in Tarbet, on the shores of Loch Lomond, living in their studio and producing various sculptures and paintings that all would admire and none would buy.

Alpin Buchanan, the youngest of the three and Cate's father, had been a poet by nature. He had not been a terribly good poet, but he had certainly been enthusiastic. He had, too, along with his blue-blooded wife, possessed an intelligence and generosity that had drawn many of Scotland's great artists and writers to their home. As a child, Cate had been bounced on the knee of Robbie Burns, and as a blossoming adolescent had been painted by Henry Raeburn. The portrait hung still on her bedchamber wall, one of her few legacies from her beloved parents.

Yes, Cate mused, life in Tarbet had been warm, lively, and filled to the brim with the passions of art. It had not, however, been profitable. Alpin's poems went to print only at the expense of his more affluent friends—and had sold only to those same friends.

Angus did manage once to sell a bust of Persephone to the Duke of Roxburghe. His Grace had promptly installed the hapless maiden in his hunting box, where she was seen by men far more interested in guns than sculpture—and not in the least concerned with promoting the work of the eccentric sculptor.

Ambrose's surface of choice was tabletops. His favorite subject was bloody scenes of the Trojan Wars and their ilk. Needless to say, the ladies who might be counted up to purchase little painted tables preferred to have their tea served above angels and roses. Ancient carnage was not conducive to good digestion.

So the Buchanan Brothers had not made their fortunes as artists. Instead, the need for such luxuries as food and clothing had led them to found Buchanan, Buchanan, and Buchanan, Architects. They had designed a few forgettable houses in New Town, Edinburgh, elaborately modernized one medieval manor house for a Lothian baron with more money than taste, and created countless marble follies for Border estate gardens.

The years immediately following the deaths of Alpin and Mary Buchanan in a boating accident had been lean ones. There were a few more follies, a very squat bank building in Aberdeen, and one more Edinburgh house, which had, Cate mused regretfully, ended up resembling something out of an Egyptian pharaoh's nightmare. Then, three years earlier, had come the commission to completely redesign a country house for the disgraced wife of Lord Maybole.

That one, an experiment in blending the Italianate style of architecture with contemporary design and ancient Scottish tradition, had been a smashing success. And while Lady Maybole was persona non grata in Town, she was a vastly popular figure with the young men of the *ton,* and entertained them splendidly, if not appropriately, when they traveled north for the hunt. Word of her now-lovely home had eventually reached London. The architects, now merely Buchanan and Buchanan, had followed.

Lord Tregaron was their first client. And, Cate thought wearily as she scanned the narrow street through the parlor window, perhaps the last. Her uncles had been scarce of an afternoon since arriving in Town. In fact, since seeing the marquess's vague requests—communicated to them through a terse letter handed over by an indifferent solicitor—onto paper, they had been home only for the occasional meal and to sleep.

It was hardly an efficient way to run a business, Cate knew, but she also knew her uncles. If they remembered their meeting with Lord Tregaron, they would attend him with charm and helpful persuasiveness. If they did not remember, there would most likely be a weary return trip to Scotland. Cate thought they had just enough money left to get back to Edinburgh and live frugally until the next commission for a marble folly.

Straightening shoulders bowed by the weight of familiar worry, she collected several discarded coats from the furniture and headed for the stairs. She could sit and wring her hands until her uncles returned, certainly, but her time would be much better used at other efforts. First among them would be to find items in her uncles' wardrobes that were appropriate for an audience with a marquess—and not liberally spattered with plaster and paint.

Cate knew little of the marquess, only that he was recently returned to Town from his Welsh estate and determined to re-do his Hanover Square town house from top to bottom. She knew those details, and one more—that Tregaron was very rich. That was all that mattered. With any luck, he would purchase the designs and the first pickaxe would be swung before anything could cause him to change his mind. With a bit more luck, the house would be a smashing success and other commissions would follow.

All of that depended, of course, on no one ever learning the Buchanan family secret. On that matter, Cate lost a good deal of her natural optimism. Great secrets, she firmly believed, were always the first to be discovered. And as far as Cate was concerned, fate had already been tempted far too long.

Chapter 2

Cate was vastly relieved to find Hanover Square all but deserted when they arrived the following morning. London was a big city, certainly, but she'd quickly learned that Mayfair was essentially a tiny village in the midst of it. There were, she assumed, few secrets among the *ton* and nothing approaching anonymity.

"Daresay your Grandda' kept a house round here, Catey," Uncle Ambrose announced as the hackney rolled to a rough halt.

"He probably did at that." Cate shrugged. She had never known her mother's father; he'd taken no interest in Mary's life after she had disobeyed him and wed Alpin Buchanan. The old man was long dead now, his baronetcy passed to some distant relation, and Cate had far more important matters to attend. Once on the ground, she gave a last twitch to her uncle's cravat. "Ah, you look grand, sir."

Ambrose grinned and patted her affectionately on the cheek. The gesture, made with a ham-sized fist, nearly rocked her head back. "Aye, grand enough for this place even, I daresay."

He turned his hoary grey head to survey the very large, very elegant exterior of the Greek Revival town house belonging to the Marquess of Tregaron. He looked, Cate thought whimsically, like a Highland warrior of old surveying a Grampian castle. With his massive frame and craggy face, Ambrose Buchanan appeared the most unlikely painter of delicate tables.

He didn't look much like an architect, either.

"Damn, but the place seems to have grown since we were here last." He turned his fierce Buchanan blue gaze to his brother. "Are you certain 'tis the same house, Angus?"

Angus clambered from the carriage and peered up at

the marble facade. "Aye, one and the same. I remember the nymphs."

He pointed one bony finger at the figures decorating the pediment. Cate took the opportunity to brush a bit of lingering plaster dust from his cuff. The coat sleeve, she noted, would need patching soon. As frail and narrow as his brother was brawny, Angus was forever poking his sharp elbows through his coats. It was a wonder, his nieces thought, that he was able to heft the clay and stone of his art. He himself seemed no more substantial than a Hebridean mist.

Cate took a last critical look at her uncles. They were garbed in freshly brushed coats, had managed, with her help, to fashion acceptable cravat knots, and as far as she had been able to ascertain had removed all vestiges of paint and plaster from beneath their fingernails. Perhaps Ambrose's wild grey hair needed a trimming, and Angus's vast eyebrows were a bit more weedy than usual, but they would do.

"Have you the designs there, Ambrose, lad?"

Ambrose brandished the silk-tied portfolio. "For the third time, what does this look to be, you daft haddie?"

"Ah, but did you look inside?" Angus gave a smug smile as his brother cursed.

"I looked before we left the house," Cate announced. This was hardly the time or place for a bit of familiar, affectionate one-upmanship. Resisting the urge to remind Angus that his small triumph would have been vastly diminished had the designs, in fact, not been between the portfolio's covers, she gently turned him in the direction of the steps. "Everything is there for the marquess's perusal."

"Good lass!" Ambrose grinned at her. Then he tugged at his cuffs and ran a hand over his hair, sending both into greater disarray.

Well, Cate mused, Lord Tregaron lived in Wales, a wild place for all its reputed beauty. Her uncles' slightly untidy appearances should not startle him overmuch. She expected, too, that his man of affairs had passed on more than just the preliminary sketches from the architects. A report on the men themselves would almost certainly have been included.

The marquess might well, however, be somewhat taken aback by Cate's appearance. Or at least by her presence.

Young ladies were generally not welcome at such meetings. But this meeting was a matter of great importance to the Buchanans, and Cate was taking no chances on her uncles' making any mistakes.

Lord Tregaron, she thought somewhat smugly, would be too entranced by the designs for his house to cavil at her presence. Cate intended to hold her tongue, to blend into whatever ungodly ornate portraits or elaborate tapestries decorated his stately home. She had no intention of saying anything at all—unless she had to. Brilliant as her uncles were at their respective work, they were rather poor at explaining the details. After years with them, Cate was more than adept at subtle prompting.

The uncles would wax aesthetic, the marquess would nod his grey and balding head, agree upon the price, and disappear to White's or Boodle's or wherever he chose to rest his gouty legs. With luck, he would then stay disappeared until the work was complete. It made the Buchanans a bit twitchy to have their clients constantly hanging about. Far better to deal with the occasional visit from some lackey and generally be left alone to the task at hand.

Cate had every confidence that the task at hand would be completed easily and well. She had not yet been inside the house, but her uncles, with their sharp artists' eyes, had described it top to bottom. A bit of muscle, some paint and some plaster, a smidgeon of heavenly protection, and the Buchanans would be on their way to fame and fortune. Cate was sure of it.

With that in mind, she smoothed her neat, ink-spared blue skirts and approached the town house's steps. The cast-iron railing was loose and its design broken away in spots, she noted, and upon closer inspection she could see cracks in the door's faded paint, cracks in the door's leaded glass fanlight. Looking down, she noticed entire panes missing from the lower level's windows, the curtains in every window sagging or torn. There was a large chip in the bottom marble step; the standard boot-scraper was missing entirely but for a ragged bolt, as if it had been torn away by a giant hand.

A wee bit worn, her uncles had said of the house. *Neglected.* From what Cate was seeing, the noble, pale stone facade fronted more than neglect; it fronted a state of ruin.

She turned to comment on the matter, but Uncle Angus was already thumping away with the tarnished brass knocker that hung loosely on the door. Almost immediately, there was the sound of a dog barking inside. It rose in volume, a deep, rhythmic woofing, and the Buchanans each took an instinctive step backward. Cate thought she detected the sound of heels ringing against stone, but couldn't be certain behind the hellhound's noise. Then, suddenly, the barking ceased. Just as suddenly, the massive door swung inward.

Cate's first thought was that, of the two figures standing there in the dim foyer, the man would be more likely to go for someone's throat than the dog.

The latter, large voice aside, stood only as tall as the calves of the man's boots. He was a funny little creature—mustard-colored, bat-eared, pointy-faced, with a stocky body a bit too long for his solid little legs. He looked, Cate decided, rather like a stout fox who'd lost his tail. He was grinning at her now, an irresistibly friendly expression that quite belied his initial greeting, and she would have bent to pat him had his companion not looked full ready to bite.

"May I help you?"

The voice was deep and cuttingly sharp at the edges. It certainly went with the rest of the package. Tall as Uncle Ambrose and nearly as broad of shoulder, if rather slimmer all around, the man had the bearing of a classical god and the face of a satyr, all juts and crags. It was not an ugly face. On the contrary, the eyes beneath the sweep of midnight hair were a stunning amber, the bold nose and wide mouth hewn by the hand of a master sculptor. But there was a hardness to the whole, a chill that Cate felt beneath her skin.

"Well?" he demanded, eyes swinging between the uncles. Apparently they had been staring, too.

"I, er . . . We . . ." Angus began. "Ah, er . . ."

Ambrose elbowed him out of the way. "We're here to see the marquess, lad." His sheer size precluded most timidity, not to mention a few manners. "Trot off and tell him the Buchanans are here."

The man stood, unblinking, for a moment. Then, "You'd better come in," he announced, turning on his heel and striding away from the door. "This is the last time I will be in the house until the work is complete, so make the most of it."

As Cate watched the impressive, elegantly tapered back recede into the shadows, she understood. No butler or man-of-affairs, this. No, the stone-faced, harsh-voiced man walking away from them was Lord Tregaron himself. Thirty years younger and ten times more forbidding than she could ever have imagined.

Her uncles, too, had caught on and were hurrying after their prospective employer. Angus, now in charge of the designs, bobbled the portfolio in his haste. Cate saw Ambrose slap at his own forehead with a meaty hand, no doubt cursing himself for having spoken to the marquess like a servant. As if he could possibly have known.

Misgivings and ill opinion rising, Cate followed. The house, she noted, as they ascended marble stairs to the first floor, was in poor repair indeed. Beneath a heavy coating of dust and grime, the floors and walls alike were cracked. There was an unmistakable smell of damp about and, unless she was very much mistaken, an odor of vermin as well.

Tregaron stalked along the hallway, odd little dog at his heels, stirring the cobwebs that hung from picture frames and draped furniture. He halted abruptly and shoved at a door. It resisted for a moment, then gave with a dismal groan. "This," he announced, "is my library. I don't give a damn what you do with the rest of the house, but I want this room left as it is."

As it was, Cate decided when she took a peek inside, it would suit a vampyre—dark, dank, shrouded. The shredded leather of one wing chair peeked out from a poorly draped drop cloth; books lay scattered over the floor and other flat surfaces, spilling their innards and a musty smell throughout the room.

"What a sad, sorry mess," she said without thinking. "It will require cleaning. New furnishings and paint, certainly a new carpet if not an entirely new floor. You would be wise to have new windows as well, with six panes over six, to replace those. Pity, those are exemplary crown glass . . ."

Her voice faltered. Her uncles' pencils, which had been scrabbling away inside their little pocket notebooks stilled. Tregaron, without saying a word or moving an inch, had dropped the temperature of the room like sudden hail.

"Who are you?" he demanded. Then, before she could reply, to Angus, "Who is she?"

It was Ambrose who answered. "This is our niece, my lord. Miss Catherine Buchanan. She is—"

"Outspoken." Tregaron studied her for a moment, granite face expressionless. Then he turned his back on the trio and gazed out the grime-streaked window. "I will decide what little work is necessary, and I will inform you. Now, are we finished?"

They'd scarcely begun, Cate thought, and decided she would like nothing better than to end the ghastly interview. She was reeling slightly from the marquess's curt insult and dismissal.

He would not be hanging about during the renovations, he'd said. Thank the Lord for small blessings.

Cate had relatively little experience with the nobility. Her own family's ties had been stretched nearly to the snapping point, and the aristocratic denizens of Tarbet were rarely in residence. Lady Leverham was a sweet enough creature, if a bit dizzy; her husband a quietly pleasant shadow. True, Deirdre Macvail and Sibyl Cameron had married impressive titles, but neither had been intimates of Cate's before their marriages, and she'd had almost no contact with either since.

From what little she knew of the more lofty peers, she carried the image of elevated noses and bored sneers. She had no reason to expect Lord Tregaron to be anything other than arrogant and dismissive. That didn't mean she wouldn't be imagining him impaling his aristocratic posterior on the loose springs she expected could be found sticking from every piece of furniture in this room. She did not care in the least for being insulted and dismissed.

"But what of the plans, my lord?" Angus queried nervously. "The . . . er . . . arrangements . . . ?"

"I have seen what I need to of the plans." Tregaron graced the Buchanans with his hatchet profile. "And all arrangements—which, I assume, means matters of money going from my pockets to yours—will be handled by my solicitor." Even as Cate was wondering why he had bothered to be present at all, he continued, "I am satisfied you will be able to manage the work. I simply thought it best to have a look at the men who will be dismantling my home, such as it is."

"Oh, we won't be dismantling, precisely," Ambrose protested.

Tregaron waved him off. "Have at it. I do not care. Now, I am leaving. I expect you'll want to have a wander through the house. There is a key stuck inside the front door lock. Take it when you go." With that, he sketched the briefest of bows. "Sirs. Miss Buchanan."

Then he was gone, his little dog trotting behind him.

Cate did not realize her jaw was slack until she tasted dust. She heard the front door thud shut, felt the very air settle as if in the wake of a brief and vicious storm. Turning to her uncles, she saw that both of them were staring at the empty doorway, their own mouths in lax O's.

"Well." Cate shook her head bemusedly. "A true charmer, that one. What a joy it will be to be in his employ."

"Now, Catey—" Angus began.

"No need to go all stiff-necked," was Ambrose's contribution. "We need—"

"Yes, yes. We need the money." Cate managed a tight smile. Bending down, she collected a warped, leather-covered book from the floor near her feet. It was a collection of Herrick, "Neutrality Loathsome" the poem beneath her fingers. "Not to fear. I've no intention of spoiling the arrangement. As long as the high-and-mighty Lord Tregaron keeps to his lofty London entertainments and leaves us be, I daresay we'll all walk away satisfied."

Neither of her uncles appeared terribly convinced, and, glancing down, Cate noticed she was slowly shredding the corner of the book's wrinkled page. Appalled by the destructive action, she hurriedly dropped the thing onto the desk, where it raised a formidable burst of dust.

Wearily waving a hand in front of her face, she announced, "Well, I suppose we ought to explore the rest of Hades now. Shall we?"

They were a somber trio as they filed from the room.

Tregaron's long stride was carrying him rapidly away in the direction of Piccadilly and the Albany, where he had taken rooms, when he slowed. Gryffydd, his short legs untaxed by brisk walks, bumped his nose with affectionate impatience against his master's ankle. It was his herding behavior, honed by centuries and, in the absence of cattle, meant to steer Tregaron toward his rooms and whatever food he might be inclined to share.

Gryffydd bumped again. Tregaron stopped and, much to the little animal's disappointment, turned back to face the way he'd come. He did not walk back toward the house, but instead stared up George Street. He ignored the tidy homes, the finely dressed inhabitants, the rolling carriages. His mind was behind the sooty stone facade of his house, just visible now on the far side of the square, in the dim ruin of his library.

Miss Catherine Buchanan. What a smart-mouthed, sharp-eyed harpy she appeared to be. It was rather a blessing, Tregaron thought, that it was her uncles he was employing and not the lady herself. Despite having no intention of hanging about the accursed Hanover Square hovel while it was being restored, he did not like the idea of Miss Catherine Buchanan striding the moldering halls on her long legs. No doubt she could strip the peeling paper from the walls with a mere glance, hence saving him the expense of other means, but he wouldn't be at all surprised to learn she stripped the paneling and plaster away, too.

Women like Catherine Buchanan belonged in the distant climes of Scotland, from whence she'd descended, stalking robustly over hill and dale, spouting moralistic proverbs and doing such good deeds for the unsuspecting poor that raw-boned Scots gentlewoman were wont to do. There was no place for her in London.

Nor room, he thought. Miss Buchanan was taller than many men of his acquaintance, not so very many inches below his own six-and-a-quarter-foot frame. Garbed in yards and yards of unattractive blue muslin, long and lean with no breasts or hips to speak of, and a mass of bronze-ish hair, she was something of an oddity.

True, that wild and abundant hair had caught what meager light the house offered, and caught his eye. True, also, that her narrow face possessed decent enough features—a tip-tilted nose, gently rounded chin, wide mouth, cheekbones high and bold enough to rival Dover's cliffs.

Miss Catherine Buchanan, of the bumbling uncles and heedless tongue, was not a beauty, not even close. She was, however, arresting and impossible to overlook, and the Marquess of Tregaron could still feel the disapproval that had been aimed at him through those slightly tilted, startlingly blue eyes.

So she did not care for the state of his house. Too bad for her. It was the very state of his house that had inspired him to hire her uncles. For what he would no doubt be paying Buchanan and Buchanan, the woman should have been curtsying those long limbs out in all directions, thanking him for his generosity. Not that Tregaron could be bothered by her lack of gratitude. He had no time to give to pondering long-of-tooth Scottish spinsters, especially those who were equally long-of-limb and wind. No, he'd not be turning his thoughts again to Miss Catherine Buchanan.

"Come along, Gryffydd," he commanded, spinning on his heel. The little dog trotted happily at his heels, canine thoughts turned as always to food, giving him an occasional nudge to keep him on the right path. "The house will be seen to. Now to find a woman to put in it."

He had given a certain amount of thought to the matter, more certainly than ever before. He didn't particularly want a wife, but his Welsh tenants wanted a secure future of some sort, and Tregaron was reasonably certain that Edgar St. Clair-Wright, his second cousin and heir presumptive, was not the man to see to it. Beyond not liking Edgar overmuch, Tregaron did not trust him. Any fellow who favored spotted waistcoats and attended the Turf with the religious zealousness of a pilgrim to Canterbury was not to be put in possession of thousands of acres of Welsh land.

True, he had not seen his cousin in some years. Edgar, like many people, might have changed. But then Edgar, like most people and things in life, had altered little over the years Tregaron had known him, and was quite probably the same creature he had always been—ignorant, indolent, and prone to undeserved pride. He had certainly not been expected to travel to Wales during the years of the marquess's mostly self-imposed exile from Society, and he had not appeared. Tregaron had always assumed the man had gloated from afar and raised debts on his expectations of attaining the marquessate and all that went with it.

Well, Tregaron mused, he would find out soon enough

if Cousin Leopard had changed his spots. As much as he disliked the prospect, he would have to appear in Society eventually. The Season was commencing; Parliament would soon be in session. The Marriage Mart would be in full swing in no time. And Tregaron was duty-bound to lead himself to the delightful abattoirs known as polite entertainment.

"God help me," he muttered. Gryffydd, thinking any word that was not a command to him implied dinner, grinned up at his master, tongue lolling, and lifted his solid little feet a bit higher with each step.

Tregaron had not intended to walk down Bond Street, a thoroughfare he avoided whenever possible. But between Scottish spinsters and marriageable mademoiselles, he hadn't been paying attention and now found himself amid the hustle and bustle of Mayfair shopping.

He quickened his pace. There was little on the shopping streets to interest him. He knew he would have to pay a visit to Messrs. Schwarz and Noble eventually, to Hoby's and Plimpton's, to Locks, all the various purveyors of gentlemen's costume and accoutrements. Eventually, too, he would need to find a jeweler to reset some of the Tregaron jewels. But that would not be for some weeks yet, and his own items would wait at least until the following day. Being a bit out of fashion did not bother the marquess. The clothing he had sported during that last Season in Town was hardly worn. He'd had no need for elegant garb in Wales. Beyond that, he knew Schwarz, Noble et al. could have a complete wardrobe on his doorstep within days of his orders. Money, again, and marquessates had a way of assuring such things.

He did pause at the window of a bookshop. That was something he had missed—the instant availability of all things printed. Despite the materials he had been able to order, he had wished for more, for the simple smell of new books every week, the tart commentary of the *Edinburgh Review,* the cheerful crush of patrons awaiting the latest bit of printed adventure or scandal.

Oh, it had smarted, seeing Miss Catherine Buchanan's face as she had surveyed the ruin of his library. Yet no amount of censure could come close to that he aimed at himself. The rest of the house be damned, Tregaron could not forgive himself for having allowed his sanctuary to suffer so ignoble a fate.

The only excuse he could muster was that he had been half out of his mind in those final days eight years past.

Not wanting to remember, he stopped before the bookshop's window and peered in. He could see row after row of new books waiting to be bound, and a few already in their glossy leather-and-gilt jackets, waiting to be purchased or collected. He imagined Byron's latest was there, and Southey's, and Wordsworth's, along with Plato and Cervantes, Thomas Aquinas, other long-dead voices from faraway shores. Tregaron stepped closer to the door and contemplated entering. Then he caught a glimpse of his reflection in one shadowed windowpane.

He had been avoiding mirrors for several years now, had begun looking into them as little as possible when he had stopped recognizing himself. Now, with his image skewed slightly by the glass, he flinched. He did not know the hard mouth, the empty eyes, the hatchet jaw. They were part of him, he understood, permanent and real, but he did not know them.

A second image appeared beside his, a boy—a sweep, Tregaron noted. As with much of his ilk, the child had adult eyes in his cherubic if soot-smeared face. He was small, his tool sack covering much of his back, various sticklike implements protruding like arrows from a quiver. At Tregaron's perusal, the boy flashed a gap-toothed grin and tipped his shabby cap.

Tregaron reached into his pocket for a shilling. The minute the child had it in hand, he flew off down the street, a grubby little imp among the city's most elegant denizens. That was London.

"Come, Gryffydd," Tregaron muttered to the delighted animal, and hurried away from the shop.

He was forced to stop again some hundred yards along when a large gentleman burst through the door of a tailor specializing in hunting gear. His reflexive "Pardon me, sir," was met by a fierce gaze that went from annoyance to awareness to disgust in an instant.

"Tregaron," the man spat.

"Earith."

The arrogant, intolerant, powerful Duke of Earith, always a fiery figure, appeared dangerously so now that he had thundered into middle age. There was some white in the flaming red hair and far too much flame in the pale-skinned face. The man appeared ready to combust on the spot.

"I'd heard rumors that you'd come back," he was growling now, the tip of his nose going slightly purple. "Couldn't believe it."

Tregaron gave a single, inward sigh before replying coolly, "I have a house here, and a seat in Lords."

He could see the thoughts and epithets roiling behind the duke's eyes and wondered what would come pouring out. He was only mildly surprised by the words Earith finally chose.

"Stay away from my daughter, Tregaron! I swear I'll have your head on a pike if you so much as breathe on her."

Tregaron sighed again, aloud this time. "I was under the impression that Lady Zilvia was already wed," he drawled. "Perhaps you would be so kind as to pass on my much belated felici—"

"Not Zilvia, you blackguard! Chloe."

"Chloe?" For a long moment, Tregaron was genuinely baffled. Then, suddenly, he recalled the lovely Lady Zilvia's younger sister. He vaguely remembered blindingly bright plaits constantly in motion as the child bounced about, and a voice to rival squalling barn cats. "Chloe?"

"I swear to you, Tregaron, one word—"

It was all he could do to keep from laughing. He raised a weary hand. "I doubt you will put much store by this, Earith, but I give you my word of honor that I have no designs upon your daughter, and certainly will not develop any." Before the duke could protest, no doubt to insist that the words Tregaron and honor meant nothing when put together, the marquess tipped his hat. "Good day, sir," he managed and, stepping around Earith's mountainous form, continued on his way.

Only then, as he navigated the final row of Bond Street shops, did he realize how much attention he had attracted. Whether it was merely his encounter with the duke or whether it had begun earlier along the street, he did not know. But he saw them now, the faces turned to follow his progress. Some were curious, more were cold, and several were outright damning.

Yes, the Marquess of Tregaron was back in Town, and it appeared he was destined to bear his dark past like an indelible ink blot on his white linen shirt. He had hoped for better from his peers, his former familiars, hoped for some tolerance if not forgiveness. All things considered, he mused as he turned the corner into Piccadilly, he really ought to have known better.

Chapter 3

Cate gingerly poked at the adipose bottom of one of the nymphs painted into the plaster of the first-floor drawing room ceiling. The plaster crumbled instantly, showering her with discolored dust. God only knew how so much moisture had gathered in this spot, but it had, and would have to be dealt with.

"This will have to go, too," she called down from her precarious perch atop a ladder. "It's rotted."

Below her, Calum MacGoun muttered under his breath. Cate suppressed a grin. MacGoun, the pinch-faced Glaswegian hired as foreman for the job, liked to grumble. The Buchanans let him. Behind the grim face and the grumbling were a good heart and a dedication to the work that would have put both Angus and Ambrose to shame had they seen their disinterest in houses as anything but appropriate for the artists they were.

"Man ought to be shot," MacGoun muttered.

"I would agree." In the fortnight since their meeting, Cate had had altogether too much time to think about the disagreeable marquess, about his deplorable arrogance and fierce, intriguing face. MacGoun's continuous, very vocal response to the state of the house had given her a perfect outlet for a bit of righteous condemnation. "As should whoever painted this disgrace."

The design, a collection of poorly painted and undeniably ugly nymphs and satyrs, wasted what was a very good space. The ceiling at this spot was a gentle, elegant dome and would, Cate was certain, do very well with the new "starfish" design created by the incomparable Sir John Soane for his own breakfast room. *Very well.* Not only would the multisectioned, vaulted ceiling look splendid when completed in the gold and crimson tones selected for the room, but it would help to bring the house firmly into the nineteenth century, into the modern world.

Satisfied, Cate thumbed her nose at a particularly overblown water nymph.

"You'll come down from there now, lass," MacGoun commanded, not caring in the least who was paying his wages. "I won't be asking again. Next you'll be cracking your crown and running to me for sympathy. You'll get none."

Foreman and workmen alike had taken Cate's presence in the midst of things very well. They hadn't balked, either, at taking orders from her. Ambrose and Angus trundled in and out often enough, bearing endless good cheer, paint spots and plaster splashes, various portfolios. But it was Cate who truly knew what needed to be done, and how to explain it.

She credited part of the men's easy acceptance to the fact that they were mostly Scots, familiar to MacGoun, and less inclined to dismiss women than their English counterparts. Then, too, Cate was the Buchanan who walked with her head firmly on her shoulders and her feet firmly on the ground. The men respected that. They tipped their caps to the uncles, gazed in respectful if slack-jawed admiration at Lucy when she deigned to visit, but they listened to Cate. And talked to her.

"We've a bit of a problem with this picture, Miss Cate," one said now from the doorway. "Jamie's to see to the floor and he can't make heads nor tails of it."

Cate nodded and prepared to descend. Both men politely turned their backs as she did, charming but unnecessary as she was well used to going up and down ladders while keeping her skirts quite decently close to her legs. In the country, she had often worn old breeches that had belonged to her father. Here in the city, much as she would have liked to disregard protocol, she knew better.

She'd worn breeches during the Maybole job. That had been rural Scotland, after all, and she had assumed in her man's garb, hair tucked away and skin forever dusted with something or other, she would attract no attention whatsoever. She'd been wrong. And she had paid for her wide-eyed naivete.

Shaking her head now to prevent the memories from

going too far down that path, Cate set her jaw and climbed down to the floor. There, she shook out her very proper skirts to be certain they were not clinging anywhere they ought not. There was no way of knowing who might come through this front door.

For some reason, privacy appeared to be a vague concept to the residents of London. She'd heard of Londoners trooping through the houses of people they did not know to view the aftereffects of fire, important birth- or deathbeds, even the victims of murder. None of that, of course, in Mayfair. But in Mayfair, she was learning, curiosity was just as avid and ill-contained, if slightly less lurid.

A good half-dozen times in the past sennight, well-dressed ladies and gentlemen, residents of the Square and its environs, had knocked at the door—and in several instances simply walked through it—and demanded to see the house. Politeness had nothing to do with the Buchanans' acquiescence. A smart businessman or woman knew when to court potential clients. So while her uncles, on whom she could always count to charm these potential fleece-bearers should they be present, entertained the nosy visitors, Cate faded grumpily into the shadows. Appropriately skirted, of course, lest she be noticed.

Now she followed Gordie, MacGoun's second-in-command, into the foyer. There, squatting among the shattered and pulled-up remnants of the original floor, was the aforementioned Jamie. The little Highlander, as seemingly unlikely a hefter of Portland stone and marble as Angus Buchanan, was rubbing at the crown of his bald head and squinting at the designs spread before him.

He glanced up, then jumped to his feet as she approached, top drawing in hand. "Sorry, miss, but I canna tell . . ." He broke off, shrugged helplessly, and pointed to the paper. " 'Tis stone here and marble there? Or there?"

Cate looked over his shoulder—and sighed heartily. Not only was the design upside down, but it was liberally spattered with both tea and paint. *Oh, Uncle Ambrose!* she scolded silently, then removed the drawing from Jamie's work-roughened fist. She rummaged through her pockets for the stub of pencil she knew was there, then strode over to the wall. Propping the paper there, with the two men to hold it, she repaired the damage as best she could, making the lines darker with her pencil so they could be seen again through her uncle's spillage.

"Here," she said, pointing, "the large squares, is the Portland stone. Bright white. Here, the smaller squares in the center, is the black marble. And here, at the edge, all around"—the *pièce de résistance* of the design, of the whole floor—"are the colored tiles."

It was difficult to see on the smudged drawing, but the colors were there, the alternating rust and gold and deep forest green. It was a daring concept, using color there and in ceramic. It was even more innovative. To the best of the Buchanans' knowledge, there were but the merest handful of London homes with colored floor tiles. As far as Cate was concerned, there would be more, many more, and not so far in the future.

"They'll break, I tell you," came MacGoun's dour pronouncement from the doorway. He wasn't deliberately being the voice of doom, Cate knew, a knowledge that often kept her from throwing pencils, sketchpads, and even hammers at his glowering head, but rather stating a simple fact.

"They will not," she insisted, more stubbornly determined as to the tiles' future than confident of it. "They are being hand-made in Kent now and will be in this floor, intact, when the Marquess of Tregaron has been six feet under for a century."

She jumped when Gordie suddenly slapped his open palm against the wall. "That's it!" he declared, smacking the wall again. "I've remembered!"

"Remembered what, lad?" MacGoun demanded.

"Why, what he did, o' course, the marquess. To get London all riled-like."

Cate had no idea that Tregaron had ever riled Society, but considering their brief encounter, she was hardly surprised. She was, however, curious. Gordie, Grampian born but a longtime resident of London, had been working in Mayfair houses for a good decade and had proven to be a marvelous storyteller. "So what did he do? Tell us," she urged.

To her amazement, the man flushed to the roots of his wiry black hair and actually scuffed his feet. "Sorry, miss," he mumbled, "but I can't."

"Can't?"

"Well, you see, it's this way. I never speak ill of him who's paying m'wages while he's still paying them. 'Tis bad luck. Last time I did, when I mentioned to my mates that Lord Pickering wanted me to build him a game room with cheaters' mirrors and pockets, I dropped a load of bricks on my foot. And before that, when I mentioned George Reynolds's fondness for the drink, I fell off a ladder into the neighbor's rose garden. And before that—"

"Never mind, Gordie," Cate insisted far more patiently than she felt. "We understand."

Oh, but her curiosity was piqued. What a terrible shame, she lamented, that she did not have anyone else to ask.

"I will say one thing for the marquess, though." Gordie's neck was still a bit pink, but he had stopped shuffling. "He must be a clever bloke to have hired Buchanans, Miss Cate, rather than Nash or one of those other lads."

Cate managed a tight smile. "I don't think his lordship even approached those other lads," was her reply. "Buchanan and Buchanan was available, eager, and came cheaply. But we'll show him, won't we, gentlemen, what a wise fellow he is?"

MacGoun grunted. Jamie grinned. And Gordie declared, "Aye, we will at that, Miss Cate."

Cate needed to get back to her ladder. "One more thing. Make certain I am warned should our wise marquess choose to drop in. His presence is quite enough to cause anyone to have an anxious fit of the heart."

Though not Catholic, she was tempted to join Jamie when he crossed himself before trotting back to his place at the center of the floor. As far as Cate was concerned, a little heavenly intervention could always do the Buchanans a world of good.

Tregaron silently wished Sheraton, Chippendale, and all men of their ilk into the devil's hands as he shifted in his grandmother's tiny and dismally uncomfortable parlor chair. He was always concerned he would break something on these visits, including his grandmother. No matter that he knew she was tough as a cut diamond and just as sharp; she barely topped five feet even in the built-up heels of her generation's fashionable shoes, and could not weigh much above six stone despite the profusion of precious family stones she tended to sport.

At the moment, she was peering at the floor through an elaborate quizzing glass that hung about her neck on a jeweled chain. "Have I not asked you before to refrain from bringing this slavering beast into my home, Colwin?"

"You have," he replied mildly.

"Yet you've chosen to ignore the request."

"I have." He glanced down at Gryffydd, who, rather than slavering, was grinning up at the dowager marchioness from his place beside her chair. It was, Tregaron knew, the prime location for the dog to receive the biscuits the dowager would pass down when she thought her grandson was not looking. "Shall I have Wills remove him?"

She promptly waved a hand that seemed far too fragile to support the collection of rings it bore in his direction. "No, no. The creature is already here, and my butler has better things to do than chase it about the house."

"As you wish." Tregaron glanced casually at the clock on the mantel. From the corner of his eye he saw the first sugar biscuit disappearing into Gryffydd's jaws. When he glanced back, the dog had crumbs on his nose and the lady was patting her immaculate white hair. "You are looking well, madam."

"You said that already," was her retort, "when you arrived. And I do not look well. I look old."

"I don't see that."

"You need spectacles. All the St. Clair-Wright men need spectacles and refuse to acknowledge it."

"Grandfather once shot a feather off your hat from a hundred yards away," Tregaron reminded her, half horrified as always by the tale and half intrigued by the passionate, devil-may-care connection the pair were reputed to have shared. "I would say that required better than adequate eyesight."

"He was aiming between my eyes," his grandmother snapped, the sudden mistiness of her own eyes belying the words. "And the very fact that that day was more than forty years ago tells you just how aged and decrepit I am."

Sarah, Lady Tregaron, nee Lady Sarah Granville, sister to the late Earl of Heathfield and aunt to the current, was of something of an advanced age, her grandson supposed.

She certainly would not see five-and-seventy again. She was, however, spry and sharp, and still possessed of much of the beauty for which she had been so famed in her youth. The years had left a gentle pattern of weblike lines on her face and turned the once ebony hair to white. The pain of surviving not only her husband but also her son had dulled the sparkle in the amber eyes. But she had never stopped living, and never stopped making her existence very much known, and often of central importance, to those around her.

She was vain. She was demanding, vinegar-tongued, and unabashedly haughty. She was also the only person on earth who cared a fig for the ninth Marquess of Tregaron.

During those years of his seclusion in Wales, she had been the only person from his family or Society to visit. Tregaron had not asked her to come, had not wanted her to come. But she'd arrived nonetheless, bouncing over the deplorable country roads in her antiquated traveling coach every three months, braving the gamut of Welsh weather and by-ways, tolerating a country she had always loathed—loathed to the extent that, when her husband had departed this life some quarter century earlier, she had emphatically vowed never to set foot in the dismal land again.

She'd changed her mind, perhaps the only broken vow in her life, when her grandson cloistered himself within his Welsh estate. Finally, after the third visit, when it became clear she was going to continue blessing him with her irascible, determined presence whether he wished it or no, Tregaron had offered to come to her in Sussex, to the tidy little estate she occupied when not in London—an estate that bordered on the one where she had grown up and that always seemed to be filled with saintly, cheerful Granvilles paying visits. Distant cousins who would have been polite enough to the marquess's face, no doubt, but winced at his approach and smiled at his departure.

Lady Tregaron had refused, insisting her grandson's ever-muddy boots and filthy beast of a dog, merely a pup at the time, would only ruin her fine possessions. She had, however, accepted the sleek and modern coach he had purchased for her, and the visits had continued through the long years.

Upon his return to London, Tregaron had come immediately to see her, and came now every second day for overly strong tea, lashes from her sharp tongue, and an hour or so of the simple, unspoken acceptance they gave each other. By tacit agreement, they never spoke of the events of eight years earlier. However, despite Tregaron's constant requests that she desist, the dowager marchioness constantly reminded him of his duty to the title and lands.

"You," she was saying now, "are not getting any younger, either. Forty at your next birthday, isn't it?"

"Seven-and-thirty," he corrected, aware that she damn well knew how old he was, right down to the hour of the day of the month and year in which he had been born.

"Seven-and-thirty. High time to be getting yourself an heir. Now don't you be scowling at me, Colwin. You don't want to be kicking off at a tragically young age like your dear papa, leaving the responsibility to a mere snip of a boy. It was not good for you to succeed to the title so early, and would do no good for your son."

Tregaron held his tongue. It wouldn't serve much purpose to mention that he did not have a son and, intent notwithstanding, was not likely to beget one in the immediate future. It would certainly do no good to mention that his dear papa's death, though tragic, perhaps, and unquestionably at a young age, had been preventable. No man of five-and-thirty should have been so arrogantly feckless as to chase after the wife of a notoriously suspicious, bitterly jealous, and famously violent army colonel. Especially when there had been no love involved, merely boredom and lust.

But the St. Clair-Wright men had never been either saintly or righteous. They'd been a misguided, ill-reputed lot for centuries. Tregaron was hardly unique in his infamy. He was merely another apple from a gnarled tree.

"Honestly, Colwin, one would think you had not the slightest care for me. At this rate, I shall die never having held my great-grandson, never knowing the fate of the name and estates so dear to my heart."

Tregaron suppressed an amused snort. The old virago was hardly on her last legs. Nor did she give a spit about the name and estates. She had lost interest in both the moment her beloved husband died, reverting almost wholly to being an eminently respectable, well-admired Sussex Granville.

To be fair, he had to admit she showed her care for him, if sometimes in odd ways. She never used his Christian name, for which he was extremely grateful. Instead, she continued to call him Colwin, the courtesy title he had borne until his twelfth year, when his father had died, and he had become the Marquess of Tregaron. For that alone, he felt she deserved better than a sarcastic response. He gave her the stock one.

"If you will endeavor to stay in this earthly realm for the time being, madam, I shall endeavor to find some unsuspecting creature to bear the next generation." When his grandmother gave a very unladylike snort and dropped a biscuit into Gryffydd's waiting maw without bothering to hide the act, Tregaron couldn't help but give a faint smile. "For now, I will set my house to rights and see to trading these rags for something Brummell would not scorn."

"Addled, impertinent fellow," the dowager marchioness muttered, not making it clear whether she spoke of the famous dandy or her grandson.

"That's as it may be. But as it happens, I have an appointment with my tailors. Apparently the half-dozen waistcoats I've already collected are not sufficient. I have another batch waiting."

His grandmother's disinterested expression faltered for an instant. "You are leaving so soon? I was hoping you might stay for supper." Recalling herself, she stiffened her ramrod-straight spine that scant bit further. "I believe Cook is preparing an entire haunch of something or other," she announced vaguely, fluttering her fingers in a very good semblance of disinterest, "and you know how it vexes me to have so much food thrust at me."

"Grandmother—"

"I cannot think how you manage to get a decent meal in those dismal, poky rooms you have taken. Disgraceful, if you ask me. Don't you come running when you begin to starve, asking for succor here."

His suite at the Albany provided quite as much room as he needed, and had sufficient facilities for perfectly adequate meals. The rest he took elsewhere—including this house. Had he not been convinced that both he and his grandmother would run mad within a fortnight, he might have stayed with her. But the situation suited him as it was.

He had much-needed freedom; she knew she only had to send a footman and he would be by her side in a quarter hour.

"Grandmother—"

"Colwin, you know it does not matter to me in the least where you dine . . ."

He could see the plea in her eyes. He had never intended to disappoint her. "It has not yet gone three. I shall return well before dinner."

She nodded once, crisply, almost hiding the brief, relieved slump of her rigid shoulders. "Suit yourself. Now, you'd best leave the beast here. My nerves are strong. I cannot say the same for the preening flocks in Bond Street."

"What a clever idea. I shall do just that."

He took his leave. By the time he reached the foyer, he knew his grandmother would have moved from her minuscule, slate-hard chair to recline on the well-stuffed sofa nearby. The plate of biscuits would be within reach. Gryffydd would be in her lap.

Tregaron descended quickly to Hill Street. The temptation was strong, but he resisted the urge to head north to Hanover Square. He had stayed away from the house for a fortnight, kept himself busy with the annoying tasks of refurbishing his wardrobe and sorting through the invitations that arrived daily. Oh, a few notable hostesses were shunning him, that much was clear, but nearly as many were requesting his attendance at their dinners, their balls, their interminable evenings of Gluck and Purcell.

Amazing, the marquess thought, what crimes a man could commit and still have any place at all in Society.

With that in evidence, and his goals in mind, he would be attending the Hythe fete the following night. He would truss himself up in fitted, fashionable clothes, sip tepid champagne, and survey the field. No doubt he would have a handful of perfectly attractive, indifferently educated, excruciatingly well-bred young ladies from which to choose—ladies and their families who considered his title and fortune just worth the risk of accepting his suit. Fortunately, he only needed one, and the Beau Monde would provide her.

Why then, he wondered grouchily as he stalked toward Bond Street, did he keep thinking of Catherine Buchanan?

Cate, for her part, was thinking wistfully of hot water, lots of it. After a long day at the Hanover Square house, all she wanted was a bath. It was not to be. Lucy had accosted her the moment she'd set foot in the house, demanding, among other things, attention and a stroll in the Park. Apparently the uncles, who had made only the briefest of appearances in Hanover Square that day, were not present at home, either.

"You cannot keep me prisoner here all the time, Cate! I must have some air, some small reminder that I have not been tossed into the oubliette of some moldering dungeon!"

Ah, the drama of it all. Such was life with Lucy. Cate could have provided the small reminder that they had been out the better part of the day before, spending money from the marquess's first advance on any number of fripperies they could ill afford but which Cate thought her sister deserved.

She could also have mentioned that Lucy had spent much of the past fortnight out and about with one uncle or the other. True, the girl was always escorted home before said uncle disappeared into a pub, but along the way she had visited such places as St. Paul's, the British Museum, Westminster Abbey, and, most recently, even a bit of Devonshire House on an art tour Uncle Ambrose had somehow arranged.

Cate, with the exception of several nearby and deadly dull shopping excursions, had seen little more than the streets between their own humble abode and the Tregaron house.

Any guilt she might still have felt at Lucy's plight—the girl did, as it happened, spend much of her time at home with only books and the meager staff for company—was forestalled by her appearance. Lucy was garbed in her newest dress, a frothy confection in white muslin, her hair carefully coiffed in classical twists and curls, and what Cate recognized as one of their mother's delicate gold chains and crosses glinting about her throat.

Beyond this unusual display of late-afternoon splendor,

Cate knew her sister loathed strolling anywhere one was likely to encounter dirt, grass, or low-flying birds.

"Hyde Park?" she demanded suspiciously. "Now?"

"As soon as you have changed your dress," was Lucy's reply, accompanied by a sad glance at Cate's work-dirtied skirts. "I am positively suffocating here!"

Again, Cate refrained from suggesting she try a day spent with falling plaster and rising dust. Instead, she glanced past her sister to the pile of newspapers spread over the large table. Lucy never paid the slightest attention to the news of the Realm. A quick glance at the top sheet banished Cate's surprise. A more thorough perusal, which Lucy tried to prevent with a quick grab at the paper, answered the question of why the girl was so eager to go walking.

" 'Among those personages late returned to Town and often to be seen taking the air in Hyde Park at the five o'clock hour,' " Cate read aloud from the social column, " 'are Lord Aubert, their Graces the Duke and Duchess of Conovar—' " She darted a sharp glance at her sister, but Lucy was gazing nonchalantly out the window. " 'Lord and Lady St. Helier. By all reports, Lady Jersey's new curricle—' Oh, Lucy!"

"What?"

"I do hate to disappoint you, truly I do. I also hate to repeat myself. Thrusting oneself upon Deirdre will not do at all. Nor will encountering Lady Jersey in the Park bring you a voucher, dearest, no matter how prettily you behave nor how lovely you look. We are not Almack's sort of people, and the sooner you accept the fact, the better."

A quick, hot flush rose into Lucy's cheeks. There was a blast of temper coming, and Cate steeled herself for it.

The door knocker clacked loudly.

Lucy went into motion like a whirlwind, her anger swept away. She scooped up the newspapers and stuffed them under the settee, then moved to the other cluttered tables. Before Cate could so much as lift a hand, the room was ready for visitors. Not that she would have lifted anything in a hurry. She was bone-tired and certain whoever was at the door had come to see her uncles—who couldn't even be bothered to be home.

"Lucy," she said wearily, "it will only be—"

The maid, cap askew, appeared in the doorway. "Lady

Leverham, miss," she announced. Lucy took just enough time to direct the full force of her smug smile at Cate before bouncing into the hall.

"Lady Leverham!" she cried. "How perfectly lovely of you to call. I have been thinking of you, hoping we should meet from the moment we arrived . . ." Cate flinched. Then sighed. "Tea, Becky!" Lucy commanded. "Now, dear madam, you must tell me how everyone is getting on in beloved little Tarbet since we were last there . . ." A moment later, still chattering away, the girl all but dragged their Tarbet neighbor and meager acquaintance into the room.

Cate's first thought was that Lady Leverham never changed. The matron's hair was still improbably dark around her plump face, her eyes still a bit vague, and her smile utterly sweet. If she were at all disconcerted by Lucy's overfamiliar greeting, she did not show it.

As soon as Lucy paused for breath, having finished the list of Tarbet residents she so hoped to meet since she had arrived in Town, Cate stepped in. "Lady Leverham," she said politely, gesturing their guest to a seat, "how lovely to see you." She'd noted with relief that the lady's notorious pet, Galahad, was not present. "You are most welcome."

"And you are a perverse girl!" Settling herself and her copious, filmy wrap into the proferred chair, Lady Leverham shook a plump finger in Cate's direction. "You ought to have informed me of your intention to be in London!"

Cate caught another smug look from her sister. "I did not wish to impose, madam. I did not think—"

"Impose? Rubbish! How can one impose on friends?"

Cate could think of countless ways to impose on friends, countless more on mere acquaintances, but apparently Lady Leverham had set her mind on their closeness. The woman was renowned for three things: her pet, her passion for all matters medieval, and her sweetly faulty memory. The third seemed to be at work now. Cate, faced with her determined neighbor and delighted sister, couldn't be bothered to correct any fantasies.

"Sibyl wanted ever so much to accompany me," the lady went on, referring to her niece, now a countess, and never a companion of either Buchanan girl, "but they are presently being bombarded with plants and glasses and chairs and the earl would lose a carton of those musty old books he insists on hauling about . . . Well, no matter. The box will turn up, the chairs will go where they must, and Sibby made me promise to bring this."

She unearthed her reticule from the folds of her wrap and withdrew a slightly bent card. Lucy all but snatched it from her fingers. "Oh, Catey, it is an invitation! To a soiree at the home of Lord and Lady Hythe tomorrow night! Now you must come shopping with me. My new blue dress will suffice, but only with some lace and gloves and perhaps a new shawl to bring it up to snuff . . ."

Lady Leverham smiled indulgently at the girl. "That's the spirit, child! I will send you to my mantua-maker, although perhaps you will find her a tad antiquated." Recalling the various medieval-looking ensembles the lady favored, Cate thought it likely they would find her favored shopkeepers antiquated indeed—and expensive.

"Oh, goodness. I very nearly forgot!" Lady Leverham said suddenly. "Sibby heard from Tarquin who heard from Conovar . . . or was it Tarrant . . . ? Holcombe?" Bold mahogany curls bounced as she shook her head in impatience. "No matter. Am I correct in understanding your dear uncles have been so gracious as to offer their services to the Marquess of Tregaron?"

"They have," Cate replied absently, wondering just how many precious shillings it would take to bring Lucy's dress up to snuff for Sibyl Hythe's party. And whether, with the help of that lady's chairs and plants and perhaps a drape or two, she herself would be able to disappear into the background.

"Well. I had heard he'd come back, but did not quite give the rumor credence. With a reputation like his, one would expect him to stay in his shadowy keep a sight longer than eight years! Scandalous, I say."

Cate, who had been feeling rather like a shuttlecock between her sister and guest, snapped back to attention. "Indeed, madam? I was not aware the marquess had been . . . er . . . in exile."

"You didn't know?" Lady Leverham demanded, sweet face slack with surprise. "Well, of course you might not have, tucked away in Scotland as you have been for all these years." She leaned forward then and lowered her voice. "It was never proven, but neither was it ever questioned, not really. Few ever doubted the matter."

"What matter?" Lucy demanded, having no scruples in displaying the rampant curiosity her sister tried to suppress.

Lady Leverham's reply, when it came, could not have been farther from anything Cate would have imagined.

"Your uncles, my dear," the lady nearly whispered, "have granted their services to a man with blood on his hands. Eight years ago, Tregaron killed his wife."

Chapter 4

Tregaron had never been inside the Hythe house before. The earl had been unmarried until recently, and had not entertained. He had also been dull as dirt, which was precisely why Tregaron had chosen this fete for his re-entrance into Society. Any party thrown by Hythe, and whichever eminently proper, demure miss he'd married was bound to be well attended, underwhelming, and so respectable as to make a man's bones petrify.

Such an event, Tregaron had decided, was the perfect place to make his appearance. He would attract a certain amount of unwanted attention, no doubt, even if few persons actually spoke to him. He would also be surrounded by just the sort of young lady for whom he was searching, a lady like the new Countess of Hythe was sure to be: prim, decorous, and solemn.

He'd received quite a shock upon entering the house.

Everything not moving was covered either with candles or some form of colorful vegetation. Music from an enthusiastic and, by the sound of it, full-size orchestra poured lustily through the ballroom doors. There were pink-cheeked, red-nosed revelers raising glasses and voices over every available inch of floor. And, unless Tregaron was very much mistaken, the furry blur bouncing from chair back to sconce to chandelier, keeping up a shrill chattering all the while, was a small black monkey.

Beyond that, it took a full ten minutes for anyone to notice his presence. Even then, the buzzing that followed his progress through the house was somewhat less in volume than he had expected. That might well have been due to the volume of all other sounds, he thought, but perhaps it also meant that his eight years of exile had worn away some of the tarnish on his name. Unlikely, but considering that the staid Earl of Hythe himself had just wandered by, typically sober-faced but sporting a floral garland atop his regal head, anything was possible.

Tregaron felt slightly encouraged. Until the first matron, upon spying him, spun on her heel and presented him with her rigid back, followed by another, and another. Well, he mused, it was no more than he had expected. He was not even surprised that the pinch-lipped Lady Broadford had seemingly forgotten that he had once pulled her son, sniveling and slightly blue, from a hole in the ice of a Sussex pond. Her gratitude at the time had been excessive. Her nose-in-the-air pivot now, causing not a ripple in her champagne, was impressive.

There were those who did not give him the cut. Perhaps none looked especially welcoming, but he saw bland interest in some eyes, outright feminine speculation in others, and took both as a good sign.

He had purposely arrived quite late. The receiving line was long over, but he followed Hythe into a crowded parlor. There, the man removed the garland with a grimace and tossed it in the direction of a hovering footman. Just as Tregaron was ready to approach the earl for a public chat, hoping a degree of acquaintance and Hythe's legendary sense of propriety would preclude rudeness, chaos erupted.

The monkey came careening into the room, using furniture, wall fixtures, and various persons to hasten his arrival. Ladies' shrieks rose above the music and conversation. Several fans and numerous glasses went flying into the air. The monkey launched itself into the melee. Chattering loudly, it landed on another footman's shoulder, curled itself into a furry ball, and leapt into the air. Hythe, his expression a combination of extreme distaste and resignation, took a quick, military-precise step backward.

The monkey barely brushed his lapels, then slid downward, fast, hitting the floor with a small thump and loud squawk.

Any concern that the creature had injured itself was quickly dispelled. A pretty young lady with glossy brown curls and an engaging smile broke away from a knot of revelers and hurried to where the monkey sat.

"Oh, Galahad, not again!" she lamented, bending over the hunched little form. "Will you never learn?"

With that, she reached out a slender arm. The monkey, with obvious familiarity, swung to her wrist, then scampered up her arm. It came to rest on the lady's shoulder, where it promptly pulled a shiny hairpin from her curls and began to chew on it.

"Sibyl," Tregaron heard Hythe mutter.

The lady shrugged. The monkey protested the motion. "I am sorry," the former offered as the latter chewed away. "I thought Aunt Alfie had him."

"Aunt Alfie," came the earl's dry response, "is not especially reliable in such matters, is she?"

"No, she most certainly is not," Sibyl, as she appeared to be named, replied, clearly undaunted by Hythe's annoyance. "But she does try." Blessing the earl with a saucy grin, she turned away, monkey aloft. If Tregaron was not mistaken, the beast actually thumbed its little nose at their estimable host.

Tregaron watched them slip into the crush. Yes, he thought, there was something undeniably appealing about the lady. But she was just the sort of woman he was not looking for. His marchioness would not be pert. She would not be saucy. She most certainly would not possess a wild, ill-behaved monkey. Or a well-behaved one, either, for that matter. He was all for pets; Gryffydd, after all, had been his constant companion for more than seven years. The line had to be drawn, however, at any animal liable to chew on one's fripperies or cause a disturbance at a polite gathering.

Just as Tregaron was pondering the realization that this gathering was far more lively than expected and, perhaps, far more lively than polite, he felt a tap at his shoulder. He turned to meet the smiling face of a smartly uniformed young gentleman who was just familiar enough to make him search his mind for a name.

"It *is* Tregaron," the fellow cried. "I heard as much, but needed to see with my own eyes. Damme, it must be ten years or more."

Yes, the man was familiar, his dark hair and laughing eyes bringing to mind their host . . . Tregaron blinked. "Julius?"

Hythe's younger brother grinned broadly. "Yes, yes, I

know. All grown. It happens to the best of us. Here now, you haven't a glass of anything . . ."

As Tregaron watched, bemused, Julius Rome snared a glass of champagne from a passing footman and pressed it into Tregaron's hand. He then grabbed a second, passed it on, then a third and fourth, leaving them each with both fists filled.

Tregaron's contact with the earl's brother had been limited; too many years had separated them for real friendship. Their mothers had been fond of each other, however, and the *ton* was small enough that their paths had crossed frequently as youths. Tregaron remembered young Rome as being cheerful, clever, and not in the least miserly with his goodwill. Apparently he had not changed much.

"Good old Tarquin," Julius announced after he contentedly drained one champagne glass. "Always the very best of everything. Being married has made a world of difference to him. He was always a good fellow, my brother, but stiff as a board. Have you met his wife? I daresay not, as I hear you're just back in Town."

Tregaron wondered what else the man had heard. Rome would have been tucked away at university, barely out of school at the time of the scandal, but certainly flapping tongues would have brought him up to snuff by now.

"I have not yet had the pleasure of meeting Lady Hythe," Tregaron said carefully, gauging the younger man's expression. "I should very much like to."

"Of course you would," was the cheerful reply. "I expect you're hunting for a wife, yourself. God only knows why you would have come to one of my brother's dos otherwise. Poor fellow had the pomp and propriety down fast, but never was much for entertainment. And you couldn't possibly have known how he has improved. Now where is . . . Ah, yes, there she is now. Come along. I'll introduce you to Sibyl, then Sibyl can introduce you to any number of suitable young things."

"Sibyl?"

"My sister-in-law. Splendid girl."

There couldn't be two. Tregaron spied the monkey, still perched on the lady's—Lady Hythe's, he corrected—shoulder. This was the woman dull-as-dirt Hythe had chosen. This was the woman he himself had hoped would contribute the breath of respectability to his foray into the Marriage Mart.

He decided it was time to rethink that plan.

Tregaron scanned the assembled misses. Most were pretty, even if it was no more than their relative youth making them so. All, he assumed, were well bred and reasonably well behaved. Some would be heiresses, although he had no need of money. A handful would be truly clever. One or two among them might actually suit him.

He spied Chloe Somersham in the crush and couldn't help but note that she had grown into a perfectly lovely creature. She was far too small for his taste, of course, and it appeared she still had a predilection for bouncing in place. But neither flaw came close to the utter distaste Tregaron had for her father, the wild and windy Duke of Earith. No, Lady Chloe would not be receiving his attentions, but it was through no fault of her own.

His eyes traveled over a sea of topknots: blonde, brunette, titian, raven. And suddenly, jarringly, came to rest on a very bold, very familiar chin.

"We will not disturb Lady Hythe just yet, I think, Rome," he announced. "She appears . . . occupied." Then, at the younger man's unconcerned shrug, Tregaron, drawn by some odd and powerful impulse, began weaving his way toward Catherine Buchanan.

He would never have expected to see her at such a gathering, would not have expected her to have been invited. But there she was, tucked into a far corner between a curtain and a potted plant, impossible to mistake as she stood a good head taller than most of the women and a good number of men, her hair blazing red-bronze in the candlelight. She was garbed in white, Tregaron could see as he approached, a rather odd design that skirted what he perceived as current fashion while somehow quite missing it. The fabric was dense, drapey, and rather looked like a costume one would expect of a Sophoclean drama.

In it, Catherine looked very much as the marquess assumed Diana might, or Hera. A goddess, but one whose glory had nothing whatsoever to do with delicacy, demureness, or celestial beauty. Catherine Buchanan needed only a bow or lance in hand to complete the image. Even as he made his way toward her, Tregaron wondered if armor might not be advisable.

Cate felt his approach even before she saw him. Maybe it was nothing more than the crowd parting before him, a waft of fans, skirts, and coattails, but she felt something. And when she looked up, there he was, all black hair, black evening wear, black scowl. No, she corrected herself, he was not scowling. In fact, his satyr's face bore no readable expression whatsoever. It merely seemed dark and twisted because of . . . well, her imagination, she decided, and Lady Leverham's words.

That lady had been terribly vague with her story. *Unhappy marriage,* she'd said, describing the late Lady Tregaron as *too young, too pampered, too beautiful,* the marquess as *always a dark one, not a laugh to be found in him.* Then there had been a *few joyless years,* some *terrible public rows,* and finally the Jermyn house party, that horrible early morning when the beautiful young marchioness had been found broken on the hard stone terrace thirty feet below the balcony of the bedchamber where she had been staying.

Tregaron was nowhere to be found, Lady Leverham had breathed, one plump hand gripping a vinaigrette that she had not actually employed. He'd gone back to London and was just sitting in his library when the messengers finally banged on the doors of the house.

No one had seen him leave the party near Windsor, nor had so much as noted his absence. No one had witnessed his wife's fall. None could disprove his fierce, pale-faced claim that he had departed for Town, saddled his own mount, and gone, even before the al fresco supper and had most certainly been well settled in his Hanover Square house, already deep into a bottle of port by the time the clocks had chimed midnight. And since Lady Tregaron had been very much alive at midnight, a gay whirl of gossamer skirts and laughter, the matter had not been pursued.

But a few sensible people knew better, Lady Leverham insisted. *People knew.*

Cate watched the marquess approaching now and wondered if he was the sort of man who could commit murder. Anyone could kill, she thought, if the stakes were high enough. Cold-blooded murder, however . . . Could an unfaithful wife—and while lady Leverham had not actually said the words, they had hung over those she did speak—have pushed him that far? Adultery, apparently, was a small matter as long as it was done with discretion. It would seem the marquess might not have agreed. And it would seem much of the present gathering thought him guilty of responding in a heinous manner. They parted before him, stared coolly after him.

She could not believe him a murderer. Surely one could tell . . .

"Miss Buchanan."

She swallowed, instinctively lifting her chin a notch. "Good evening, Lord Tregaron."

She cursed the unhappy chance that had allowed him to spot her. She'd hidden herself so carefully, after all, in the corner. She'd chosen a white dress, too, knowing many of the women present would be in white. By all rights, he ought not to have seen her at all. As soon as she had been dutifully introduced to Lord Hythe and a handful of disinterested fellow guests, she had faded into the background. And, she told herself firmly now, she was ever so grateful that not a single, solitary being had approached her since.

Now here was Lord Tregaron, bearing down on her like one of the Four Horsemen. She'd had no idea that he would be present. It was merely bad luck that he'd spied her and simple logic that had her wishing he would take his large and unmistakable form elsewhere. Beyond her stomach doing a jittery little dance—courtesy, no doubt, of being so close to a man who might or might not be prone to violence—a person would have to be blind not to notice the steady swivel of heads in their direction.

Somehow, telling the marquess to go away didn't seem the thing to do. Nor did asking him if the rumors were true, if he'd shoved his beautiful wife from a balcony in a fit of jealousy.

She was spared that decision by his cool, polite, "How do you do, Miss Buchanan?"

"I am quite well, thank you," she replied after a moment. Her "And you, sir?" was somewhat lacking in enthusiasm.

"I am tolerably well. And your uncles? Are they here tonight?"

A polite question, Cate thought, even if the marquess knew himself more likely to be passing an evening with the mad king than a pair of Scottish architects. No, Tregaron and his sort would not really be so sanguine about the likes of Angus and Ambrose Buchanan rubbing elbows with dukes and bishops.

"We are in the company of Lady Leverham," Cate replied, seeing no reason to inform the marquess that, although Lady Hythe had been gracious enough to extend the invitation, Ambrose and Angus had opted instead for entertainments of a slightly less elegant sort. Cate thought she'd heard whisperings about dice and Covent Garden. "My uncles did not attend."

"Ah. Well. I trust they are in good health and spirits."

It was too silly, this little exchange. Cate stared into the hard face, trying to understand why he was speaking to her at all, let alone exchanging pleasantries that, while they might well be proper, seemed sorely out of place considering their one previous meeting—and his reputation. She dared a sharp glance into the amber eyes, looking for answers among the enigmas.

She was too long in responding this time. One of the marquess's black brows lifted into a slow, sardonic arc. His wide mouth twisted into something that could not quite be called a smile. "So it goes."

"I beg your pardon, sir?"

"Merely a comment on the predictability of some things, Miss Buchanan. No matter. I will assume your uncles are in fine form."

"Oh, they . . . I . . ."

"I will also assume that you do not dance."

Confused, Cate blinked up at him. "My lord?" Even unnerved as she was, she has to look *up*—a rarity for her because of her height. She looked up at so few people.

"Either you do not dance as a matter of principle, or your sets are all bespoken for the evening. Perhaps you have just this day turned your ankle, or you are in the very final hour of mourning for some distant departed relation. Have no fear, Miss Buchanan. I shall not ask. Nor will I require an explanation should I see you on the floor later. I understand perfectly."

Cate prided herself on her quick mind. This time, however, she was lamentably slow in comprehending his meaning. When she finally did, he was continuing, "I meant only to be civil. But then, my . . . renown has little to do with my being civil, or even civilized, so I will not pretend to be surprised. I will, however, express my hope that you will enjoy the remainder of your evening. Good night, madam."

He took a step backward. Cate, despite her better judgment, felt a sharp tug at her conscience. She knew she was often curt, rarely gracious. But she hoped she was not often entirely without manners, even when the person with whom she was conversing was fiercely disquieting. She was, too, smart enough to know that a deliberate insult to the person putting food on one's table was not among a woman's wiser choices.

"I do not dance, sir," she informed him, quite honestly, "but I thank you for"—he had *not* asked, she recalled, and before she could ponder that too deeply, continued—"for your good wishes and inquiries. Please, rest assured the work on your house is progressing well. I think you will be pleased."

Cate had never been one for toadying and wondered if she'd done it up a bit too brown. Well, there was nothing to be done about that now.

Tregaron said nothing for a few moments. Instead, he fixed his gaze on her face. Cate suddenly had a very good idea how a hen, even a scrawny one, felt in the presence of a fox. She felt a faint prickling that went from her toes to her cheeks, her nerves alight. And just as she began to imagine a balcony, nighttime, soft summer air, and a current of emotion . . . he spoke.

"I don't give a damn about the house, Miss Buchanan. But then, I imagine, neither do you, really. It's not your concern, after all. So"—he sketched a brief, perhaps mocking bow—"I bid you good evening once again."

In an instant he was gone, striding through the crowd, which moved away from him as he approached, then closed ranks behind his back. As more curious faces turned to Cate, more eyes scanned her from the towering top of her head to the tips of her not-small, well-worn slippers, she pressed herself back into her little corner and wondered if her fiercely thudding heart could be heard by all present.

Cate Buchanan, who prided herself on her iron core and

fearless front, was more than a bit unnerved by the Marquess of Tregaron. And she wasn't at all sure just why.

Her instinct now told her that it was time to depart. She would bid the Ladies Leverham and Hythe—both of whom had been all that was welcoming and charming—good night, collect her sister, and leave. It hardly mattered that they had arrived in Lady Leverham's carriage. She and Lucy would walk the few blocks home. It would not be seemly, perhaps, but it would be expedient.

Even as she took a half step away from the wall, Cate knew she would not be going anywhere just yet. Lucy, whom she could just see through a knot of young men, was having a marvelous time. She glowed, she flirted, her silvery laugh ringing out over her admirers. Heads turned; the crowd surrounding her thickened. By all appearances, Lucy Buchanan of Tarbet, daughter of nobody-in-particular, possessed of little more than her beautiful self, was on her way to becoming the belle of the ball, if perhaps not the toast of the Town.

Cate would sooner walk through fire than spoil her sister's evening by dragging her away from her brightest moment to date.

She feared Lucy would be disappointed soon enough. Gentlemen, even noblemen, payed attention to a pretty face or clever tongue. They flirted, offered their arms for picturesque strolls, and gave flowers. But they never married girls like Catherine and Lucy Buchanan. Not when their hemispheres were sprinkled with other young ladies whose pretty faces and clever tongues were delightfully accompanied by fortune and status.

Perhaps, Cate thought, if her sister could fall in love with an ordinary fellow, she would avoid the disappointment. But she knew Lucy, and knew Lucy had eyes for but two types of gentlemen—the Byronic poet and the lofty peer. The girl's daily perusal of the *Times* and the endless gossip pages would have made that evident, even if her regular rhapsodies over the merit of rhyme and entail made her sentiments perfectly obvious.

Every peer, with the exception of Lady Leverham's sweet if distant husband, had his eyes at a level that went right over even Cate's Maypole head. Every poet Cate had ever met had stars in his eyes and dust in his pockets. To be fair, she was fond enough of poets; her beloved father, after all, had been one, but they were a woefully unreliable lot as far as financial stability was concerned.

She was not fond of the peerage at all.

Tregaron, with his granite face and looming figure, was no different. Just because he had set her firm opinions wobbling a bit with his attention, with his perfectly civil words and whiskey-edged, goldmine-deep voice . . .

" 'Pon my word. Here's a face I hadn't thought to see in Town!"

Cate went still as stone. She did not have to turn, in fact she was loathe to do so, to identify the speaker. She knew that voice. She'd heard it often enough, sometimes soft as silk, sometimes harsh with mockery, sometimes when it had been too dark to see the handsome face that went with it. He was there—on her very first foray into Society. He was there and she shouldn't have come. She'd known that from the beginning, but Lucy . . .

Blood roaring in her ears, she turned slowly. Her limbs protested each inch, but she'd been discovered. He had found her, and there was nothing to do but face the consequences head-on.

There he was—lean, smooth, handsome, and fashionable, and so polished that, had he been a gem, he would have been blinding. Nothing had changed save perhaps the pattern of his cravat knot. He looked exactly the same.

And he was not looking at her at all.

The others were there, too, not ten feet away, grouped around a man Cate did not know, alternately thumping him on the back and peppering him with questions about his time on the Continent. Cate stood, frozen, for countless minutes, desperate to sit down but terrified to so much as twitch lest she be seen.

Then, just as she thought her knees might fail her, a new voice spoke, quietly, just beside her—cultured, pleasant, completely unfamiliar. "I say, Miss Buchanan, as we've not been properly introduced, you will probably think me the most impertinent fellow. But you look as though a bit of quiet wouldn't be unwelcome. With your permission, I will escort you to a private chamber."

She'd been too frozen to even notice someone approaching. The face, when Cate turned to look at it, matched the voice—attractive, friendly, and unfamiliar. She could not allow this man, a man she did not know, to take her away from the party. But, oh, it was so tempting.

"Julius Rome, ma'am. Your servant." He offered his arm. "My brother, he's Hythe, you know, would tell you I'm a trustworthy fellow, if something of a scapegrace. My mother would tell you I'm a veritable prince among men."

Again, against better judgment, but trusting her instincts—and heeding her desperation—Cate took his arm and allowed him to lead her on her jelly-weak legs, skirting the walls and keeping behind whatever blind was available, from the room.

Tregaron watched them until they were out the door, then resumed his conversation with Charles Vaer. He had never much cared for the man, who in middle age had settled into a stout pomposity, but Vaer had approached him in an almost friendly manner. The matter behind the manner, of course, was that Vaer had a daughter who, despite her ample beauty, respectable portion, and unimpeachable reputation, was still very much unmarried. If Vaer, who possessed the subtlety of an inebriated bull, were to be believed, darling Elspeth had been on the verge of understandings with both the Duke of Conovar and the Earl of Hythe—at different times, of course—before her place had been unscrupulously usurped by, respectively, an Irish-born upstart widow and a mannerless Scottish spinster.

Vaer had not been quite so obvious as to list all his daughter's charms to Tregaron as if he were a potential bidder on a horse. The man had not been far off, however. For his own part, Tregaron had not especially cared. He did not know either Conovar's wife or Hythe's. Vaer had pointed out his Elspeth, who was, in fact, lovely and surrounded by only the finest of Society. She very probably possessed a fair number of the attributes with which her fool of a sire credited her. Beyond that, the man's mention of a mannerless Scottish spinster had served quite effectively to turn most of Tregaron's attention right back to Catherine Buchanan.

He'd watched her from the corner of his eye as she did absolutely nothing at all. She'd stayed right where he had left her, wedged between wall and plant, attracting scant attention, but still as conspicuous as an armored Amazon at Almack's. She appeared neither happy nor discontent. She simply *was,* and Tregaron had been struck and somewhat horrified by how fully she was occupying his mind.

Now, in the wake of certain decidedly odd events, he listened to Vaer drone on while he waited with fast-rising impatience for Rome's return. It had been at least a quarter hour, probably more. When the younger man at last appeared, Tregaron excused himself to Vaer with strained politeness and followed Rome to a corner of the parlor.

"What in God's name took you so long?" he demanded. "You saw her to a quiet place?"

Rome, rather than taking offense or showing any of the curiosity most men would have, shrugged. "Not the quiet place I'd intended. I was all set to tuck her up in Sibyl's sitting room, but as soon as I got her into the hall, she scarpered. Barely stayed long enough to offer thanks and ask me to let Alfie Leverham know she was going before she made a dash for the door. She was halfway down Mount Street before I caught her."

It didn't surprise Tregaron to hear Catherine had bounded into the London night. He would have expected as much. In fact, he very nearly smiled at the image of Miss Buchanan striding through Mayfair on her stork-long legs, scattering the neighborhood's bantam residents as she went. "I take it you escorted her home."

Rome did draw himself up slightly then, as if to protest any hint he might not have instantly performed such a task. "I did, of course. Binney Street. Pokey little house, actually . . . Ah, well. She's a curious creature, your Miss Buchanan. Pale as a sheet, the whole time, but she chattered away about the weather as if we were at a sunny luncheon party. Curious, but somehow rather delightful."

Tregaron had noted Rome's use of the term *his* Miss Buchanan, noted too the *delightful,* but made no correction. For some reason, he didn't think it a good idea for the younger man to look for Catherine's delightful qualities. If, in fact, she possessed any.

"I don't suppose you'll tell me what sent her haring off into the night," Rome said conversationally.

"I am not certain, myself."

But he had seen her go pale, alarmingly so. And he had taken note of the clutch of gentlemen whose arrival had coincided with her pallor. Gramble, Reynolds, Fremont, and several men he had seen only from the rear. An idle, unappealing bunch, to be sure. He would not ordinarily have expected Catherine to have known any of them, but some instinct told him that she did indeed. Somehow. And had, despite being the least likely damsel in distress he could imagine, been badly in need of rescuing.

He'd imagined what her response would have been had he arrived at her side, ready, if tarnished, lance aloft. She would have said something cool and cutting at the very least, perhaps even trodden on his toes as she stalked off. So he had opted for an alternative, and the passing Julius Rome had served his purpose admirably.

"Thank you," he murmured now, grateful. "You're a good man, Rome."

Julius grinned. "Yes, well, there are a few of us left, aren't there?"

Tregaron assumed an answer was not required. He also assumed, perhaps with the optimism of idiocy, that there had been a dash of friendly support in the younger man's words. Of course that camaraderie might be nothing more than the result of Rome's natural, childlike optimism. No matter. One ally in London was more than the Marquess of Tregaron had had in eight years.

Chapter 5

"Honestly, Cate, I cannot believe you did not tell me!" Lucy swiped her lacy little parasol through the air for emphasis, nearly clipping her sister on the chin. "How could you have said nothing at all on the matter?"

Cate wearily handed a sheaf of ceiling designs, with their recent changes, to the waiting MacGoun, who promptly stomped off. The man was scowling, as usual, but Cate had a very good idea that it was Lucy's presence on the site that had his hackles up on this occasion. While the other workmen seemed to regard Lucy's calls as something akin to a heavenly visitation, the foreman found them a dismal nuisance.

Cate agreed. She loved her sister, but wished the girl would keep herself away from Hanover Square. She prattled, distracted the men to the point that a plasterer had, only minutes before, got his foot stuck in his bucket, and kept Cate from getting much of anything done. And now, on this visit, she was insisting on discussing matters Cate would just as soon not, all involving the Hythe fete of the night before. Thus far, she had prattled about Cate's untimely departure, the glory of the decorations, and the elegance of the attendees, most notably the gentlemen.

"How?" Lucy demanded again when Cate did not respond.

"It never occurred to me," was her nearly truthful reply. It earned her a hearty snort.

"The man is not so old as to be wholly unacceptable, not at all unpleasant to look at, rich as Croesus, and a *marquess,* and it did not *occur* to you to mention it to me?" Incredulous, provoked, but not truly angry, Lucy stomped one tiny foot, sending up a formidable cloud of plaster dust.

She fluttered a hand in front of her face. "Oh, why can you never work in *clean* places!"

That got a wry smile from Cate. "I always try, keeping you in mind, dearest, but I cannot seem to manage it, even for you. And as for Lord Tregaron, you knew perfectly well that he was a marquess and a wealthy one. Our opinions of acceptable ages vary so that I have long since given up trying to understand precisely where you place your limits, and I cannot say I find the man at all pleasant to look at."

That was not entirely true, perhaps, but when one lived among any number of half truths, one learned not to split hairs over one more or less.

She continued, "Beyond that, Lucy, he has a dismal character, and an even worse reputation."

"Mmm. Yes, I know he does"—her sister's eyes actually went a bit starry—"but he has such lovely shoulders. In such a stunning coat. I daresay it cost more than all my wardrobe and yours combined . . ."

"Ah, you actually admit the rags with which I adorn myself and hence torture you qualify as a wardrobe, then."

Lucy ignored her. "I found myself wishing he would ask me to dance last night. How exciting it would have been! Certainly he might have wished it, too, but sadly, did not take the opportunity."

"You were introduced?" Cate demanded, surprised.

"We were not. But Mr. Rome would have seen to it."

"Mr. Rome," Cate murmured, shuddering as she recalled certain events of the previous night, "is very much the perfect gentleman." She was more than grateful to him. Without his assistance, she might have been forced to face a far less pleasant prospect than Lord Tregaron's company.

"Yes, he is rather sweet, isn't he? He was ever so gallant to you, Catey, seeing you home when you took ill." Lucy had certainly accepted that half truth Cate had given her about her sudden departure from the Hythes'. "What a shame he isn't likely to ascend to the earldom. He might have done as a husband."

"For you or for me?" was Cate's wry query.

She got no answer. Lucy was wandering off, doing an airy circuit of the mostly bare and gutted drawing room. Only the floor remained intact, the intricate parquet waiting to be restored to lustrous glory. Lucy ran a gloved finger along the top, grimacing at the large smudge left on the pale doeskin. Then she did a pretty pirouette, causing one of the workmen who were stripping the damaged paper from the walls to drop his heavy scraper with a clang.

"Pale green," Lucy announced after a full scan of the room. "I would do it all in green. Silk on the walls, I think, brocade on the furniture. Yes, pale green and gilt. And the rest of that"—she waved vaguely at the remaining molding that connected walls to ceiling, searching for a word she'd heard a thousand times and would never, her sister knew, remember—"fungus has to go. It's far too plain."

Cate had every intention of seeing it replaced with something far plainer, a design without a ribbon or curlicue in it. She had also meant to go from the drawing room to the master bedchamber suite, where the ceilings required her perusal. She was changing her mind, however. Lucy's newfound interest in decoration was hardly subtle. The widgeon was envisioning herself elegantly ensconced in the drawing room, no doubt dressed to suit both the pale green-and-gilt decor and her new title of marchioness. Cate didn't particularly want to hear her ideas for the boudoir. There was already a profusion of fat plaster cherubs—which were not long for their places.

As she became more familiar with each inch of each room, Cate was having a more difficult time imagining Lord Tregaron living in this house. Too much of it spoke of female taste, and extravagant female taste at that, an extravagance that had been indulged and allowed to swell throughout the entire house. Rather like a storm, it had left its share of detritus behind: pink velvet drapes in the drawing room, gilt on every medallion and cornice, the never-ending supply of unattractive ceilings.

With the exception of the ravaged library, and Cate had not set foot inside that room since the first day, there was no indication that the saturnine marquess had ever inhabited the house at all.

Everywhere she turned, she encountered the ghost of the late Lady Tregaron. The marchioness's personal belongings had been cleared from the house, she'd noted, along with all of the marquess's with the exception of his books. The workmen had taken some furniture and a few bits and pieces to the attics. Cate had no idea if the rest of the removal had taken place recently, or all those years earlier, before the house was closed up and allowed to rot into its sad state. Either way, had Tregaron ever put his stamp on any of the rooms in which he had lived, it had been erased. Lady Tregaron's hand, however, was everywhere, spread thickly from floor to ceiling.

"Catherine!" Lucy's voice cut into Cate's musings.

"Hmm?"

"You have not heard a word I have said, have you?"

"Gilt," Cate said with a sigh. "Fungus."

Lucy snorted again. "I asked if the marquess could be expected to attend the Wardour fete."

"How in heaven's name am I supposed to know that? I am not his secretary, Lucy, nor do I have any insight whatsoever into London's social calendar. I had not even heard of the Wardour fete before now."

With that, she rolled the remainder of the papers she held into a tidy tube, tucked it under her arm, and stalked off toward the rear parlor, where the afternoon's work would center. Lucy, uncowed, skipped prettily to keep pace. Behind them, the sound of pounding hammers, thumping doors, and the cheerful whistling of the workmen combined for a lively symphony.

"Of course you have heard of it, Cate. We are to attend with Lady Leverham, Tuesday—"

"No."

"I beg your pardon?"

"No," Cate repeated. "You may attend. I will not." Images of the night before flashed through her mind, defying all the morning's effort to keep them at bay and bringing the same flush-to-chill sensation to her cheeks. "As you no longer have need of my presence, and as I have less than no interest in propping up more walls or swilling tepid refreshments, I will be suiting myself and staying home at night."

"But, Catey, the Wardours—"

"Do not know me from a Highland sheep. I am certain, however, they are acquainted with Lady Leverham, which is all the better for you."

"The theater," Lucy persisted.

Yes, Cate thought, she would be sorry to miss perhaps the only chance she would have to see Mr. Kean, Mr. Braham, and Mrs. Porter. To see *Pamela* and *School for Scandal. Macbeth,* which she so loved reading, each blood-soaked Scottish scene, but had never once seen performed. "All drivel," she snapped.

"Vauxhall Gardens."

Acrobats and fireworks and music under the stars. "Noisy and crowded, I'm sure."

"My chance to meet the marquess!"

This brought Cate to a quick halt in the rear parlor doorway. "Lucy . . ." Heeding the steady stream of workmen in the hall, Cate motioned her sister into the stripped, plaster-dusted room. "You must not develop an interest in the marquess."

"And why not, pray?"

"Because marquesses and their sort do not marry ladies of our sort." They offer other attachments, perhaps, Cate thought, but not marriage. "Like weds like in this little corner of the world."

"Oh, pooh. That is fustian. Both Lord Newling and Mr. Faringdon-Smythe have perfectly good titles, or will have someday"—Lucy held the edge of her periwinkle wrap against the stripped wall and squinted at it—"and both made very pretty proposals. Yes, this color might do nicely here."

"Who are—" Both Cate's jaw and tidy roll of designs dropped. She left the latter on the floor. *"Proposals?"*

"Proposals. I have had two thus far. And after but one night. Lady Leverham says she does not know of any other young lady who has had the same yet this Season."

"How splendid for you," Cate said tersely. "I assume you were in Lady Leverham's company when these proposals were made."

"I was not. I've only just come from her house. The gentlemen came to ours. Almost one atop the other. How very awkward it might have been had they arrived together. Offers of marriage ought not, I think, to be heard in multiples. They brought flowers as well. Very pretty. Orchids from Lord Newling . . . or were his the roses?"

Flowers. "And chaperons, perchance?"

"Oh, that. I wrapped Becky up in some shawls, sat her in the far corner of the parlor, and told the gentlemen she was my dear, deaf old Aunt Rebecca. Neither of them so much as looked her way once they'd done their bows."

"Lucy!"

"Well, what was I supposed to do? You are never home, and the uncles were nowhere to be found!"

That, Cate mused, was true enough. She was gone early, never at home until evening, and the uncles had chosen that very day to arrive before noon, hale and happy and actually ready to do a spot of work. In another place and time Cate would have heartily commended her sister for being resourceful. Turning the maid into old Aunt Rebecca had been inspired indeed.

"But, Lucy, still . . ."

"Have no fear. I declined both proposals. I am waiting for a far better prospect. Newling is a sweet fellow, but he cannot seem to finish a sentence without tripping all over his own tongue, and Mr. F-stroke-S has the most noisome mama. I should quite loathe having to share a table with her, let alone a house. I wonder, does Lord Tregaron have a mother? He must have done at some point, but perhaps not now. And of course, she need not live with him, or even dine . . ."

Feeling rather as if she had been buffeted by a stiff wind—not an unfamiliar sensation when dealing with Lucy—Cate wearily rubbed one hand over her brow. "I do not know if he has a mother, Lucy, but I do know he possesses a rather vile degree of arrogance, boorishness, and condescension that would make sharing a table with him something of a trial."

"So you do not like him." Lucy fixed her with angelic blue eyes.

"I do not."

Now the girl actually giggled. "Honestly, Catey. If I were to dismiss every person you do not like, my circle of acquaintances would not number above a half dozen."

Cate did not dislike most people. She wanted to tell her sister that, to shout that there was a world of difference between dislike and distrust. A world of difference.

Instead, she squared her shoulders and announced, "The man is rumored to have disposed of his wife. If nothing else strikes you as a reason to avoid his company, that must."

With that, she moved to retrieve the roll of designs from

the floor. It had rolled several feet away before uncurling. She bent, gathered the sheets, and was just straightening when a movement outside the door caught her attention. Slowly, her eyes rose past the grinning, tongue-lolling, foxy face of the yellow dog to plaster-dusted boots to breeches, waistcoat, and cravat. In the shadows of the hallway, she could not see much of the marquess's face, but she expected she would have recognized him in a pitch-black cave.

For his part, Tregaron could see every inch of Catherine, including her face. It had gone quickly from flushed to pale and now was set in dismayed lines that did nothing to improve her looks but spoke volumes. She'd been caught slighting his character and was both mortified and terrified that he would send her entire family packing.

As far as he could ascertain, from what he had heard, she had not said anything that did not possess at least a kernel of truth.

He made his decision in an instant. "Good afternoon, Miss Buchanan. I hope I am not intruding on a private conversation."

He saw her gingery brows snap together as his own gaze slid to the other young lady in the room. He assumed Catherine was confused, uncertain now whether he had, in fact, overheard her cutting comments. The other woman did not appear to be particularly confused. She appeared simply, staggeringly perfect—an angel, haloed by sunlight and dancing dust motes.

The angel, with all the subtlety and discretion possible under the circumstance, prodded Catherine with the tip of her lacy parasol. Catherine flinched, straightened, then cleared her throat. "G-good afternoon, my lord. I did not . . . you were not expected."

Tregaron expected she received another poke as she flinched again. "I trust your uncles will forgive the intrusion. I was nearby and thought I would stop in for a moment." He turned his attention to the other woman, with no subtlety whatsoever and waited.

"Ah, yes. Of course. Lord Tregaron, allow me to introduce you to my sister, Miss Lucy Buchanan. She is . . . we are paying a visit to our uncles."

"Already we possess like thoughts." His words and attention directed ahead of him, he strode forward and, when the angel promptly curtsied and offered her tiny hand, bowed over it. "It is a great pleasure to make your acquaintance, Miss Lucy."

Perhaps the girl did not possess her sister's innate, fierce vitality, but she certainly did not simper. And even if she had, a man might forgive any number of flaws in such a flawless package.

"The pleasure is mine, Lord Tregaron." Her voice was slightly higher pitched than Catherine's, completely missing that faintest of Scots lilts. Deliberately? Tregaron wondered. As artless as Lucy Buchanan appeared, he detected an amusing and not unappealing hint of the performer in her.

From the corner of his eye, Tregaron saw Catherine bending to pat Gryffydd. The little sod promptly rolled over onto his back, his stubby legs straight out, and offered his belly for rubbing.

The angelic Lucy breathed, "I have been admiring your home, my lord."

"Have you?" All he could see was dust and brutally bared rooms. A vast improvement as far as he was concerned. "I must confess I would not have recognized it."

There was a hole the size of a dinner platter in the middle of the wall. Through it, Tregaron could see the adjoining room, which, before its transformation to hovel, had been his wife's beloved dining room. Ah, how she had loved to entertain. There was a hole in that far wall, too, opening into the drawing room, where, he had noted, the pastoral fresco on the domed ceiling had been reduced to a few pastel splotches. The central, gauze-clad nymph, whose face had been that of his wife, painted by the besotted artist she had never actually paid, had been wiped away like so much spilled paint.

It had never occurred to him to leave any instructions whatsoever as to the disposition of the frescoes. It certainly did not matter now.

There was wood or marble missing from every floor, enough in the foyer that he would have gone tumbling into the abyss had not an odd little man with both grey skin and hair shouted out something unintelligible. It might have been a warning; it might have been a comment on the weather. Either way, it had caught Tregaron's attention, and he had not gone tip over tail.

The ghastly expensive wallpaper his wife had chosen was gone from the walls, only the odd strip here and there giving any hint of what had once been. Pieces of moldings and medallions were scattered over areas of the remaining floor. There was dust and dirt everywhere else.

Tregaron could only imagine what had been done to the upper floors.

"Lucy." Catherine's voice cut into his musings. "Perhaps you could go find the uncles. I am certain Lord Tregaron would like to speak to them."

And so he did, if only to commend them on a splendid job and tell them to keep on with the good work. Lucy, however, obviously did not think it such a good idea. Her delectable rosebud mouth turned down into a very pretty pout, and she tossed her glossy, titian head.

"Oh, Cate . . ."

Catherine said nothing. She must have spoken silent volumes, however, because a mere few seconds later, after charmingly excusing herself and promising to be back in the flutter of a cherub's wings, Miss Lucy glided from the room—leaving Tregaron alone with Catherine. *Cate,* he recalled her sister's use of the sobriquet. *Cate.* It suited her.

"Miss Buchanan," he began, even as she was saying, "Sir . . ." Both fell silent.

"Please." He gave her a brief nod.

She was garbed in yet another unattractive dress, he noted, yellow this time. It did nothing for her maypole form or unruly red-bronze hair, which had sprung free of a few of its pins. Nor did it speak well for whatever hand had designed it. It was ugly, unfashionable, and none too tidy. In it, Miss Buchanan rather resembled a gangly-limbed, wild-headed urchin.

At the moment, she was twisting pleats into the grime-streaked skirts even as she looked him steadily in the eye. "My lord, I fear I have been . . . most impolite. Last night, I . . . Well, I was rude, and feel I must apologize."

Had she opened her mouth and announced, "T'the divil wif you, guv," he would not have been terribly surprised. An apology, however, startled him. It wasn't that he thought Cate Buchanan ill-bred. He simply expected her, like Juno or Boudicca, or any of the woman warriors she brought to mind, to stand firm, right or wrong, and never give an inch of ground.

He was also certain that it had never once crossed Cate Buchanan's mind that she might have done more than merely insulted his aristocratic pride. That she had pricked at his emotions more.

Nor did she make any apology for having very recently stopped just short of calling him a vile, supercilious murderer. But then, he mused, a wise man took what was offered. And was patient in waiting to take the rest. Beyond that, and the realization startled him, standing as he was in a house he had grown to hate, with this woman's vitality striking him almost as forcefully as an open-handed slap, he was unable to feel his wife's presence at all.

"Think nothing of it," he replied gruffly.

"Oh, but I feel I must—"

"Enough!" He winced at the momentary loss of composure. "Please," he added as evenly as possible. "We will not speak further on the matter."

He could see Cate's confusion in her mobile features and couldn't help but wonder what she would say were he to tell her that he very likely felt as unsettled as she. She wouldn't believe him, probably. The villains of the gothic romances so popular these days were never unsettled.

Having no idea what to say, not a common occurrence in his life, he was relieved to hear the angel's dulcet voice in the hallway. It heralded the divine creature's reappearance, and Tregaron found himself thinking that a man could, without a doubt, get a great many months of pleasure simply watching Miss Lucy flutter in and out of rooms. Even with the salt of the earth rolling in her ethereal wake.

He saw her wobble as one of her uncles, the large one, patted her narrow back. "Good lass!" the man boomed, then, arm extended, tromped across the floor. It was rather like being approached by a walking oak tree. Gryffydd wisely scuttled out of the way. "Good day, my lord!"

Tregaron held his ground. "Buchanan," he greeted the fellow, not knowing whether it was Angus or Ambrose, and not particularly caring either way. He accepted the ham-sized fist, flinched when his shoulder nearly exited its socket, and glanced past the fellow to see the second architect hopping cheerfully in the background. "Sir."

Both, plaster-dusted and clearly in the midst of a day of hard work, appeared perfectly delighted to see him, as delighted as Miss Lucy. A far cry from the po-faced maypole who had, Tregaron noted, withdrawn to a corner of the room. There was something that did not fit with Cate and her family. Tregaron found himself surmising that she might well be the millstone about the collective, ebullient Buchanans' necks. He only hoped she did not dampen her uncles' obvious enthusiasm for taking apart and reforming his house.

He gave an inward shrug. "I am sorry to intrude, gentlemen—"

"Not a bit of it," the huge Buchanan announced magnanimously. " 'Tis your house, after all."

"Quite," Tregaron agreed, "but I did not want you to think—"

"Oh, we Buchanans never think," came from the little fellow. "Nothing worse for the client than us going about thinking too much."

"Ach, Angus, you daft twist of haggis. His lordship'll be wondering if we're to be sending his fine home tumbling into a pile of rubble."

Tregaron eyed the various holes in the walls and cleared his throat. "I, er . . . yes, well. I did say I wouldn't be skulking about, peering over your shoulders—"

"Skulk all you wish, m'lord."

"Peer away, though you'd be best to do the peering over me, as Ambrose's bloody great shoulders block the very sun."

"Aye, well, peer over Angus, then, but ask your questions of me. I'm your man for the talk . . ."

Cate wondered how on earth she was to stop the blathering before it took a turn from foolish to dangerous. As it happened, Gordie chose that very moment to come trotting into the room. MacGoun's second-in-command was a sight, dusted from head to foot in a grey powder that gave him a distinctly ghostly appearance. For his own part, he seemed as wholly unconcerned with his state as the uncles. Other than repeated swipes at his brow with the back of his hand, he appeared to be going about as if nothing were unusual. Which, Cate thought, was perfectly true.

What she did not consider was that Gordie might not see Lord Tregaron standing by the single window. He didn't.

"We've a problem, Miss Cate," he began, a familiar refrain. He didn't see her give a quick shake of her head, either. "The glass for the windows here—"

Cate coughed.

"Ah. Sorry, miss." Gordie took a hasty step backward. "I oughtn't to have come barging in like this. Not in my state. I've given you a snootful o' dust now, haven't I?"

"Gordie—"

"Nay, nay. My fault, miss. Here. I'll just open the window. As for the glass, 'tis late arriving . . ." He skidded to a halt halfway to the window, eyes wide in his plaster-pale face. "I . . . er . . ."

Cate took a quick glance around the room. Her uncles were suddenly as wide-eyed as Gordie and just as speechless. Lucy had her fingertips pressed to her lips. Tregaron was regarding the stammering Scot as if he'd bounded into the room sporting body paint rather than plaster dust and spouting Gaelic rather than perfectly understandable, if untimely, English. She did not think he would appreciate an introduction.

"Perhaps you ought to talk to *Uncle Angus* about the glass after Lord Tregaron has departed," she suggested. "We don't want him to have to listen to such mundane matters."

Gordie reached up to scratch his head, sending down a new torrent of dust. "I . . . er . . . aye, to be sure." He made a jerky bow. "Beggin' your pardon, m'lord. Sirs. Miss . . ." Spinning on his heel, he made a quick dash for the door.

"Stop!"

Tregaron's voice cracked like a whip. Gordie froze.

"My lord—" Cate began.

He stalked away from the window. "I believe I comprehend what is going on here."

Cate's fingers tightened in the worn muslin of her dress. She felt a tiny tear open. "You . . . you do?"

"Indeed." The face, so like marble, gave nothing away. "And I must say it is not well done of any of you."

"Oh . . . my lord, please . . ."

"I did say I would not be visiting. Perhaps I should have informed you of my change of plans. However, as has been mentioned, it is my house and I will come and go as I please."

"Of course, my lord, but . . ."

He shot her a stony glance. "I will not have you thinking you can duck and dodge around me."

Oh, we Buchanans don't think, flashed into Cate's mind. And now they would finally pay for it.

"I will not have you thinking I have absolutely no interest in what you are about here. I find myself curious and will not have you saving all discussions for times when I am not present. Is that clear? As it happens, I would like to hear about the glass." With that, he stalked to the middle of the room, where he stopped, facing the connecting wall. "And about this very interesting hole. Ventilation?" he demanded, his voice dry as sand.

Cate's heart, which had first threatened to stop entirely and had then raced at alarming speed, thudded back into some semblance of a normal rhythm.

"Ventilation? Not a bit of it," was Angus's jovial response. "We're to have the wall down entirely."

Ambrose rubbed his hands together and grinned. "The next as well. In fact, you've come at just the right time. We've been waiting all morning to get on with it."

True enough, Cate thought. They had arrived bright and early, urged into workmanly vigor by the promise of the day's activities. Only the combination of MacGoun's peppery command and Cate's foresighted hiding of certain tools had kept them from going at the demolition job like eager schoolboys.

Apparently Angus had found the massive hammers.

He retrieved a pair now from where he had propped them outside the door. One he jauntily swung as if it were nothing more substantial than a walking stick. The other he passed to a blank-faced marquess, who, to his credit, neither flinched nor dropped the thing onto his foot.

He propped the heavy head on the floor. "And this is meant to . . ."

"Go through the rest of this wall here," Uncle Angus

announced as if it were nothing more than common sense. The marquess's brows shot up into impressively high arcs.

Again, Cate debated stepping in, but Uncle Ambrose forestalled her. When he explained, " 'Tis a new innovation, this, running rooms together like a grand mole hole," she relaxed a mite.

It wasn't precisely how she would have opted to describe the concept, but at least Ambrose seemed to have the idea firmly in his head. She decided to let him go on with the explanations.

She regretted that decision not a minute later.

"Mole hole. I see." Tregaron nodded. "You mean to say that it will be one long room."

"Aye."

"From here all the way to the front of the house?"

"Ah . . ." Ambrose peered uncertainly through the hole to the one in the next room's far wall. "Er . . ." Waving her arms to get his attention, hoping she would not attract the marquess's as well, Cate nodded vigorously. "Aye!"

"Completely open one to the next?"

"I, er . . ." Ambrose shoved one hand into his already wild hair and twisted. Cate swept her arms inward and out like a mad orchestra conductor. When that didn't seem to work, she pointed at the room's entrance. "Door!" Ambrose bellowed. "Oh, aye. There will be sliding double doors joining the rooms. With the grand windows at this end and a . . . er . . ." Cate held one hand, palm in, in front of her face. "A mirror at that end. You leave the doors open during the day for . . . ah . . ." Cate rolled her eyes as she gestured to the window. "Light! Close 'em for privacy, warmth, and so on."

Cate had belatedly recalled that this particular alteration might not have been altogether clear in the drawings. And that the lack of clarity had perhaps been rather deliberate—in case the design had seemed too odd and been rejected by the marquess before he could see how very perfect it was for his house.

Tregaron, whose hammer handle had been waving beneath his fist like the tail of a bad-tempered cat, was utterly still now. Cate found herself holding her breath. The uncles were both staring at the marquess, rapt. Gordie, eyes wide, stood like a statue in the doorway. Even Lucy, who had been posing and fidgeting, hating not being the center of Tregaron's attention, was still now. Waiting.

"You are going to knock down my walls," he murmured. "All the way down." Then, after an agonizingly long pause, he actually smiled. It wasn't much of a smile, to be sure. More a quick baring of very nice teeth, Cate noticed. And she decided it was rather a nice smile for all its brevity. "What a marvelous idea. Yours, sirs?"

For an instant, Cate thought her uncles were going to take credit for the innovation. She realized almost immediately that the pause was due only to the fact that Ambrose had completely forgotten the name of the brilliant man who had actually created the concept.

"Repton," she said soundlessly. Ambrose blinked at her. *"Repton!"* she mouthed again.

"Reptile!" Ambrose shouted.

The marquess blinked.

"Repton," Cate said wearily, aloud this time. "You have been painting Cleopatra again, haven't you, Uncle. You have asps filling your head. Uncle Ambrose," she announced to Tregaron, "does marvelous classical studies in what little spare time he has away from here, my lord."

"Indeed? Perhaps you will allow me to commission a work from you, sir," Tregaron offered. Cate assumed he was being polite and that whatever table or canvas her uncle produced would go the way of most of his art—into the attics. Ambrose was grinning like a madman.

Angus was bouncing on the balls of his feet. "Have you the need for a sculpture or two, m'lord? Cate . . . er . . . *we've* thought it best to do away with the cherubs."

"Have you?" This time, Tregaron's flashing smile lasted a full second. Cate's pulse gave an odd shiver. "Fancy that. Well, Mr. Buchanan, if I am correct in assuming you sculpt, we shall discuss the matter at another time."

Angus joined his brother in beaming from ear to plaster-dusted ear. Then he shouted, "Go fetch us another hammer, Gordie! There's a good fellow. We're to take a wall down." As the younger man scuttled off, Angus turned back to Tregaron. "Well, off with the coat, lad! You'll get no decent work done with that thing on you."

If anyone had commanded the Marquess of Tregaron to disrobe since his infancy, Cate would have been very much surprised. She was fairly certain no one had *ever* pressed him into work. And by all appearances, he was going to both refuse and give Angus, who truly believed he was bestowing a gift upon the much younger man, something of a set-down. Tregaron's brow had furrowed dangerously, his mouth thinned.

"I do not think . . ." he began. Then, "If the ladies would be so kind . . ."

It took Cate a moment to realize he was very politely telling her and Lucy to remove their delicate sensibilities and female posteriors from the room so he could remove his coat. Her jaw dropped. He was going to do it. He was going to take off that obviously expensive coat and attack a plaster wall with the uncles.

She wanted to refuse, didn't want to leave him alone with Angus and Ambrose. Then Tregaron cleared his throat, fixed her with those fierce eyes and she knew she had no choice. "Come along, Lucy," she said, her reluctance even greater than her now leaden-footed sister. "We'll leave the gentlemen to it."

She might have been mistaken, but she thought she felt the marquess's eyes on her as she walked from the room. She certainly did not mistake the odd tingling that went running up and down her spine. Shaken nerves, she told herself. Only to be expected after that little drama.

Gordie met them in the hall, massive hammer in hand. "Watch them," Cate commanded. "Do not leave them alone with the marquess for a minute. I'll be in the drawing room if I am needed."

"Aye, miss." Gordie dragged his hand across his forehead in a familiar gesture. " 'Twas a close one, that."

"It was indeed."

Cate made her way down the hall on slightly unsteady legs. Lucy followed. "I thought I would quite die with the giggles back there, Catey, first when Gordie nearly spilled all and then when Uncle Ambrose—"

"Lucy." Cate gave her a quelling glare.

"Well, I did. It was ever so diverting." At her sister's hiss, Lucy shrugged. "You could tell him. Perhaps he would not mind."

Cate stopped in her tracks. "Perhaps he would not mind," she repeated. "Perhaps not. Perhaps, unlike any man I have ever met outside our family, he would not mind knowing that it was not two men responsible for the fate of his house, for every inch of the designs, but one woman. Me. Perhaps, upon learning that fact, he would not mind having been deceived. Perhaps, unlike the likely rest of the arrogant, dissolute bunch among which he moves, he would not send us packing home to Scotland or, more likely, tossed into gaol for fraud. Perhaps . . ."

Whether it was the concept of imprisonment or being sent back to Scotland, Cate did not know, but it certainly touched Lucy. "Oh, you mustn't tell him, then, that it's you who is Buchanan and Buchanan, Catey! You mustn't tell anyone! It will remain our family secret."

"Yes, our family secret."

The problem, of course, was that Cate had little faith in a Buchanan secret staying so. She was not a natural pessimist, but she'd gone too long, since she'd taken over the business with the Maybole estate to be precise, expecting several walls of secrets to come tumbling down on her head, on her family's heads. They'd had more than their fare share of reprieves.

She flinched as the first hammer thudded lustily into the wall behind her.

Chapter 6

Tregaron was convinced he had little bits of wall down the back of his trousers. How the stuff had made its way there defied explanation, but he was certain that there were very few inches of his skin that had not been dusted. And other than his face and hands, he had not been able to clean much of anything. He itched.

Several feet away, Gryffydd was stretched in utter contentment, belly on Lady Tregaron's plush parlor rug, legs pointing straight out in front and back in a position Tregaron had never seen managed by any canine but these little Welsh herders called *corgyn*. The animal was snoring lightly, happy as a stoat.

Tregaron's grandmother had refused to touch Gryffydd, insisting that not only was the beast's newly grey coat rather alarming to view, but that it would do untold damage to her clothing and furniture. Tregaron had done his best to dust the animal off, but only a bath would remove the detritus of the afternoon's interlude. Not wanting to disappoint his grandmother by forgoing their regular visit, he had opted to call on her first, stay only long enough to explain, then head back to the Albany and countless ewers of hot water. This scheme, like so many other, had promptly gone awry.

Lady Tregaron was having none of it. She'd rolled her eyes, clucked her tongue, and insisted that a maid spread a bath sheet over the chair before Tregaron sat. She had not, however, allowed him to make a hasty exit. She had also refused to have Gryffydd too close. And she'd complained with impressive lyricism when the *witless gudgeon of a girl,* as she'd phrased it, set a plate of ginger biscuits on the floor, rather than the table. Her grandson opted not to comment that such complaints were much better made promptly and to the offending party, rather than when the maid was long gone from the room and the plate had been summarily emptied by one delighted dog. He'd hidden his smile and held his tongue.

"Two walls?" the dowager demanded now, for the third time. "You?"

"I did not do it alone," her grandson informed her once more. "The Misters Buchanan did a great deal of the actual destroying."

Lady Tregaron sniffed. "Outlandish, I say. Architects and marquesses side by side, going at walls with hammers. In my day—"

"In your day, madam, you would have hefted a hammer and joined in."

A faint smile crossed the lady's lips. "Well. I might have done. Perhaps."

"It was rather alarmingly entertaining."

"Yes, I expect it was. And I suggest you remind yourself of that thought tomorrow when you feel as if someone has taken a hammer to *you*."

Tregaron smiled. "Ah, Grandmère, you wound me with your conviction that I am such a weak creature, a veritable soft custard."

"I think you no such thing, and you well know it. You are a fine specimen of a man, Colwin, if a rapidly aging one."

He felt too generally pleased with himself to argue over his age yet again, or to agree that yes, he quite probably would ache like the devil the following day. He'd had an absolutely marvelous time, hammering away at the walls, and did not care to sully the memory with logic.

It was time, he'd decided, to find some sort of physical activity. In Wales he had walked and ridden relentlessly, not having much else to do. But he would become soft in Town if he did not change his ways. He could walk and ride extensively here, too, he supposed, but it was all so stop-and-start in the London crowds that much of the healthy benefit was lost. Perhaps he would purchase a spot in one of the duelling or boxing clubs. If they would have him, of course.

"I must say, I am glad to see you becoming involved in something." His grandmother's voice cut into his musings, which had turned just grim enough to spoil the pleasant glow left from his entertaining and strenuous attack on the wall. "So, tell me about these Buchanans. Three brothers, you said?"

"Two. And two nieces."

Tea arrived then. It had amused Tregaron that his dog's comfort had been seen to before his own, but he did not begrudge Gryffydd the attention. He was, too, so pleased at the prospect of a cup of tea that it hardly signified that he'd had to wait. He was convinced there was a coating of plaster dust on every inner surface as well as outer, most notably his throat. Gordie, the funny little Scot with the apparent nervous condition, had provided ale, but it had only temporarily washed away the grit. It had served much better to further flame the Buchanan brothers' enthusiasm for the whole destructive process.

His grandmother eyed him shrewdly as she poured the tea. "Nieces?"

"Mmm." The first swallow was heaven. "The Misses Catherine and Lucy Buchanan."

"And they are to be found in your house every day?"

"Oh, I think not." Tregaron eyed the sugar-dusted tarts and decided against taking one. It looked altogether too dry for his taste. "I believe they drop in every so often to visit their uncles. I imagine there cannot be a great deal of daily entertainment available to two country ladies of moderate birth and limited means."

"Poor, are they? And not in the least pretty, I daresay. Scotswomen can be so terribly reminiscent of small rodents."

Englishwomen, in Tregaron's opinion, were just as likely to be reminiscent of large equines.

"As it happens, the younger Miss Buchanan is possessed of very good looks." An understatement, to be sure, but Tregaron did not care for the look in his grandmother's eyes. His going into raptures over the fair Lucy's glories would not be wise. "Someone contrived to get the pair of them invited to the Hythe fete. I wager the girl will find herself married to some well-heeled young buck by the end of the Season."

Apparently reassured that her grandson would not be shackling himself to a young lady of beauty but little other merit—and Scottish to boot—Lady Tregaron queried, "And the elder?"

"Catherine. She is . . ."

He was not particularly surprised, but was displeased nonetheless, to find he was at a loss for words with which to describe Cate. He could picture her well enough, those endless limbs, sparking eyes, and masses of wayward hair. What he could not seem to do was get a firm grip on her character.

"Catherine Buchanan is most certainly not a beauty."

"Ah, well, a sweet and clever girl, then, I should imagine. Plain creatures with beautiful sisters usually are."

Tregaron gave a bark of laughter that startled him as much as it did his grandmother and the sleeping dog. "Cate? Clever, yes. Sweet? Good Lord, what a concept. She is as sweet as a green lemon."

She was tart, indeed, sometimes positively sour, but to be fair he had to concede that she was also intelligent, vibrant, and anything but dull. A man was never bored in Cate's presence.

"I do not believe I have ever met a young lady quite like the elder Miss Buchanan."

There was a sharp *snick* as his grandmother's teacup met with its saucer. "You admire her."

Did he? Tregaron rubbed thoughtfully at one knee, where he'd somehow managed to make a hole in the fine wool of his new breeches. "Perhaps. As one admires a tenacious pit bulldog or the sheer presumption of a summer rainstorm. I should not choose Miss Buchanan as a friend, I think."

"Hmph," was his grandmother's inscrutable response.

It occurred to Tregaron that Cate would most certainly not choose him as a friend, either. In fact, he had caught the better part of her opinion of him in general, as a suitor to her sister in particular.

Possesses a rather vile degree of arrogance, boorishness, and condescension, she'd said of him. *Rumored to have disposed of his wife.*

He wasn't sure which statement was worse.

Nor did he understand why he cared. He had lived for so long now with his grim reputation. And once he had ascertained that there would be no trial, that his peers, much as they might want to, would not openly accuse him, he had stopped even contemplating asserting his innocence. He wasn't actually innocent, and the unpleasant truth would not serve much of a purpose at all.

He'd found that not caring much was convenient, if not always comfortable. Better to be feared than loved, old Machiavelli had told his prince. Well, that made perfectly good sense to one marquess. He simply found being feared and reviled something of a bore. Merely a bore.

He yawned. "So, am I invited for dinner tonight?"

"As a matter of fact," Lady Tregaron replied, "Georgiana Otley has organized an impromptu dinner party and has requested my presence. I would so like to attend, but you know how I cannot abide the London streets at night. Always so crowded, and heaven only knows what sort of ruffian one might encounter lurking about, ready to dive through one's carriage window."

Danger of ruffians or not, the dowager did not often venture out at night. Truth be told, she limited her day excursions as well, citing the terrible crowds and undesirable persons treading upon one's toes and leering at one's jewelry. Her grandson had always thought the inconvenience more pertinent to the matter than possible robbery. True, she did adorn herself with more jewels than the average queen, but she also did not set foot outside the house without her filigreed, primed, perfectly deadly little pistol. Which she quite enjoyed possessing.

Tregaron knew Lady Otley was one of his grandmother's oldest friends. They had made their own bows in London more than fifty years before, made their highly approved marriages, made their moves to distant estates in Derbyshire and Wales. Tregaron was aware, too, that they saw each other rarely, that each occasion was precious and too short.

He also knew that Lady Otley's son was Charles Vaer. Meaning Miss Elspeth Vaer would almost certainly be present, coiffed and costumed and glossed, fully prepared for the perusal of a marriage-minded, if poorly regarded, marquess. Tregaron thought he could take on another set of walls with relative ease. He was not certain he possessed the requisite stamina to endure the attentions of the collective Vaers.

"Fine," he announced, knowing he could no more disappoint his grandmother than fly to Hanover Square. "I will be more than happy to escort you to the Otleys' this evening."

Lady Tregaron clapped her hands in delight. "Splendid. I am so pleased. You are a good boy, Colwin. And"—she leaned forward in her seat, eyes alight—"you were very nearly convincing enough to make me believe you wouldn't rather be walking shoeless over a path of bent nails."

"Given that pair of options," he returned with no small amount of irony, "I daresay I am safe in asserting my social merit. I would certainly choose the Otley dinner."

"How very upright of you, Colwin."

"Yes," he drawled, shifting in the diminutive chair to dislodge some of the persistent plaster particles within his clothing, "Isn't it just?"

Several minutes of companionable silence elapsed. Then, "Colwin."

"Yes, madam?"

"Your beast is scratching."

True enough. Gryffydd was having an enthusiastic scratch at a spot behind his dusty ear. His almost-human grin showed how very much he was enjoying the experience. There were times, Tregaron mused, that one could do far worse than to be a dog.

"Colwin."

"Yes, madam?"

"You are scratching, too."

Tregaron removed his hand from the small of his back and tried to ignore his grandmother's highly disapproving stare. This, apparently, was one of the times when there was much to be said for being canine.

Cate was debating hiring a rat terrier, if one could do such a thing in London. In Tarbet, there was always one about, easily borrowed. The postmaster had Billy, the elderly Misses MacDuff had Marigold and Pansy, the blacksmith had Magnus. True, Cate wasn't absolutely certain there was a rodent population still living in the house's walls—the daily pounding being enough to send even the hardiest creature scuttling for quieter climes—but she'd heard enough suspicious scufflings during the rare quiet moments to make her wary.

It was one of those quiet moments now. Lucy had collected "Auntie Rebecca" from the lower foyer hours past and had decamped for home; the uncles had disappeared as soon as the second wall was down; and the workmen had left for the day. Cate had emptied the house, sending off her usual escorts by telling Gordie that MacGoun would be seeing her home, telling MacGoun that Gordie would.

She was seated inelegantly on the salon floor just inside the doorway, her back propped against the wall, shoes off and legs in a comfortable sprawl. Her tea had long since gone cold and bitter in its jar, but it was heaven to her tongue. A day full of dust made for a very parched mouth indeed. So did a day full of jangled nerves.

She'd thought the marquess would never leave. In fact, after he'd gleefully joined her uncles in demolishing a sizeable portion of his home, she had half expected him to ask MacGoun to add him to the daily crew list.

It had been nerve-wracking, indeed, lurking about the periphery, trying to remain unseen while not missing any of the action—or interaction between Tregaron and the uncles. Nerve-wracking, exhausting, and a waste of too many hours that would have been far better spent at any number of activities.

It had also been eye-opening. The marquess had become a different creature during that time in which he had wielded the hammer. His face had lost that dramatic stoniness, taking on instead a satisfied concentration when he was working and a very nearly genial series of expressions during the rest breaks. He had joined her uncles in inconsequential banter. He had shared the crew's inexpensive ale.

He'd displayed a rather appealing, sweat-dampened, linen-covered expanse of arm, shoulder, and torso.

Cate had tried not to notice, had commented to herself that any man who could hammer away at a wall with such force and satisfaction was one who might very well take satisfaction in forcefully damaging other things. But there hadn't really been violence in his movements. There had been an earthy resoluteness and an aristocratic grace.

He had won over her uncles in a heartbeat. Lucy had done all but swoon into his well-sculpted arms. Of course,

Cate reminded herself now, neither uncles nor sister had ever been the land's best judge of character. An annoying little inner voice promptly reminded her that she herself had had her notable lapses in that area. Gordie had ended the day wholly impressed with the marquess's hard work. Even MacGoun had grunted his approval.

For a reputed murderer who'd been cold-shouldered by many of his peers for nearly a decade, Tregaron had made quick work of becoming a grand fellow in the eyes of the Hanover Square Scottish contingent.

Having forgotten all about the possible Hanover Square rat contingent, Cate nearly leapt from her skin when something furry brushed against her hand. Only her determined self-control, honed by a life among devil-may-care loved ones, kept her from leaping all the way to Windsor when a wet black nose poked at her chin.

It took her a moment to identify the dusty creature with its paws propped on her lap as Lord Tregaron's dog. By that time, the animal had taken several enthusiastic swipes at her chin with his tongue and was grinning up at her with delight.

For some odd reason, she felt compelled to commend him for having scared ten years off her life, climbed into her lap uninvited, and thoroughly wetted her face. "What a marvelous fellow you are," she said as she scratched behind the large, batlike ears. The dog, lacking a tail, wriggled his bottom and grunted. "Yes, you are."

"Gryffydd!"

Woman and dog both turned to face the door. Neither got up. Tregaron stood there, looking, Cate thought, much as he had when he'd departed some two hours earlier. He was still wearing the same clothing, was still liberally coated with plaster dust. The difference was that he did not appear quite as gratified as he had upon his departure. The granite mask was back, with all its immutable planes and angles.

"Gryffydd," he repeated, his voice managing to drop a seemingly impossible level lower than usual. The dog removed himself from Cate's lap. He did not, however, appear alarmed or cowed. He was simply obeying. "I apologize, Miss Buchanan. He can be mannerless at times."

"I . . . I do not mind." And she didn't. The dog was as

appealing as his— She shook her head quickly. "I did not expect to see you again today, my lord."

Realizing she was at more than one disadvantage, seated as she was, she shoved her feet into her shoes and quickly if not especially gracefully clambered to her feet. Tregaron offered a hand, which she politely refused.

"I had not expected to return," he said once she stood facing him, "but I seem to have left my stick behind and wished to collect it before the evening."

Cate had not seen a walking stick, but she was more than happy to go in search of it. The sooner the marquess left again, no doubt for some expensive if not necessarily respectable entertainment, the sooner she could collect her scattered self and go home to her family for a predictable if not restful night. "If you would wait here, my lord, I will go—"

"Please, do not concern yourself. I will—"

They were both standing in the doorway now, stuck, shoulder to shoulder, and had Cate not suddenly felt rather breathless, she could have laughed at the farcical squeeze. Tregaron inclined his head and waved a hand toward the hall. Cate assumed there was little humor to be found in this man. Otherwise she might have thought the flash in his eyes had been one of amusement.

"After you," he murmured. With nothing else to do but go, Cate did, leading the way toward the rear room, where the demolition had begun earlier that afternoon.

She felt a bump against her ankle as she went, then another. Glancing down, she saw Gryffydd push at her again with his nose. She stopped. The dog stopped. Behind them, Tregaron stopped. When the dog merely grinned up at her, Cate, feeling foolish, resumed walking again.

She had gone no more than three steps before Gryffydd was at it again, nudging her almost as if he wanted her to turn and walk into the wall. She stopped. The dog stopped. Tregaron stopped. And sighed. "Miss Buchanan?"

She pointed downward. "He was pushing me." Feeling even more foolish now that she had tattled on a poor, dumb animal, she bit her lip.

To her great surprise, the marquess smiled. "He was herding you,."

"I beg your pardon?"

"Herding. It's what *ci-llathed* are bred to do."

"Ci . . ." Cate repeated, her tongue tangling on what was obviously a Welsh word.

"Yard-long dogs." At her raised brows, Tregaron smiled again, that fast vanishing, startling flash of teeth. "An ancient Welsh yard, I've always assumed. A short one. Gryffydd was trying to herd you toward a place likely to hold food, and away from the house. He doesn't much care for the place."

Neither, Cate thought, did Tregaron. Bad memories? Or too many happy ones?

"Ci—" she tried again, deciding a try at tongue-twisting, mind-bending, impossible Welsh was far safer than pondering this man's inner thoughts. And far less complicated.

"Also known as a corgi. Simpler on the English-speaking tongue."

The door to the drawing room was open. As they entered, Cate took in the huge, open area that had not so long ago been three separate rooms. She darted a glance at Tregaron, hoping with all she was that he could see how wonderful it would be when completed. He'd been agreeable enough about the idea, had certainly been a full participant in the downfall on the walls. But now, damage done, it might well look very odd.

He looked wholly disinterested.

"Light," she blurted. "Space." Then, cursing this sudden stammering over concepts she knew and liked so well, she continued, "Mr. Repton's design calls for a conservatory at one end and a large mirror at the other. We . . . my uncles have ordered large panes of glass for the rear of the house—"

"The glass that is late in arriving, I assume."

Cate winced but said nothing. Better for Tregaron to think her ignorant of the matter than for her to be explaining that the glass was not merely late, but not coming at all. A problem with the factory, MacGoun had snarled. Knowing the foreman, trusting him, Cate had not pressed. They would simply have to take their business elsewhere, hope little or no money would be lost in the transaction, and pray the new glass would arrive before her overzealous uncles had taken it upon themselves to create the necessary space in the rear wall.

Needing to get away from the subject of glass, Cate announced, "There will be large mirrors . . ." *Glass* mirrors of course. She gave an inward sigh. ". . . between the drawing room windows. When the sliding doors are open, you will have both real light and space and illusional. It will be glorious."

Tregaron gave a noncommittal grunt. Cate followed him this time as he stalked into the dining room through the massive opening he had helped create. "That," he muttered, gesturing to the bare space around the fireplace, "was a perfectly decent mantel not five hours ago."

"It was *scagliola,*" Cate said immediately.

"Heavens," came the dry retort, "not *scagliola,* certainly!"

"Plaster and marble chips," she explained, ignoring the sarcasm, "used to make fake marble. The mantel was chipping. This house deserves better."

"Mahogany?"

"W—my uncles have chosen colored marble. Green, from Ireland. Wood warps."

Tregaron propped one shoulder in the place where the chipping, fake marble used to reside and regarded her through dark and unreadable eyes. "You are very knowledgeable, Miss Buchanan. Forgive me in advance, for I mean no offense when I say surprisingly so."

Cate bit her lip. How easy it would be to say too much. "I have spent my life among architects," she said, her eyes fixed on the fraying piping at one cuff as she worried at it with the fingers of her other hand. "Some of it was bound to slip into my head over the years."

"You make yourself sound very simple and very old."

"I am six-and-twenty," she retorted, instantly embarrassed to have given any personal information at all.

"Hardly an aged crone."

"Perhaps. But hardly in the first blush, either." She resolutely straightened her shoulders and lifted her chin. Truth be told, she'd never had much of a blush, first or otherwise. "Shall we look for that walking stick now, my lord? I would not want to detain you from your evening's pursuits."

Tregaron trailed her through the second space, which had once been a wall, with some regret. The Scots spinster was back, thin-lipped, dry, brusque. Moments before, Cate's face had been animated, almost pretty as she talked about plans for his house. For those few minutes, they had been easy together. He sighed.

As expected, his stick was propped in the corner of what had been the breakfast room. He had no idea for what purpose the Buchanans intended the chamber. Ultimately, it would be decided by the next marchioness. The last one had been a glorious sight in the morning light, all glistening golden hair and glowing skin. She had never failed to dazzle him.

There would be even more light, more windows, according to the Buchanans. Tregaron tilted his head and tried to imagine sunlight falling on old crystal and a new collection of glossy curls.

"It truly will be wonderful when completed."

Tregaron blinked and turned to face Cate. She was hovering in the doorway, dust dulling her wild hair, hands clasped tightly at her waist.

"Truly," she repeated, and Tregaron realized she was agonizing over his opinions on her uncles' work. For the first time, he wondered about Cate's role in the family. He'd thought of her as a damper on the other Buchanans' high spirits. Perhaps the truth was that she was the voice, albeit dour, of reason and practical matters.

"Don't fret," he replied tersely. "Short of knocking down the outer walls and painting everything inside purple, I cannot imagine there is anything your uncles could do that would bother me overmuch." When Cate's eyes—smoky blue now, he noticed, in the early evening light—widened, he demanded, "What now?"

"Well"—her hands were clenched tightly enough that Tregaron could see white at her knuckles—"w . . . they actually will be knocking down this exterior wall. Part anyway. For the bigger windows."

Images of Angus and Ambrose Buchanan going at a supporting wall with their hammers flashed before Tregaron's eyes. He felt his jaw shift.

"Each section six panes over six," Cate announced, the words tumbling over the words. Tregaron closed his eyes. "They'll go all the way to the floor, with narrow, amber glass panels at the border to create gold light . . . My lord . . . ?"

He'd just had a very good image of the Buchanan brothers grinning out at passing Mayfair traffic as they peered through a massive hole they'd made in the *front* wall. It was too much. Unable to help himself, Tregaron chuckled. It was a rusty sound, even to his ears, a truly amused chuckle. God help him, before long he'd be laughing.

Cate was staring at him as if he'd sprouted horns.

With some effort, he composed himself. "Ah, Cate," he murmured, completely forgetting the cool propriety that was so much a part of him now, "I am overwhelmed. Tell your uncles to have at it. I honestly couldn't care less."

She merely stood gaping at him, and for the first time during the encounter, Tregaron realized she really was a woeful mess top to bottom. Her hair had all but vanquished the last pin, springing outward from her head like an overgrown autumn garland. Her dress was a bit shabby, and far dirtier than it had been earlier, bearing a veritable plethora of stains, many of which he did not think he could identify. There was soot on her nose, flecks of plaster on her hands, and what appeared to be mud up to her ankles.

She looked rather as if she had been dragged backward through a hunt course. She made him look nearly tidy.

"Have you been here all day, Cate?"

There was a long pause, then she nodded. "Yes."

"For God's sake, why?"

"I . . . ah, I wanted to watch the walls come down. It seemed a most . . . diverting exercise . . ."

"Rubbish." Tregaron saw her flinch. "You were here to make certain nothing disastrous happened. Yes, I believe I am finally beginning to understand the situation."

He couldn't decide whether she actually paled, or if it was merely the play of light on her plaster-dusted face. He went on, "You know a great deal about your uncles' work. In fact, I expect you do a bit of it. Well, of the supervising, anyway. Yes, Cate, I have come to the conclusion that your uncles are very fine architects indeed, but rather poor organizers. Hardly surprising, really. The ones who can do the brilliant designs often falter at the more practical aspects."

He gave her an approving nod. "You see to the simpler matters, do you not? I imagine my appearance here today threw everything out of balance."

Later, when thinking on the matter, he would have to

conclude that it had been no more than his imagination. In the moment, however, he was convinced Cate turned into an entirely different woman right before his eyes. Her rigid spine, rather than making her appear more the flagpole than ever, gave her a fully regal posture. Above her lifted chin, the light caught the bold angles of her cheekbones and glinted in her coppery hair, a bronze bust of some mythic warrior queen. And when those wide lips parted, Tregaron half expected a flow of imperious Latin to spring forth.

"So I assume we are not to expect you at the house tomorrow, my lord?"

Not Latin, but imperious enough, and more than clear. "No," he replied, knowing—and not bothering to dispel the conviction—that he was the trespasser at that moment, the visitor in the house. "Not tomorrow."

She nodded. "Good night, then, my lord. You will lock up behind yourself?" With that, she spun on her heel and hastened from the room. Her footsteps sounded first in the hall and then on the uncarpeted stairs.

It belatedly occurred to Tregaron that he had neither heard not seen anyone else in the house. He stalked through the open rooms to the front windows and peered down into the street. Cate had just descended the last stair and was hurrying away from the house, her long stride carrying her quickly away through Mayfair. Quite alone.

Tregaron shook his head and grunted, wondering where the woman drew the line for proper deportment—if she drew it. He was just about to quit the window when he saw Cate skid to a halt. What he saw then made his fist clench painfully over the hard, carved head of his walking stick.

Chapter 7

"'Pon my word. Here's a face I hadn't thought to see again!"

Cate heard a rushing, like fast-moving water, in her ears, and for an endless moment actually thought she might swoon. But she was not a swooner, had never succumbed to the vapors in her life. The moment passed.

Willing her jaw not to tremble, she fixed her gaze on the middle of the three men in front of her. "Nor I yours, Lord Fremont," she managed through stiff lips. She nodded coldly at the other two. "Mr. Gramble. Mr. St. Clair-Wright."

Fremont, as she'd noted at the Hythes', had not changed. He was still very handsome, as long as one did not look too closely into the pale green eyes. His blond hair was still abundant and deliberately touseled, his tall frame draped in the most fashionable clothing someone else's money could purchase. Taking in the plush silk waistcoat, glossy pantaloons, and perfectly tailored superfine coat, Cate wondered who was footing the baron's bills these days. When they'd met, it had been Lady Maybole.

"Ah, fie on my memory," he was drawling now. "I'd remembered the fire, Catey, but fully forgotten the ice."

His companions chuckled. Cate stiffened, but held her tongue. She hoped her gaze was icy indeed as it swept over two of the other men who had made those last weeks at the Maybole estate so memorable—and so very hard.

Lucius Gramble had not weathered the three years as smoothly as Fremont. He possessed the money his friend did not, but had never possessed any of the appeal, no matter how deceptive Fremont's appeal might be. Even under the foolishly top-heavy hat, Cate could see that Gramble's receding brown hair had thinned further, bringing his unprepossessing features—close-set eyes, small, soft mouth—into prominence. And while the fact that Fremont padded both shoulders and thighs was known only to a select few, Gramble could never hide his use of cotton batting and horsehair.

Cate had disliked him on sight. He had known that, and never forgotten.

Edgar St. Clair-Wright was, in retrospect, the best of the bunch. Not that that was saying much. While the others had ultimately been deliberately, cleverly cruel, he had simply been lazy, selfish, and stupid. Where other young ladies had seen the dark eyes beneath the shock of midnight hair as slumbrous and poetic, Cate had eventually seen the sort of dull disinterest one usually found in cows and overfed hounds.

Several men were missing from the unwelcome little tableau: Freddie Fortescue, Charles Reynolds, Beau Graham. Cate assumed they could not be so very far away. Fremont's set always moved together. Together, in Scotland, they had appeared dashing, dramatic, blessed with the sort of heavy-lidded ennui that seemed never to fail to challenge the female heart. Apart, Cate realized now, they were as appealing and interesting as a heap of coal.

Ah, the clarity of hindsight . . . the ever-frank inner voice taunted her. *How much of your own stupidity can you ignore, Catherine?*

"You're looking . . . much the same," Gramble announced, his rodent eyes skimming from the tip of the formidable half boots she wore when working to the top of her dusty, disorderly head. His companions chuckled, no doubt remembering how easily she had once taken veiled insults as compliments. "You certainly haven't lost your . . . er . . . impressive stature."

Holding herself stiffly, she murmured, "Not everyone is fortunate in the passage of time, Mr. Gramble. It leaves some persons with rather less than what they once possessed."

His quick, then quickly stilled reach toward his hairline was some balm to her pride, weak and several years late though it might be. When St. Clair-Wright bluntly offered, "Don't recall you being quite such a Long Meg," she refrained from commenting that he'd favored much higher heels on his shoes when they'd last met. Mocking the short and pinheaded had never been a choice activity of hers.

Nothing had kept the lot of them from making a mockery of one naive young woman. "I do not recall much at all of you, sir," she lied, and felt slightly better for it.

Then she gasped as one of Fremont's gloved hands suddenly shot out to circle her wrist. Had she been prepared, she could have resisted. But off-balance as she already was, it took only the slightest tug for him to have her standing nearly up against his chest. To anyone watching, she would appear willing, even eager. He was a master at that, at the illusion of affection while his eyes glittered and his hands squeezed too hard.

"Don't tell me you've forgotten *me,* Catey." He actually sounded amused. "Not after we were such . . . good friends. Why, I do not think I could bear it if you did not have the same memories I have of our time together."

Not for the first time, Cate wondered if there were no end to his callousness. Apparently it was not enough that he'd bruised her, made a fool of her, very nearly ruined her. He needed her to remember the humiliation of it all, beginning to sad, sorry end.

She knew why. He had spent those weeks amusing himself by pursuing her, a woman who had not instantly fallen at his feet, eventually capturing her attention and at least a piece of her heart with his pretty words and discreet embraces. When it had all gone wrong, when she'd learned how he'd toyed with her to entertain himself and his wretched friends, she had struck back, albeit weakly. She'd ignored him in those final days, refused to acknowledge him at all. And that was something Lord Fremont could not abide. Now he was going to make her hurt again. She wondered just how far he would go.

"I am afraid I haven't time to stand and reminisce," she managed between clenched teeth, trying to pull her arm free. "I am too late as it is. Good-bye, sir."

He did not release her. Instead, he rubbed his thumb in an intimate little circle over the inside of her wrist. His hands were gloved. Hers were bare. She suppressed the unpleasant shudder and stood firm, face deliberately blank. One of his pale brows lifted, and he smiled. Cate did not think it was in admiration.

"So cold, Catey. And so formal. Don't you remember—you used to call me Raphael so sweetly."

So she had. Raphael, her golden angel. How soft if had sounded on his lips when he had begged her to use it, to be so familiar as to use his Christian name. Of course she had.

His name, as she had learned much later, was Gerard.

"Good-bye," she repeated, not bothering to call him anything at all, and tugged harder with her arm.

"Tsk, Catey. You insult me. As it appears you are alone, you must allow me to escort you home. What sort of gentleman would I be to do otherwise?"

His companions, to whom the question had glibly been addressed, grinned and replied, "No gentleman at all," and "None, sir!"

"Come now, my dear. Do not deprive me of the opportunity to play the gallant. And to have a bit of a coze. You will tell me what you are doing here in Town; we will relive our halcyon days."

Cate would sooner lead a pack of slavering wolves to her door than this trio. However, despite whatever horsehair was packed discreetly into Fremont's coat, his grip was impressively strong. It tightened now. Cate's mind whirled, searching for any escape.

"As it happens, Fremont, the lady is not alone."

No one had heard Tregaron's approach. But there he was, tall and austere in the late afternoon light. Even the dusting of plaster he wore could not dull the aura of power and, yes, danger that he wore as other men wore greatcoats, layer upon complicated layer making up a dramatic whole.

Only minutes before, though it seemed a lifetime, he had made her feel as insignificant as the lowest drudge. Now, suddenly she was Andromeda, facing the sea serpent, and Perseus was about to unchain her from her rock. Then again, she thought somewhat giddily, not certain if she had imagined the peculiar, undefinable flash in his amber eyes, there was something of the leviathan in him, the dragon . . .

"Gentlemen," came his clipped greeting. "Cousin."

Cousin? Cate's jaw dropped at St. Clair-Wright's mumbled, "Tregaron." She would have found a blood connection between Prinny and the Emperor of China less surprising.

"I had heard you were in Town," Edgar muttered, his gaze fixed on his cousin's boots. "I was certain the reports were mistaken."

"Yes, well, such is the problem of relying upon gossip for news of close family members," was the cool reply. "One can never be certain what is true." Then, to Cate, the marquess said, "Forgive me for lagging, Miss Buchanan. Gryffydd seems to have gotten it into his head that there is vermin about. Shall we continue on our way now?"

He stepped forward, elbow crooked. Of course she could not take his arm until Fremont released hers. He would know that. And his eyes were fixed on the other man's face. The challenge there was so subtle that most would have missed it. But Cate knew that Fremont, for all his unfortunate characteristics, was not stupid. What she didn't know was whether he was possessed of more cowardice or arrogant bravado.

His response didn't give her an answer. He *did* let go. Cate rubbed her wrist with her other hand to restore feeling in it. Fremont inclined his fair head in Tregaron's direction. "I was not aware our Catherine was in your . . . company, sir. One must always be concerned for the ladies in this Town. There are so many villainous characters about. And altogether too often, one cannot detect them from their respectable counterparts."

"Amazing, is it not?" Tregaron drawled. "London used to be such a comfortable place to be a villain. No one ever mistook one for a gentleman."

His elbow brushed against Cate's. It wasn't much of a nudge, certainly not on a par with his dog's habitual herding prods, but it got Cate moving. Chin up, jaw set, she took his arm. It was warm and so very solid beneath her hand. "I am ready, my lord."

"Splendid. Gentlemen." With the briefest of nods and a short whistle to bring his dog to heel, Tregaron led her away toward Oxford Street. She didn't look back at the trio, not even when Fremont's voice called out loudly,

"Do not despair, sweet Cate. We shall have ample time to relive our days together in Scotland!"

The entire encounter could not have lasted above five minutes. To Cate, it seemed to have gone on for years.

Tregaron seemed to know his direction. He was certainly

heading toward Binney Street. He said nothing as they went, and Cate was grateful for it. She should thank him for the rescue, she knew. She could offer him an explanation for the scene from which he had effectively rescued her.

She didn't dare try. If she so much as opened her mouth, she knew the floodgates would open. The tears that were only just pooling in her eyes would turn to a torrent. And God only knew what revelations she would pour out with them. No, better to stay silent and let this odd, inscrutable man see her safe. See her safely home, that was.

A sennight later, Tregaron could not comprehend how so much time had passed since he'd last seen Cate. He had watched as she'd let herself into the tiny house in Binney Street, heard her muffled thanks and good night—painfully polite, or simply pained—and assumed they would meet again soon, if not the very next day.

He hadn't intended to stop by his own house the following day, but he had. And the day after and the day after that. There had been no sign of Cate on either occasion, although he'd thought he heard the lighter tread of feminine feet on the bare wooden floor at one point. No willowy female form had appeared.

The Buchanan brothers had been absent, too. Off checking on the status of glass, marble, and tile, the twitchy Gordie had informed him. MacGoun, the sour foreman, had offered tours, explanations of the day's work, but there had been no real welcome, certainly no invitation for Tregaron to take off his coat, roll up his sleeves, and pitch in. Of course there hadn't been. He was the house's owner, after all, a marquess. The afternoon of pounding at the walls with a hammer had been a matter of madness, of being caught up in the enthusiasm of the moment and the Buchanans. So Tregaron declined MacGoun's offers and took himself off to do things better suited to a peer of the realm.

He'd been fitted for the last, excessive waistcoat. He'd found a boxing club that readily welcomed him, though he was discovering that none but a few witless young cubs and the proprietor himself hurried forward to spar against him. He had attended a sale at Tattersall's with Charles Vaer, shared a companionable bottle or two with Julius Rome, and attended a fete at Lady Holland's with his suddenly socially inclined grandmother, who had promptly disappeared into a corner with Henry Brougham for a mutual lambasting of the Government Gazettes—leaving her grandson to the fish-eyed gazes of half the guests and the slightly drunken and amorous attentions of one attractive if a bit glassy-eyed widow.

He'd declined her not particularly subtle suggestion that they explore their host's upper chambers. He had never been one for hurried gropings in unfamiliar houses. Beyond that, the top of the eager Mrs. Langston's head barely reached his top waistcoat button. Hurried gropings tended to be on the rough side, and he had no desire to send his partner home in any sort of damaged state. Tiny women, he believed, were rather more trouble than delight in general.

So he'd seen his tiny grandmother, rarely a delight but beloved nonetheless, home, returned to his rooms and, as seemed the way of things since he had returned, shared a plate of fine cheese with his dog and had half a bottle of finer Madeira for himself.

He was looking forward to the same now. He wasn't quite sure why he had accepted the Hythes' offer of a seat in their theater box. Boredom, perhaps, appreciation for their welcome, and the knowledge that if he was to find himself a wife before the typical pairings of the Season thinned the field, he'd better increase his efforts. Thus far, he hadn't been overly impressed with any of the young ladies he had encountered. True, he had attended few entertainments. True, he supposed Elspeth Vaer would do in a pinch, perhaps even better than that should he actually get to know her. He could make an effort to get to know as many eligibles as possible. The trickle of invitations was constant if not overwhelming. Yes, he decided, he would simply pay more attention to important matters.

Beside him, he heard Sibyl Hythe sigh. Apparently she was finding the production of Sheridan's *The Rivals* as uninspiring as he. Even the marvelous performance of Margaret Porter as the determinedly, misguidedly noble Lydia Languish could not rescue a lackluster production. And it was only the third act of five.

It was a familiar if convoluted plot involving concealed identities and the search for love. The women were easily fooled; the men not what they seemed. Rather like life, Tregaron decided, except he had far more experience in the realm of foolish men and deceptive women.

He and his beautiful young bride had certainly fit the bill. And had continued to do so during the three ill-fated years of their marriage.

"What I wish to know," Lady Hythe murmured to no one in particular, "is why it always takes so much effort to discover that one's perfect mate is right in front of one's nose."

On her far side, her husband chuckled. Then shushed her. She shushed him back. Below, Lydia Languish nearly rapped her perfect mate, disguised of course, in the nose with her fan.

"Well?" Lady Hythe demanded. Clearly she was past bored. Tregaron sympathized.

"Keeps things interesting," her brother-in-law offered. He had been reading the day's turf report for the past half hour. Tregaron was impressed. Rome had even brought his own candle for the purpose, and had thus far managed not to spill so much as a drop of tallow on either his paper or his knees.

"Keeps one in a constant state of near apoplexy," was the tartly whispered retort.

"You survived, Sibby. Old Tarquin found you soon enough."

Old Tarquin grunted. His wife muttered, "Indeed. It only took him fifteen years."

Tregaron saw the earl take the countess's hand and lift it, gently, to rest over his heart.

Interesting. In all the years he had been acquainted with Hythe, Tregaron would never have thought the man to possess a single romantic thought. Of course, he hadn't known the earl very well, but still . . . Romance held so little place in their world. He'd learned that in a most painful manner.

But that was neither here nor there. He was older, wiser, and determined to do far better. Hythe had managed well. For all her pert irreverence, Sibyl Hythe was a delightful creature. Pretty, clever, warm, she complemented her husband's reserved austerity. Were it not for the high-spirited spark that never seemed to leave her eyes, Tregaron might have thought her a fine model for his own search. He was not, however, in the market for high-spirited.

"Dull as dirt, if you ask me."

His head snapped around. "I beg your pardon?"

"This whole blasted evening. All of this." Rome waved a languid hand over the audience and yawned. "I cannot think what possessed me to come tonight. A wise man would close himself up in Watier's till dawn every night except Tuesday."

"Dare I ask what a wise man does on Tuesdays?"

Rome gestured at his sister-in-law and grinned. "Best not, for courtesy's sake. We'll trot over to Covent Garden Tuesday next and I'll show you."

Tregaron caught on. And found himself considering the possibility of an actual Tuesday night outing. He could certainly do with a night of uncomplicated entertainment. With a woman who was pretty, welcoming, every bit as high-spirited as she wished to be, and wholly unlikely to expect declarations and devotions in return.

The act ended then, with something of a whimper. Julius promptly leapt to his feet. "Thank God. I'm off, then. Care to join me, Tregaron?"

Oh, it was tempting. But he had no desire to give offense to the Hythes. "Thank you, no. I shall . . ."

"Turn to stone, most likely. Ah, well, I wish you the joy of it." The younger man bade an unapologetic good night to his brother and sister-in-law and, with a jaunty salute, trotted from the box.

Tregaron was halfway to his feet, thinking that he could, at least, offer to go for refreshments, when the curtain was jerked open.

"My goodness, what a lot of nonsense!" The feather attached to Lady Leverham's turban bobbed in time with her words as she swept into the box. "Who wrote this piece of drivel?"

"Sheridan, Aunt Alfie," Sibyl replied. "It is certainly not his best work, but—"

"Drivel. Not a knight or minstrel to be found." The lady lowered herself with a huff into an empty chair." And the actors speak their lines so loudly. I ask you, how can a body possibly hope to have a civilized conversation with *that* going on in the background?"

Tregaron was eyeing her off-center fur collar with suspicion. He was fairly convinced it was not a collar at all. When he glanced up, it was to find her eyeing him with some interest.

"Tregaron."

"Lady Leverham." If he remembered correctly, she had never actually snubbed him, but he'd always assumed she had been rather vocal in her opinion of his poor character. Come to think of it, however, he realized she hadn't thought particularly well of him before the scandal. Nor had she held much of an opinion of Belinda. "This is a . . . pleasure."

He thought he might have heard her snort. Of course, it might have been Hythe, who was now staring intently into the gallery. But Hythe would never snort.

"Are you enjoying the play?" Lady Leverham demanded.

He debated praising the dismal piece to the rafters. "Not especially."

"Well." Apparently that earned him a point, or at least half of one. "What do you think of the Season so far? I would imagine it is all very different for you now. After all, you did dispose yourself of your—"

"Aunt Alfie," Sibyl cut in, shooting Tregaron a dismayed glance that he felt was entirely unnecessary. He would have been more than happy to let her aunt say whatever she bloody well pleased. "Was not Miss Buchanan with you?"

He snapped to full attention.

The older woman glanced about vaguely. "Oh, dear. Have I lost her again? She was right behind me not a minute ago. One must not take one's eyes of the girl for an instant. She is forever being waylaid by some breathless swain or another."

Tregaron was hauling the curtain aside before she'd stopped speaking. Indeed, Miss Buchanan was there. Only he was not certain if she were the Miss Buchanan he'd expected to see.

"Miss Lucy."

"Lord Tregaron!" She stepped lightly toward him, eyes bright, a celestial vision of floaty ivory gauze and titian curls. "How very delightful to meet you here."

She certainly appeared sincere, if a bit breathless. Her

swain, on the other hand, seemed decidedly unconcerned with the sudden shift in her attention. "Tregaron." There was no censure in the man's eyes, merely a wry amusement. "It appears the years have not altered you in any unfortunate manner."

Tregaron wasn't certain that was true, but he was certainly as wealthy as he had been, guaranteeing him a certain amount of attention from unmarried ladies. Evan Althorpe rarely had two guineas to rub together. "Nor you, Althorpe."

The man had never seemed to mind his aristocratic poverty overmuch. He had a title, a house, an estate that more or less sustained itself, and a decent collection of wealthier friends who could be counted upon to buy the grog. Tregaron had always admired Althorpe's resourcefulness, and had been entertained by the his utter lack of concern for much of anything. He rather expected he would have *liked* the man had he ever been given the opportunity.

Althorpe, ever fair and angelic in appearance, gave a wicked smile. "I daresay a bit of heavenly intervention might change me . . . but probably not." As Miss Lucy's delectable visage was still pointed in Tregaron's direction, he turned his own to the other inhabitants of the box. "Lady Leverham," he announced solemnly, "you continue to outshine every other demoiselle in the land."

He bent over the delighted lady's hand. Tregaron flinched as her collar, much as expected, detached itself from her shoulder and, scampering over Althorpe's arm, got a firm grip on the man's quizzing glass. Tregaron's last sight before turning away was of Althorpe trying to tug the thing from the monkey's now distended mouth. Galahad, as all of London knew, especially liked the taste of gold.

"You are looking very well, Miss Lucy," Tregaron offered, unable to do other than admire the artfully arranged red-gold curls and the lovely creature they topped.

She giggled. "You are too kind, my lord. I fear after wading through the crush in the halls to attend the Hythes, I must resemble the veriest of hedgehogs."

Well, that was a new one, but after several acts of Sheridan's Mrs. Malaprop butchering the English language, Tregaron could only be amused. "You are the very pineapple of perfection, mademoiselle."

Lucy blinked at him. Apparently she was not familiar with Mrs. Malaprop's most famous line, declaring a gentleman "the very pineapple of politeness." But then, there was no guarantee that "pinnacle" was even in the girl's vocabulary. He was beginning to wonder if the lovely Lucy wasn't something of a henwit. Either way, it was merely one more indication to Tregaron that, no matter how piquant the impulse, he should not make jests. They always seemed to fail.

Weary suddenly, he forced a smile and returned to being the pineapple of politeness. "Are you enjoying the performance?"

"Oh, very much. I do so love the theater!"

Yes, he mused. One who was likely to be welcomed and admired and flattered at every public appearance would no doubt love the theater, regardless of what was transpiring on stage.

"And your family, they are well?"

"Quite, thank you. My sister is here tonight—"

"Here? At the theater?"

Lucy negligently surveyed the thumb of one pristine white glove. "Of course she would insist on remaining in the box, all the way at the back, no less. I ask you, my lord, where is the joy in that? I wonder why she bothered to come at all. She will not like the play, no matter what I say to the contrary, and will not put herself forward to be seen. Is she not a perverse creature?"

Perhaps a discriminating one. Among other things, he preferred the back of the box, too. Tregaron murmured a few noncommittal words. Not that what he said mattered much. Miss Lucy had found her stride and was chattering away with the enthusiasm of a small child or well-trained parrot. By the time Lady Leverham rose, indicating it was time to return to their box, the girl had informed him on the proper choice of colored paint for his house, the very best places in London to purchase fabrics, and the truly stunning picture the Duke of Conovar's barouche made as it navigated the park.

He wasn't entirely certain why she'd added the third bit of nonsense. But then again, he wasn't the best ear for the first two, either.

It took several minutes to disengage the monkey from

Althorpe's watch fobs and for Lady Leverham to gather up her yards of gauzy wrap. Lucy accepted Tregaron's offer of an escort back to their seats with a brilliant smile guaranteed to reduce most men to quivering aspic. Her chaperone gave him a long look before a regal if curt nod. The monkey was eyeing his watch chain.

It was a short walk to the Leverham box, a mere few from the Hythes'. Lord Leverham was there, dozing happily in his chair. The other seats were empty.

"She's done it again!" Lucy sighed. "Run off in the middle. How, I would very much like to know, does she plan on getting home?"

"Don't be ridiculous, dearest." Lady Leverham settled her ample self, her copious wrap, and her monkey into a seat. "She has merely gone . . . for a stroll. She'll be back soon enough."

As it turned out, soon enough did not happen before the end of the intermission. Tregaron remained in the box until that point, one eye on the entrance, one ear on Lucy's descriptions of the interiors of Devonshire House. As the play recommenced, and Lady Leverham's repeated glances in his direction made it clear that he had graced them with his presence quite long enough, he made his farewells and moved into the hallway.

He waited there for another quarter hour.

There was no sign of Cate. He did, however, get a very good look at his cousin Edgar, Lucius Gramble, and Beau Graham as the trio returned to their own box. He was fairly certain they did not see him. Judging from the volume of their voices and weaving walk, all they were seeing was spots.

The sight drew him right back to the question that had been bedeviling him for seven days: How did Catherine Buchanan know the Fremont set, and how well? He had no answer, and that bothered him nearly as much as the possibilities that refused to leave his head. Suddenly, the concept of watching the rest of the play was most unappealing.

As he descended the theater steps to the street, he was trying not to imagine his cousin and Cate having a pastoral interlude on some northern estate where Edgar was a guest and the Buchanans were working. He then tried not to recall the reprobate Fremont's reputation for seducing any number of young women who ought not to have been seduced.

Tregaron was in no mood to be bothered, so when the small figure appeared at his side, he was ready to just hand over a coin and be on his way. Only when the shilling stayed in his hand did he glance down. It was the sweep from several weeks before, just as small, just as grimy. Tregaron thought he might have seen the boy from a distance once or twice, but hadn't paid much attention.

"Evening, guv," the sweep said now, tipping his cap.

"Up a bit late, aren't you?" Tregaron demanded, then felt foolish. These creatures of the streets hardly kept normal children's hours.

He was surprised when the boy replied, "I'll be on me way home once all you fine folk have left here for yours." He jingled coins in his pocket. No doubt the theater crowd was a splendid place to beg—or pick pockets. "Me mam'll crease me if I don't."

"You have a mother?" Most of these children, as far as Tregaron knew, were orphaned. Those who weren't had been sold into virtual slavery by what parents they had. "She knows where you are, I take it. What you do with yourself."

"Aye, to be sure. Right on top of everything is me mam."

"I'm sure she is. What's your name?"

"Billy 'Arris," was the reply, "but I goes by 'Arris."

"Well, Harris"—Tregaron flipped him a guinea rather than the shilling—"I'd say it is high time to retire, at least for the night. Hmm?"

"You, too, guv. You look like someone kicked you in the b—"

"Good night, Harris."

"Just looking out for you, guv."

"Thank you," Tregaron said wryly. "You are too kind."

"Not a bit of it." With that, the boy flashed a grin and the guinea and vanished into the shadowy alley next to the theater.

Tregaron, as he waved for a hack, had to admit the imp wasn't so far off the mark. He felt rather as if someone had given him a good wallop that evening. In fact, as he climbed into the carriage, he even felt a very physical twinge between his shoulder blades.

Even the best-laid schemes, he mused, could turn out badly. Perhaps he ought not to have come back after all. Perhaps he ought to think about going home to Wales. Or perhaps, and suddenly this idea seemed the only option, he just needed to follow an entirely new direction,

Chapter 8

Cate surveyed the plasterwork in the master bedchamber with satisfaction. It had been a good week's work. Gone was the red silk from the walls, the rampaging gilt and endless plaster cherubs from the ceiling. In their place were simple moldings and vast expanses of white walls awaiting a wash of light, smoky blue paint and whatever paintings the marquess would choose to hang in his private space. He would be pleased. How could he not? Buchanans and crew were giving him a wonderful house.

Somehow, Cate had been able to avoid encountering Lord Tregaron for nearly a fortnight. And it had not been easy. Between the persistence of her sister and Lady Leverham, demanding her presence at various evening activities, and Tregaron's habit of dropping in at the house on random occasions, Cate had become a master of the side step. To avoid the demands of but not offend Lucy and Lady Leverham, she'd had headaches, toothaches, and even a three-day cold, which had oh-so-conveniently only plagued her at night. To avoid Tregaron and his sudden appearances, she'd been inside most of the tall presses and wardrobes in the house. She'd even nearly gone diving out a convenient window when she'd heard him calling to MacGoun. His voice was as familiar to her now as the nuances of his neglected, hollow gem of a house. The window had been on the third floor; he'd been on the first.

Foolish. Once Cate's heart had stopped thumping in her ears, she'd felt utterly, inexcusably foolish. The work must be sending her mad.

She and her crew were slowly changing the house. Each day, a bit of colored glass, or varnish, or a swath of rich paint brought out a new facet of the structure's Palladian glory. There was a long way to go, to be sure, but each day brought new accomplishment, a new surge to Cate's pride, and added certainty that she would be so very sad to let go once it was all complete.

Better, she thought, to do the work and leave it behind her at the end of the day. It was a good philosophy, she knew, but she couldn't quite fool herself into believing that was why she had been so determined to avoid Lord Tregaron. That, she decided, was due to embarrassment—he'd witnessed the dismal scene with Fremont et al.—and her need to keep the private matters of her life private, especially from that pair of stirring and disturbingly sharp amber eyes. He was her employer, even if he didn't know it. That was all. Absolutely all.

As for all of her sister's demands for her presence, Cate felt a twinge of guilt at her deceptions, but not enough to relent on any but the most quiet occasions. She'd attended the theater twice, one small musical soiree at Lady Leverham's, and could not resist, no matter how hard she'd tried, a night at Vauxhall Gardens. There, hidden by the generous shadows of night and their outdoor box, she had been able to watch the other attendees—from all walks of London life. Everyone, shopkeeper or servant or peer, seemed to be having a marvelous time. No one save Cate herself seemed burdened with anything more than the choice of which glittering spectacle to take in next.

She had watched the fearless acrobats with her jaw slack, gasped at the fireworks that lit the sky and made her heart leap cheerily. Surrounded and anonymous, she had been able to let go of just enough of her worries to laugh aloud and enjoy every moment. She and Uncle Angus had shared too many sugar-rock sweets and both had been slightly jittery and green of face on returning home. Lord Leverham had shared enough champagne with Uncle Ambrose that the latter had had to carry the former to his carriage at the end of the evening. Galahad had gone missing until a merry band of soldiers had gone off in search of him. Upon returning, monkey in tow—apparently he had been entertaining a group of flashily dressed lightskirts, a fact that was kept from Lady Leverham—they had demanded only smiles from the young ladies as payment. Most had fawned over Lucy, but two had settled themselves at Cate's feet and not budged until the end of the entertainments.

All in all, it had been a magical night.

Now that the Season was in full swing, there was something to do, someplace to be nearly every single night. The coveted invitation to Almack's had not arrived, much to Lucy's bitter disappointment, but there was no shortage of requests for her presence elsewhere. She flitted from day to day, ball to ball, like the loveliest, liveliest of sparrows. The uncles joined Lord Leverham at his home which, by their report, was possessed of an incomparable games room and wine cellar, or they trundled about London seeking their own amusements. Cate, relieved of any companion duties whatsoever, was in her bed by nine o'clock most nights. She scarcely noticed how quiet and lonely the house was. Scarcely at all.

Lucy spent much of her time in the company of the Leverhams and the Hythes. Sibyl Hythe was all that was kind, extending every invitation to Cate as well. No doubt the dashing young countess thought the elder Miss Buchanan something of a backward creature, a dull stick, but she was nothing but cheerful and gracious on those occasions when they did meet. And she opened her arms, her home, and her social set to Lucy, a kindness for which Cate would gladly have embraced her.

On those afternoons when not with one of the other ladies, Lucy relied on aged, shadowed corner-occupying Auntie Rebecca. Either way, Cate inevitably arrived home to find a new batch of overly fragrant flowers crowding every surface in the little drawing room, and often an overly dedicated swain or two lingering after polite visiting time was past, just to be in Lucy's presence. Considering how often the girl was out in the afternoon, Cate was never surprised to find an aforementioned swain waiting hopefully in the foyer or even on the street for her sister's return. Early on, she had taken pity on the poor fellows and tried to feed and entertain them. That had been short-lived. They were invariably polite, but they most certainly did not want to be chatting with the elder Buchanan sister. For Cate's part, after a long day in Hanover Square, she was ready for a bath, a meal, and silent time. Now she just left Lucy's ardent suitors where she found them and went about her own business.

The current favorite seemed to be a dashing young marquess, Lord Aubert, who had taken the girl driving once and cheerfully if casually partnered her in several sets at various parties. Cate had seen the fellow; he was certainly handsome, well dressed, and possessed of a very expensive phaeton. Handsome, rich, titled, and debonair. The gossip, glumly passed on by Lady Leverham, was that Aubert was in absolutely no hurry whatsoever to take a bride, much to the apoplectic distress of his father, the Duke of Earith. Surprisingly, Lucy did not seem to mind overmuch. She was having the time of her life.

At present, Lucy was visiting Hookam's with the delightful Lord Althorpe, who, the girl said, would be quite the perfect creature were he not poor as a church mouse. To Cate, of course, it did not matter that he possessed neither carriage nor vast, echoing town house. To Lucy, such things were of paramount importance. It was all well and good, she insisted, to visit a lending library on occasion. It was necessary, however, that a gentleman be able to purchase the entire stock of Hatchard's should he so desire.

Of Tregaron, she merely shrugged, sighed, and murmured what a shame it was that he was so very old and stiff. Cate resisted the urge to argue the matter.

Tonight was the Tarrant ball. Lucy would be accompanying the Hythes. Cate needed to find an excuse quickly if she were to avoid going. She had been invited to the Tarrants', of course. She had even met the viscount and viscountess. Both had been perfectly pleasant, charming even. In fact, Lady Tarrant had rather reminded Cate of Sibyl Hythe.

The piquant impulse to accept the invitation had returned more than once. Of course, half of the *ton* would be in attendance and for that simple reason, Cate knew she should not. She did not want to chance encountering Fremont and his entourage again. Perhaps their earlier meeting had not been as miserable as she had expected—courtesy, she was forced to admit, of Lord Tregaron's timely appearance—but it was one she was loathe to repeat. The basest moments of one's life, she firmly believed, were best lived only once.

"I'm off, Miss Cate." MacGoun spoke from the doorway, startling Cate out of her reveries. "Fetch your things and I'll see you home."

Cate shook her head. "I've the other bedchamber designs to check before I go. Uncle Angus is about somewhere. We'll walk home together."

The foreman grunted. "You work too hard, lass."

"Not nearly so hard as your crew. They did a marvelous job here. And ahead of schedule, no less."

MacGoun took less than a second to survey the room. "Aye, aye. No' bad." Which was, Cate knew, the man's expression of supreme delight. "No' bad at all." With that, he shoved his battered cap onto his sparse hair and announced, "You've two minutes if you change your mind about an escort home."

"That's very gracious of you, Mac, but truly, I'd prefer to wait for Uncle Angus."

"As you like. 'Night, Miss Cate. Don't you be letting the old coot keep you here till all hours."

Cate smiled fondly as the foreman stomped from the room. His manner might not be gracious, but his intent always was. He looked out for her, more avuncular, perhaps, than the uncles. In truth, she wasn't at all sure that Angus was in the house. He had taken over a sunny little room near the lower garden door and had promptly filled it with clay, plaster, and all the various tools of his art. Cate had yet to see anything complete emerge, but he seemed happy in the few hours he spent there each week, and couldn't do any damage the workmen couldn't repair when they finally got to the house's lower levels. Both he and Ambrose were chomping at the bit, ready to be done with the tedium of the house—as limited as their participation was—and left to their art. Cate sympathized.

If her uncle was, in fact, sculpting happily, she would collect him on her way out. If not, she would simply wander home alone. She'd done so often enough, leaving through the rear door and garden gate—just in case.

As it turned out, she made quick work of checking the designs for the remaining bedrooms. Monsieur Henri des-Jardin of Piccadilly, né Henry Gordon of Aberdeen, would be arriving within the sennight, his minions bearing swatches and bolts of fabric to be matched for draperies, bed hangings, and upholstery. Later, as other rooms stopped resembling ruins and began to show off the Buchanan touch, Archibald Stewart, the Bond Street rug dealer, would arrive, as would James Wallace with his silver sconces and John Paul MacQuarrie with his designs for crystal chandeliers, all to replace what had not been salvaged.

Uncle Ambrose was to paint one wall—and one wall only—under Cate's stern direction. She had relented enough to allow a lively classical scene for the ballroom, but it was to be utterly free of carnage. Together, they had agreed on a Dionysian revel: the god with his wine, Pan with his pipes, dancing sylphs. Ambrose was already planning the faces he would use for various characters. Cate hoped that, should the Duke of Wellington ever attend a ball at the Tregaron home, he would not object to seeing his visage atop a centaur's body.

As for Angus, he was busy sculpting away at God only knew what. He'd been muttering about a tribute. If his subject was his present employer and extended beyond a bust, Cate could only pray that her uncle would relent a bit from his strict traditional steadfastness and add a fig leaf.

Neither uncle's project had been approved by, or even described to, the marquess for that matter, but Cate wasn't overly concerned. Ambrose and Angus were cheerfully occupied, and their wares were as suited to a fine house as that of the old friends they had hired to provide rugs and crystal and silver.

So went the artists. And a jolly bunch they were. While the London contingent might be elegant and elite now, they would, to the Buchanan brothers, forever be the lads from years gone by and miles above the Border: Dancing Henry Gordon, Archie the Stew, Jem Wallace, and Jackie MacQ. Lord Tregaron was a fortunate man, if unwittingly so, indeed.

Smiling to herself, Cate quitted the chamber and headed for the stairs. At the landing, she rested a hand on the wonderful stair rail that curved all the way to the first floor. So many houses these days were using the Adam design of slender mahogany handrail atop intricate, delicate, painted cast-iron balusters. Not Cate. Not in this house. Nothing on earth could have persuaded her to remove the huge, heavy, amazingly graceful sweep of oak atop its solid balusters. There was nothing delicate about the design, the carvings simple, the spindles meant to stand for a hundred more years.

The wood was especially fine oak, expensive even in its day. It bore the rich patina of a century of hands and, Cate hoped, youthful bottoms. It was a banister meant to be ridden.

She stood at the top of the stairs and glanced down to the floor below. Not surprisingly, there was no one in sight. This was one of her weaknesses and, while Cate knew she had a great many, was one she did not regret. Gathering up her skirts, she settled herself on the rail at the top of the stairs, pushed off, and flew.

It was a huge thrill, a long breathless moment as she coasted along on the polished oak, gaining speed as she slid downward, around the grand curve, into the final stretch that ended with a very large, very solid finial. That's where her skill as a banister-slider of many years and fearlessness aided her. At the last possible instant, she grabbed the finial, shaped like an acorn and large enough to fill both her hands, and used it to swing herself off the banister and into a flying arc that carried her a good six feet from the base of the stairs.

It wasn't her best landing. Her heels hit the floor with a jarring thump. She managed to stay on her feet, but it took some windmilling of her arms and a few stumbling steps that had her bumping into the rich paneling of the wall. Her first thought, when she felt the wood give, was that she had somehow broken it. Then, as she regained her balance, she discovered the truth of the matter.

What had looked to be a single panel in the lowest part of the wall was actually the door to a small cupboard. Such cupboards were not unusual and were intended to hold a variety of items, but Cate had missed this one entirely in both her explorations of the house and her occasional occupation of various presses and wardrobes. Bending over, she peered inside.

There was only one object there, a painting in an ornate frame, tilted so its subject was hidden. Curious, assuming it had come from either the drawing room or the dining room, both of which were nearby, she pulled until it was free of the cupboard.

It was a portrait of a young woman, blond, green-eyed,

rosebud mouth curved in an enigmatic smile. She was impossibly beautiful, even for a creature of paint and canvas. Beautiful enough to make Cate do something she very rarely did—wish that Mary Buchanan had passed on to her even a tenth of the aristocratic beauty she had possessed.

There was little in the few visible inches of gauzy white dress to give the image a specific date. Nor did the woman's halo of pale curls help. Sometime in the last thirty years, Cate thought. A masterful study, certainly an expensive one.

She heard a step in the hall behind her. "Uncle Angus," she called, "come see. I do believe this might be a Reynolds."

"Sir Thomas Lawrence, actually. Reynolds was . . . not available."

Cate was startled enough by the unexpected voice that she promptly let go of the corner of the frame she held. The whole thing dropped with a clatter to the floor. "Lord Tregaron!"

When she turned, it was to see him standing in the drawing room doorway. "Miss Buchanan."

He was clad, as usual, in his somber colors and ever-present austerity. In the late afternoon light he looked drawn, tired. In contrast, his dog stood at his ankle, golden and grinning. Not for the first time, Cate thought them an incongruous pair and wondered what moment had brought the friendly, cheerful little beast into its master's lair.

"I suppose I could have put that somewhere else." Tregaron pointed to the portrait. "Should have."

An odd statement, Cate thought, and one she didn't understand. She did, however, suddenly comprehend something else. "This is your wife." It was not a question.

He gave a terse nod. "Belinda. The year we were betrothed."

"She is . . . was very beautiful."

Tregaron's mouth twisted into what might have been a wry smile—or a sad one. "Yes. She was. Very beautiful."

"And the work is so very fine. There is no reason to lament the fact that Sir Joshua was . . . was . . ." She could not recall the word he had used.

"Dead, Miss Buchanan. Reynolds was quite dead at the time."

Barely giving Cate enough time to scuttle backward out of the way, Tregaron stalked across the floor, shoved the painting back into its niche, and closed the panel. "Have you been seeking to entertain yourself here?"

He watched as several expressions flitted across Cate's mobile features. Embarrassment, he thought, and . . . annoyance. Cate was annoyed with him for asking, or perhaps for catching her nosing through his house. Perverse creature, he mused. It was, after all, his house. She was neither employee nor guest. And he was not going to discuss Belinda.

Finally, pulling in her endless limbs, she clambered to her feet. He didn't think she would accept his assistance, but proferred a hand anyway. She refused it. When she was on her feet, the top of her familiarly unruly head at the level of his nose, noteworthy chin lifted, she announced, "I did not intend to open this cupboard, my lord, nor any other in the house. It was inadvertent."

"Inadvertent."

Now she flushed, no doubt realizing how unlikely it was that such a portal would open of its own volition. "I struck the panel."

Tregaron sighed. In the various scenarios he had imagined, expecting to meet with her in the past fortnight, this did not come close to any of them. "You know, Cate," he said wearily, "I really do not care—"

"I struck it when I came off the banister."

"I beg your pardon?"

Now her face, from lofty Scottish brow to high Scottish cheekbones, was a red to rival the fiery lights in her hair. "I was sliding down the banister. I landed poorly."

"Landed poorly. I see." He glanced up along the curve of the rail and winced. "Do you often slide down banisters?"

"Not so much now. Truly. But as a child . . . Didn't you?"

"No," he said shortly. "I did not."

"Never?"

"Never!"

Cate seemed momentarily taken aback—either by his tone or by his very revelation. But to her credit, she did not press the matter. Instead, she shrugged. "Well, I was a fanciful child. I slid down things, climbed others, dug for treasure, and searched for faeries. I am much more sensible now."

Tregaron found his pique slipping away. He was oddly charmed by her words. Charmed, too, by the way her chin had pushed forward as if she were waiting for him to challenge her.

"What of dragons, Miss Buchanan?"

Now her jaw seemed to go just a bit slack. "What of them?" she demanded.

"Perhaps Scotland is known for its faery folk, but Wales has dragons."

He managed not to smile when she responded with a snort that might well have shot fire. "Hmph."

"You do not believe in dragons?"

"Scaled, clawed, winged creatures? Prone to devouring overconfident knights and hapless virgins?"

"Not very sensible sounding, I agree. But would we believe in seraphim if the Church did not tell us to? Or cherubim?"

"No, but neither of those are known for their viciousness. And the Church says nothing about dragons."

Tregaron admired the spark of challenge in her fine eyes. "St. George," he replied, and envisioned Cate yet again in armor, sword in hand.

"Apocryphal. No such person."

"Perhaps not," he said affably, "but perhaps there was such a dragon."

"Do *you* believe in dragons?" she asked, clearly baffled.

Only the human sort, he could have told her. But there was something so strangely satisfying about the moment, almost magical, so instead he answered, "I live in Wales. It would be churlish of me to laugh at legends, much like a resident of England laughing at tales of a majestic royal family. Now, I wished to have a word with your uncles. Are they here?"

He saw her hesitate for a moment. Then she replied, "I believe Uncle Angus is belowstairs. If you would care to wait here, I will look for him." She started to hurry away.

"Cate."

"Yes, my lord?" She stopped partway down the stairs to the foyer, but did not quite raise her gaze to his face.

What do you believe in now that you have abandoned the

faeries? he wanted to ask. *What do you dream of at night?* He suddenly wanted very much to know.

"I will accompany you."

"Oh, no," she protested. "There is no need . . ."

But he was already descending the stairs behind her. With a last backward look, she continued on her way. The house was oddly quiet, Tregaron noted. He'd become used to arriving to the sounds of saws and hammers and the occasional snatch of a Celtic tune from one of the mostly Scottish workmen. Now there was only silence, and he recalled just how quiet the house had always been. Unless Belinda was entertaining. The servants had always muffled their footsteps and voices. He had tended to closet himself in the library with his books and more silence.

He wondered when he had grown to crave the noise and bustle of a home he'd never known.

As they reached the marble foyer, Tregaron noticed that the front door was ajar. "Careless," he muttered as he stepped forward to close it.

Cate was just ahead of him, so it was her foot that landed on the piece of foolscap. When she lifted her foot, he got a clear view of the message scrawled there.

You have been deceived.

Tregaron bent and snatched up the sheet. He flipped it over, but there was nothing more to be read. He crumpled the paper in his fist. "Damned cowards," he growled.

He had no idea who had left the note, nor what it was supposed to mean. But there was no question that the message was not a friendly one. *Deceived. Deceived, perhaps, into thinking he could return to the life he'd once known . . .*

He glanced up to find Cate's eyes fixed on his face. Blue as the sea off the Pembroke coast, he found himself thinking. And wondered if the truths about his character and his past would change the look there to loathing.

You have been deceived, my dear.

He hadn't expected his former friends and neighbors to speak their minds to his face. But then, he hadn't expected cowardly and obtuse little messages, either. All in all, it was ever so slightly amusing. *Hah.*

He thought a brandy and an hour with Southey's latest might suit him at the moment.

"Can I escort you home?" he asked Cate.

She blinked at him, then replied, "No, no, thank you. I will wait for my uncle. I . . . Did you not wish to speak with him?"

Had he? Tregaron shrugged. "I have seen all I need to see. So . . ."

"Yes?"

"I will be off." He opened the door, tipped his stick over his shoulder, then tried to think of something to whistle as he went. "Good afternoon, Miss Buchanan."

To hell with whistling, he thought. He would just walk briskly all the way to the Albany—to his books and his brandy and whatever further joys the evening was going to bring.

He felt Cate's sea blue eyes on him as he went. Then he heard his own front door close behind him with a click.

Chapter 9

As far as second cousins went, Jason Granville, Viscount Tarrant, wasn't at all bad. In fact, Tregaron remembered enough pleasant childhood interludes in Sussex that he'd found himself dreading this evening far less than most others that involved a public appearance and crowds. Of course, the amount of brandy he had consumed earlier had helped a good deal. Now, comfortably propping up a wall in Tarrant's elegant Berkeley Square town house, a measure of splendid champagne in his hand and several more in his belly, he was not at all unhappy.

Of course, he thought with a wry grimace, he might be wholly *deceived* in the matter.

At the moment he had no idea where his host was, nor the viscount's charming wife. Off being charming, no doubt. The Tarrants were charming. They could have added the word to the family crest. Tregaron and his grandmother had been included in the small, pre-ball dinner party, and had been warmly welcomed and sumptuously entertained. Yes, the Season was progressing more smoothly than it had begun for him. Perhaps it would end with equal smoothness. An hour into this particular ball, he wasn't in his usual thumping hurry to depart.

He'd deposited his grandmother, who was perhaps not as charming as other members of her family but who had insisted on attending the party nonetheless, in the card room with a fond if stern warning not to relieve her opponents of too much money. He had then danced with his hostess, with Sibyl Hythe, and with Elspeth Vaer, the last under the not-quite-approving eye of the lady's mother. Apparently Lady Vaer was not as keen on the match as her husband. Neither, Tregaron wanted to tell her, was he. He'd gotten through the country dance easily enough, despite it seeming to go on forever, and Miss Vaer had said absolutely nothing of interest during the entire duration. He had then escorted her from the floor, fetched her a lemonade, and returned her to her giggling, glittering circle of friends, several of whom had eyed him with interest. He vowed to give them a similar perusal sooner or later.

He supposed he could dance with Elspeth again, just in case she was the sort of girl who eventually grew upon one like a creeping mold. He supposed, too, that two dances in an evening might imply inclinations he did not possess. And that was something to be avoided, possibility of mold or not.

He idly scanned the crowd. Not looking for anyone in particular, of course, but careful to observe all the corners and alcoves nonetheless. The better part of Mayfair seemed to be present. To be fair, the Granvilles were numerous enough to be mistaken for the population of a small Continental country, but they'd still allowed enough room for a decent crush of non-relations.

A familiar Granville voice spoke at his elbow. "How much have you imbibed, Colwin?"

He glanced down, brows going up. "Not nearly enough, probably. Why?"

"You were smiling. It alarmed me."

"Nothing alarms you, madam."

"Mmm. True." His grandmother deftly grabbed a glass of her own from a passing footman. Several delicate sips later, it was empty. "So, who is she?"

"Who is whom?"

"Please, Colwin. Obtuseness does not suit you any more than jovial drunkenness. Who is the absent female who has you smiling while you all but sweep dust from the floor with your eyes?"

"Interesting analogy," he murmured, stopping his gaze mid-sweep.

"Not especially. And now you're dodging." Lady Tregaron tapped the rim of her empty glass thoughtfully against her lower lip. "Fascinating. Is she marriageable?"

"Grandmother!"

She gave an unrepentant shrug. "Well, one never knows. I've always expected gentlemen spent rather more time thinking of their enamoratas than their more respectable counterparts."

"Grandmother, really!"

"Oh, for heaven's sake, Colwin. Since when have you been so starchy? I simply wish to know if this lady will provide me with great-grandchildren whom I may acknowledge publicly."

Completely unbidden, Tregaron was struck with an image of long-limbed, wild-haired, freckled children running roughshod through his grandmother's pristine house. "God help me."

"What was that?"

He shook his head. "No matter. I promise you that should I ever commit the unfortunate act of turning more St. Clair-Wrights loose upon the world, you will be able to acknowledge them with impunity."

His grandmother sighed. "Your enthusiasm for the prospect sends me into raptures, Colwin."

"I live to serve, madam."

As far as he was concerned, they were done with the matter. "How much did you win?" he asked.

"Oh, a paltry amount. Is it the Vaer girl?"

He ignored her question. "How paltry?"

"A few guineas. Negligible. I do hope it isn't one of Earith's chits."

"Lady Zilvia is delightful—"

"So she might well be, but her *father* . . ."

"And married. Lady Chloe is still little more than a child. Earith's chits are safe enough from me. Whom did you deprive of these few guineas?" With his grandmother, it was always wise to know, lest the losing party should prove the sort to lose badly. "Not Lady Broadford, I trust."

"She cheats. I will not play against her. Oh, dear, not *her* daughter! Please, Colwin."

The very thought of jesting, let alone an actual attempt at it, had long since disappeared from Tregaron's life. It rose now like the faintest of bells in the back of his mind.

"Lady Theresa is a delightful creature," he announced.

"She flirts."

"Ah, but with such wit and intelligence."

"The girl's tongue is ready to flap out of her head!"

"Such an extraordinarily beautiful head. She is an Incomparable."

"She has *red hair*!" his grandmother moaned. Which, apparently, said it all. "Oh, dear Lord. Related to the Red Wardours. How shall I bear it?"

"Calm yourself, madam," Tregaron advised, patting her narrow back. "There is every possibility that Lady Theresa will refuse me."

"Oh, Colwin, you have made the creature an *offer*?"

"Only a very informal one. There is every chance she mistook it for an invitation to paddle in the Serpentine."

Lady Tregaron's eyes narrowed suddenly. "You are mocking me, boy."

"I? What a propos—" He broke off, blinked, then did a poor job of muffling a laugh with a cough. "Miss Buchanan."

She had been about to walk right by. Apparently she had missed seeing him. He couldn't have missed her in the middle of an active battlefield.

Who dresses you, Cate? slipped into his mind, followed by the realization that he really couldn't care less. She was one of a kind, and what she wore hardly mattered.

Tonight it was a long column of mossy-colored fabric, complete with far too much trim that resembled sturdy cobwebs. Someone—not she, he hoped—had tried to conceal her freckles by dipping liberally into the powder pot. There was a flowery sort of ornament stuck into her hair. All in all, she looked like a fugitive from a third-rate production of *A Midsummer Night's Dream*.

"Miss Buchanan," he repeated, and she stopped at last. The stiffening of her shoulders made him suspect that she had heard him the first time. Her slow turn did nothing to dispel the suspicion.

"Lord Tregaron." She sketched a brief curtsy. He managed not to so much as flinch when his grandmother dug a sharp if discreet little elbow into his side.

"Madam, may I present to you Miss Catherine Buchanan of Argyll. Miss Buchanan, my grandmother, Lady Tregaron."

Cate dipped into a much more formal curtsy then. His grandmother took full advantage. When the girl was midbend, the dowager rested her fan on Cate's shoulder, keeping her where she was. It could not have been terribly comfortable, but it put the two of them eye-to-eye.

"The architect's niece," Lady Tregaron murmured. "The elder, I presume?"

"Yes, ma'am," Cate replied. If Tregaron reminded her of a dragon, it was clearly a family trait. This tiny, lovely woman could, no doubt, breathe fire. Cate thought she might like her if given a chance. At the moment, she was a bit terrified. "My sister Lucy—"

"Is the beauty. Yes, yes, I know all about it." Lady Tregaron lifted an ornate filigree lorgnette to her eye for a long moment before letting it drop back to her bosom, where it tangled with a profusion of jeweled chains. "I must say, you are a novelty to view. I don't suppose you are related to the Hepburns."

"Not to my knowledge, ma'am."

"They were the Earls of Bothwell, you know." As if that bit of information were likely to make Cate change her answer. "Extinct, of course."

"Sadly, Lady Tregaron," she announced, "I do not believe we have any ties to that family."

"Pity. There is definitely something of the Hepburn about you. And I have always found it most handy to be related to someone notorious, or at least noteworthy. Bandying about the names of one's kin saves one from having to speak overmuch about oneself."

Something flashed in the amber eyes, so much like those of her grandson, gone before Cate could identify it as distaste or dismissal . . . or something else. She took a deep breath.

"I fear we Buchanans are far too busy trying to muddle out how we can possibly be related to one another to look much beyond the immediate connection."

Lady Tregaron's elegant brows rose. "A peculiar group, are you?"

"Dangerously so, ma'am."

"Tell me, Miss Buchanan, is the rest of your immediate family as . . . er, clever as you?"

Cate hesitated a moment, made her decision, and replied tartly, "Far more so. Why do you think I call them dangerous?"

Again the lady's eyes glittered. She allowed Cate to stand up straight. "London beware, then." To her grandson, she announced, "I am off to coax Lizzie Melbourne into a game or two of cassino. She is not a proficient player and is wearing a very pretty emerald brooch tonight that would go quite well with my earrings."

"Grandmother—"

"Go have a dance with Miss Buchanan, Colwin. I daresay it will be a curious experience for you, dancing with a woman who can meet your gaze squarely." She fixed her own gaze upward. "Just how tall are you, Miss Buchanan?"

Cate felt herself bending her knees ever so slightly and silently cursed her weakness. She had never hated that question, never even minded it before three summers earlier. "I believe I am, perhaps not quite, just—"

"Oh, never mind, girl. It isn't as if we can measure people's stature in inches, after all. Don't tread upon her toes, Colwin." With that declaration, Lady Tregaron got a new grip on her lorgnette and marched off into the crowd, leaving Cate with the marquess.

He broke the awkward silence smoothly enough to leave Cate in no doubt of which of them was the awkward one. "Shall we dance?"

No flattering preamble, no mention of pleasure, honor, or any of the other joys men were trained to cite with their requests for a dance. Cate was all set to refuse, just as she had been set to creep past him minutes earlier.

She hadn't meant to overhear his flippant, offhand discussion of Lady Someone-or-Other to whom he was planning to make a formal offer of marriage, but she had. Given the choice, she certainly would not have chosen to hear his grandmother's succinct commentary on red hair. She had heard both, and decided to take her suddenly flushed cheeks elsewhere to cool.

Not that it would have mattered, anyway, at least not as far as appearance was concerned. She was reasonably certain that Lady Leverham's liberal dusting of face powder would hide even the worst Highland windburn.

She hadn't wanted to attend this evening. Especially after seeing the single word on the note in Tregaron's foyer. *Deceived.* She hadn't been able to see the rest, and she knew perfectly well that it could not possibly have anything to do with her family. Of course it couldn't. But it had rattled her nonetheless. Any mention of deceit at all, and both heart and head started to pound. As it turned out, she had completely neglected to come up with a good excuse for staying home. So here she was.

Several glasses of champagne, consumed immediately upon arriving, were buoying her somewhat. One more, and she might be able to forget that note, that word entirely.

"Cate?"

All it took was the simple use of her name and the offer of his arm. He'd used her name before, offered his arm before, but there was something in both now that she could not refuse. Forward, presumptuous—he was both. He was also all but betrothed to one woman and living with the ghost of another. Worst of all, he had somehow become almost . . . likeable, and it was altogether too disconcerting. Life, Cate mused, was not meant to be quite so complicated.

At that moment, she didn't care. She simply wanted to dance with him.

She could both see and sense heads turning as they took the floor. Was it his reputation, she wondered, or that he was stepping into the heart of a minuet with a grey-clad, white-faced nobody? A nobody who, upon her entrance not a quarter hour earlier with Lady Leverham, had been mistaken for that lady's paid companion.

That loudly whispered reply and following giggle from a woman she had never met had stung, but she supposed she ought to be grateful she hadn't heard the question. It had involved her identity, no doubt, and something unflattering about her appearance. She supposed she could put a bit of effort into the matter, but . . .

Who would care if I did?

"If you did what?"

Until Tregaron spoke, she did not realize she had said the words aloud. She sighed, searched for a quick and clever retort. He managed to loosen her tongue with a quick press of her fingers with his.

"My appearance has caused comment this evening," she said, lifting her chin.

"That is not surprising," Tregaron said with a shrug.

Cate tried not to be hurt by the words. She knew perfectly well that she was not the *ton's belle ideale*, and did not need to be succinctly reminded of the fact.

"So who would care if you . . . ?"

"I did not mean to speak aloud, but I hardly think anyone would care if I took to leaping through the hoops that fashion dictates. I am not likely to be improved by an hour with a modiste whose French accent is as fraudulent as her fees."

"I see no need for you to even contemplate such matters," was the marquess's polite reply, but Cate did not miss the quick head-to-toe look he gave her, nor the fleetingly quirked eyebrow.

"Toadying to fashion does not suit me," she muttered.

"Nor me."

There was a simple sincerity to the words. But as Tregaron guided her in a turn, hands alternating so they were momentarily face-to-face, she could not help but notice how well he wore the current fashion. The stark black suited him, echoed the sleek ebony of his hair. The knee breeches suited him, displaying a pair of fine legs that Cate knew she should not be observing, but that she couldn't help thinking would look rather marvelous beneath a tartan kilt. The austerity of the white waistcoat, the simplicity of his cravat knot, the single, sapphire-tipped fob on his watch chain all suited him. So very well.

"I have only so many dresses," she heard herself blurt out, "with no need of more. And Lady Leverham was intent on draping me in all sorts of ancient-looking, gauzy stuff."

"You declined, I see."

"I thought the trim on the dress was more than enough." Cate glanced down ruefully. "It appeared so . . . acceptable in the pattern book. Lady Leverham's wrap would not have helped at all, but she was so crestfallen that I allowed her to do as she wished with the powder. She does go on so about my freckles."

"Does she indeed?"

"Lucy, too. Of course she is blessed with perfect . . ." Cate broke off, appalled with herself—blathering on at the marquess like some featherbrained ninny. And he was listening with all courtesy, accepting her idiotic babbling without smirking, minding the steps of the dance without once faltering—or allowing her to.

Gracious, graceful, and cursedly appealing. Of course, Cate thought a bit waspishly, determined to banish her embarrassment, he was also thought by some to be capable of foul acts.

Gritting her teeth, she vowed to keep control of her tongue for the remainder of the dance.

"You were saying . . . ?" Tregaron said politely.

"Nothing of import." Cate smiled sweetly—and promptly missed a step.

His hand tightened for an instant around hers. In that moment, Cate knew that she could get both feet tangled in the ridiculous trim of her dress and he still would not let her fall. He was strong enough, tall enough to hold her completely steady.

For some absurd reason, she wanted to cry.

He waited courteously for her to get back into the pattern of the steps. She smiled brightly. "I have always thought there are few dances as pleasant as a minuet."

To which he flashed that stunning, gone-almost-before-it-began grin and replied, "And I have often thought that I would rather be treading barefoot over sharp stones."

Just as she decided that she'd been insulted yet again, he continued, "Come now, Cate. You cannot expect me to believe you enjoy mincing about in a minuet. Not when you stride about London as if it were the open moors."

"Well, I—"

"Do you waltz?"

"I . . . no. I never have."

"Pity. It is a dance made to suit the long-limbed Graces of the world. And, if we gentlemen are very fortunate, we are able to participate from rather closer than this." He lifted their joined hands. "We have been deprived, have we not, living in our respective distant climes?"

How nice it might have been, Cate thought wistfully, to have experienced her first waltz with a man who would not be daunted by the prospect of having all of her many inches in his arms. But there was no waltz music to be heard, and she had never fancied herself a Grace. Beyond that, whenever she danced a freer set of steps, like a Scottish reel, she was wary of knocking other, smaller dancers off the floor.

"I do not mind the minuet," she said firmly.

"Sharp stones," Tregaron said again, and guided her into the final pattern.

When the music ended, Cate expected Tregaron to lead

her back to the sidelines and leave her somewhere in the vicinity of Lady Leverham, who was holding court near the door. And he might have done just that had she not stopped dead halfway there.

Lord Fremont, resplendent in his formal garb, was striding straight toward them. His fair hair was artfully tousled, his handsome features wreathed in the brightest of smiles. He was quite probably the handsomest man in the room, arguably the cleverest, and Cate was certain that he was coming over to demand a dance. She was equally certain that his intentions were neither honorable nor amicable.

Is this not a room meant to be danced in? He had trailed her into the conservatory of the Maybole house, a sennight after he'd first spied her, breeches-clad and busy, in the gutted music room. Cate had no idea why he was speaking to her at all, and especially with such charm and civility. Later she would decide it was because she'd shown no interest in him, hadn't even looked his way on those odd occasions when their paths crossed.

He did not know that she watched him, watched for him, from beneath lowered lids all the time, awed by his fair beauty.

Was it a room meant for dancing? No, she'd replied tartly, her heart going like a drum, when he'd finally spoken to her; it was a room meant for holding ungodly expensive plants that had no place in Scotland. He'd stared at her blankly for a moment, then thrown back his golden head and laughed. Cate, certain she was being mocked and knowing better than to spit at one of her volatile employer's most treasured guests, had turned her back on him, resumed her task of measuring the windows, and answered him in curt monosyllables until he went away.

She could never have foreseen what the following days would bring—dazzling smiles, snippets of poems, hushed and repeated requests for midnight dances under Egyptian palms . . .

Is this not a room meant to be danced in?

Cate nearly stumbled as Tregaron abruptly steered her in the opposite direction, away from Fremont with his complacent smile. Right past a gaggle of sharp-eyed matrons, past Lady Leverham and her coterie, weaving through the crowded game room, into a small parlor and right out a pair of French doors. In a matter of moments, Cate found herself on a side balcony that was full of shadows and completely empty of people.

Her heart was pounding as she reached the railing. "Sir," she began, ready to pull away, to protest, when neither seemed quite the thing to do. But she realized then that he had already released her and was standing a good five feet away, just barely outside the doors. "Thank you," she said softly, honestly. "I did not want to . . . to . . ."

With what meager light came from the chamber behind his back, Tregaron's face was obscured in shadow. All Cate could see was that he was leaning against the ivy-covered brick wall, arms crossed over his chest, covering much of the white of his waistcoat and shirt. Dark, she thought. And not a little dangerous.

Dear God, she was foxed, or at least closer than she had ever been.

His voice, coming out of the darkness, was low and rough enough to make her heart do another jittery thump. "What happened between you and Fremont, Cate?"

"What ever would make you say—?"

"Do you think me stupid?"

"No," she replied, feeling foolish herself. "No, I don't."

"What happened between you and Fremont?"

She momentarily considered telling him, spilling the whole dismal tale then and there. But tempting as it was to tell someone—to finally be able to tell *anyone*—she couldn't. There was no way to explain without sounding exactly like the moon-eyed, naive creature she had been.

"We were acquainted briefly in Scotland. I do not care for him. That is all there is to it."

"All there is?"

"Yes."

He came away from the wall so quickly and smoothly that she barely saw him move. Then he was standing halfway along the balcony, halfway between her and the door. "Liar," he said softly. Then, "But keep your secrets if you need to."

Cate waited for him to join her at the rail. He didn't. She turned to stare out over the darkened garden far below. "I suppose I ought to go back inside."

"Ah, yes. Of course. We cannot have your reputation sullied by mine. By all means, go before you are missed."

Cate couldn't help it; she gave a short laugh. "I'm not likely to be missed. Not here anyway."

"Do you always do that?"

"Do what?"

Tregaron took a half step forward, then seemed to change his mind and retreated to the wall. "Deny your own value."

She thought for a moment. No one had ever accused her of such before. "I know my value," she said eventually, "and where it exists." Then, feeling the need for some levity, she added, "I simply have no pretensions about my sense of fashion or my freckles."

Of all the polite responses he could have made, she did not expect, "For what it's worth, Cate, I like your freckles."

He had meant only to be honest, not to startle her. But he had; he heard it in her soft intake of breath. He certainly did not expect a simple declaration of fact to send her running. But there she went; she very nearly got by him as she all but bolted for the door.

He reached out and managed to snare her wrist. "Cate."

She pulled back, but not hard enough. "I really must be getting back."

"Are you feeling missed?"

Her skin was surprisingly warm against his, even through the fabric of her glove. He supposed he had expected, without ever giving any thought to the matter, for her to be as cool to the touch as she was in demeanor. He really ought to have known better. There was a fire within Cate Buchanan that he had sensed. Now he was feeling it.

"Cate," he said again, tugging gently and trying to remember the last time he had encountered a woman who had met him with real warmth.

She was close enough now that he could see her features clearly. The color of her eyes was lost to the night, but they were wide in her face, her still lips parted slightly in surprise, or dismay . . . or something else. Tregaron could see a pulse beating above the deplorably high, cobwebby trim of her bodice. He imagined the bold lines of her collarbones beneath, the soft hollows beneath those.

He had never questioned that there was something stirring, undeniably appealing to him about this woman. She was vibrant as sunlight, bright as summer. He had simply never considered that she might take on the properties of moonlight as well—soft, alluring, drawing a man like the sea.

He tugged again, until their arms rested length against length. "Who would have thought it?"

Her breath was shallow; he could hear and feel it. "I should . . . I shouldn't . . ."

"Make up your mind," he commanded, surprised to hear the easy smile in his own voice. He'd had no idea he was smiling.

One more tug, or a very deep breath, and she would be flat up against his chest. A curious experience, indeed, holding a woman whose eyes were nearly on a level with his. He imagined being stretched across a mattress, eye-to-eye and hip-to-hip, and felt his body leap in response. "Ah, Cate."

"Colwin." She said the word slowly, hesitantly. "Is that your name?"

He actually debated lying, saying yes, yes it was his name. "No."

"But your grandmother—"

"It is the title I bore," he said shortly, "when my father was still alive."

"So your name, your Christian name, is . . ."

Tregaron felt his smile harden into a grimace. "Is my secret for tonight."

"Why?"

"Why on earth is it important? Tregaron will do, or Colwin. My . . . friends use those, so what should it matter?"

"It matters," came the terse reply. "But I have no right to press."

He felt it slipping away, the heated moment between them. Because of a nearly forty-year-old vagary on the part of his eccentric mother and some fierce need he sensed now in Cate.

"Will Colwin not do?" he demanded.

There was a long pause. Then, "Of course, Colwin would do as well as anything. As well as Raphael. Or Michael, or Gabriel. Or Lucifer. What are they but names, after all?"

Names of archangels, and one very infamous fallen angel. Tregaron was completely lost. "I do not understand."

"No." Cate tugged sharply, pulling her wrist from his grasp. "I don't know how you possibly could."

With that, she pushed past him, her long stride taking her from the balcony and back into the house almost before he could blink. Knowing he had just committed some grievous error, and not entirely certain it involved names, Tregaron followed. By the time he reached the ballroom, Cate was nowhere to be seen.

Lord Fremont was. In fact, the man was just leading Lucy Buchanan from the dance floor. He glanced up, saw Tregaron in the doorway, and gave an almost imperceptible, unmistakably mocking salute. Then he guided the angelic Buchanan sister into the crush and out of sight.

Throughout the remainder of the evening, the closest thing to a Buchanan that Tregaron could find was a very long draught of his host's excellent Scotch whiskey. It came to him easily, was warm and ever so slightly sweet, and left him no more muddled in the head than one long-limbed Scotswoman.

Chapter 10

"Shocking!" Lady Leverham announced after luncheon the following day, rapping a plump fist on the little table beside her chair. "Outrageous! Honestly, my dear, could you not have shown a tad more discretion than to disappear from the Tarrant affair with that man?"

The diatribe had been going on in a similar fashion for the past several minutes. Cate sat stiffly in her chair and gave silent thanks that the good lady was more loquacious than truly condemning. She scolded, but her heart clearly ran a distant second in enthusiasm to her tongue.

Cate sneaked a glance at the porcelain mantel clock. Like many of the lady's possessions it bore a medieval theme—this time a knight, lance aloft, an overly pink-cheeked damsel, and a similarly pink-cheeked dragon. Cate dragged her eyes from gilt-tipped green scales to the gold hands on the face of the clock. Half past two. She shifted again in her chair. This was one of her very rare and always uncomfortable absences from the work site. And she would not have come at all had not Lady Leverham's invitation for lunch demanded her presence as well as Lucy's.

Lunch had been perfectly lovely. The lady's post-salmon sermon was far less so.

"Now, fortunately," she was saying, "I do not believe many people noted your absence. I myself would have remained ignorant had I not observed your return, but then, he rejoined the festivities far enough behind you that no connection could be certain. Of course, the *ton* does have that rather unfortunate habit of assuming first and ascertaining later."

Lady Leverham paused to remove a silver teaspoon from her pet's mouth. The monkey chattered irritably, shaking a small fist, before scampering down from his mistress's lap to crouch at the bottom of Cate's chair. He gave her, or at least her loose hairpins, a long, considered look. She glared back. For a minute, woman and beast locked in silent battle. Then Galahad gave a faint simian sneer and scuttled off to friendlier climes.

"Well, my dear"—Lady Leverham crossed her arms and managed to paste an almost believably stern frown in her ever-pleasant features—"what have you to say for yourself?"

She was answered first with a dramatic sigh. Then, "Not a thing," Lucy replied, negligently examining the toe of her pink kid slipper for imaginary scuffs. "I have done nothing at all, save pass a diverting quarter hour in the company of Lord Fremont. We were quite surrounded the entire time."

"And so you were," the lady said dryly. "By books. Which make no more appropriate chaperons than a deserted library makes an acceptable spot to chat." She turned to Cate and fluttered her plump hands. "You say something, dearest. I have quite run out of helpful scolds."

Cate was at a wry loss as to what she could possibly say. She certainly could not take her sister to task for having wandered into a secluded part of the Tarrant house with a man. Not when she had done the same with Tregaron, had come so very close to . . . Memory washed over her with a little chill that was not unpleasant in the least. Of course, it was followed almost immediately by mortification.

She had wandered out onto a secluded balcony with the Marquess of Tregaron—consummate blue-blood, pinnacle of wealthy arrogance, former social pariah. And her employer. She had stood far too close to him, so close that she could see the odd line of silver threading through his midnight hair. She had very nearly kissed him, simply because it seemed the most natural thing in the world to do.

Cate fumbled for her handkerchief and forced a not terribly convincing sneeze. Then she silently cursed her flaming cheeks. She had not blushed with half so much regularity since her altogether too awkward adolescence, when even the sound of her name would set her to the blush.

No, she thought. She would not be scolding her sister for passing a few stolen, fascinating minutes with a gentleman. She would, however, say her twopence worth on the matter of that man.

"I do not wish to impose my tastes on yours," she announced, choosing her words carefully, "but I cannot help but think, Lucy, that you could do far better than Lord Fremont."

Apparently she had not chosen quite carefully enough. Her sister blew out an exasperated breath, sending the feathery titian curls at her forehead into a charming dance. "Oh, Catey, *really*."

"I simply mean—"

"I know what you mean. You mean *you* do not care for him. Well, you are not infallible. Look at the terrible things you said about Lord Tregaron. And he has turned out to be perfectly delightful, has he not?"

Lady Leverham sniffed loudly. Cate closed her eyes for a weary moment. She was not certain *delightful* was a word she would have chosen. *Disturbing*, perhaps. *Gracious. Unsettling. Alluring. Dangerous.*

"Well?" her sister demanded. "Has he not?"

"He has been most . . . inoffensive," Cate offered weakly.

Lucy rolled her eyes. "Inoffensive. Fine. Am I to take it you find Lord Fremont offensive?"

"I find him unimpressive." As much as Cate wanted to add *cruel*, *selfish,* and *vain*, she did not know how she could. "I cannot think what he has to recommend him beyond a pretty face."

"Ah, but such a very pretty face it is."

"Hmph. Not an ounce of chivalry in his body," came their hostess's contribution. "Four duels, and in all four he fired early!"

Cate blinked. She had no idea Fremont was prone to dueling. That he would so risk his own hide amazed her. That he would fire early, hence, she supposed, really not taking much of a chance with his hide at all, did not.

"Four times?" Lucy demanded, clearly finding this tidbit rather fascinating. "Would you not think that his opponents would have been the wiser after the first, and most definitely after the second and third?"

"Men," Lady Leverham announced, "are never quite so stupid as when they are smacking each other about the face with gloves or groggily waving pistols across a damp field. If there is any act more asinine than a duel, I am certain I do not know what it is. Now a nice joust, on the other hand . . ."

"What was the reason for the duels?" Lucy wished to know.

"Other men's wives and daughters," was the prompt response. Then, perhaps realizing that a bit more circumspection was appropriate around her young guests, Lady Leverham cleared her throat and amended, "Fremont's . . . social behavior has occasionally been frowned upon. He was even once forced to rusticate on the Continent while his third opponent decided whether or not to expire. He is not, I fear, the best companion for you, Lucy, dear." Her ordinarily guileless eyes sharpened. "You were not . . . excessively . . . entertained by the creature, were you?"

Cate, clenched fists hidden in her lap, wanted very much to hear the answer to this question. She also wanted very much to hear about these wives and daughters—or even just about the frowned-upon social behavior. She silently willed her sister to answer and to ask. But Lucy, choosing the very worst time to develop a reticence and disinterest in gossip, merely shrugged.

"It was not such a stimulating encounter that I am breathlessly anticipating the next. Among other things, Lord Fremont does not converse particularly well."

Relief that her sister did not seem to be falling under Fremont's potent spell washed over Cate. It hardly mattered whether Lucy's disenchantment came from wisdom or that the subject in question did not possess either the requisite fortune or lofty enough title. Unlike Cate, Lucy seldom changed her mind about a man. People did not grow on her like an unwelcome rash.

That did not mean Cate wasn't ready to have at her over those "other things" Lord Fremont did poorly.

She counted five instead, sighed, and casually asked, "On what did you converse?"

"Actually," Lucy replied with a delicate little yawn, "we did not. He conversed, mostly about the color of my eyes. After that, his most frequent mention was of you."

"Me?"

"Mmm." Lucy did not elaborate for a long moment, instead turning her attention to helping their hostess disentangle her lavish gold bracelet—which, Cate had noted earlier, bore a remarkable resemblance to chain mail—from the table's lace doily. "He spoke of the delightful days you spent together on the Maybole estate."

"You spent delightful days with Fremont?" Lady Leverham demanded. Then, deciding she had chosen the wrong event to grace with a reaction, "You were a guest of the *Loose Maybole*?"

"Not really. Louisa Maybole commissioned the uncles to renovate her house. We occupied a tenant cottage. Lord Fremont was a frequent guest at the house, and we became casually known to each other. He did not say we were . . . more than acquaintances, did he, Lucy?"

"He spoke very fondly of those days, adding, of course, that he must have suffered a severe knock on the head at some point not to have remembered me." Lucy rolled her eyes again and flashed her best impish grin. "He also said you were the sweetest of creatures and a trusting soul—which made it more than clear to your devoted sister that you and he were certainly no more than mere acquaintances."

If that were only true. Cate wondered if she needed to do something about Fremont. And she wondered what she could possibly do if the answer was yes. It was going to require some serious thought.

"You know, my dears" —Lady Leverham had finally succeeded in freeing herself from the doily and was now removing it from the table—"I am ever so fond of this table, but cannot be sure it is suited for this room."

Apparently she had either forgotten or temporarily exhausted the subject of Lord Fremont. Cate was perfectly happy to discuss tables.

The lady's parlor was a minstrel's dream of Gothic arches, carved mahogany furniture, and lush silk tapestries. There was even a painted wooden unicorn in one corner and two sets of armor flanking the door. The table, one of Ambrose Buchanan's finer works, depicted the fall of Carthage. His painted skies had never been smokier, his rivulets and rivers of blood redder. In a room whose four walls were decorated with an impressive collection of maces, pikes, and daggers, the little table looked right at home.

Lady Leverham patted its glossy surface wistfully. "After

all, there is little that is more distressing than different epochs of one's life intruding upon one another."

Cate heartily agreed. Such circumstances could be terribly uncomfortable, not to mention dangerous.

Tregaron grunted as a well-aimed fist thumped into his gut. He dashed what he optimistically assumed was sweat from his brow and earned himself another thump for having lifted his guard arm.

Madness. On a good day, when his mind was reasonably clear and all he wanted was some exertion for his body, this activity was foolishness. On a day like this, when he had chaos roiling in his head and all of him, tip to toe, was reeling from too much liquor, it was madness.

"Enough, sir?" his opponent asked.

"No!" Tregaron snapped, jabbing out a right hook. An image of Cate-on-the-balcony flashed into his muddled brain just then, slowing the thrust enough that a three-legged turtle could have dodged it.

An instant later, he was seated on the hardwood floor, stars in his eyes, a dent below his ribs, and no feeling whatsoever in his posterior. "Madness," he said aloud, then, "Ouch. Bloody hell."

To his credit, Rob MacDougal did not ask if he was hurt, nor did the fellow apologize. Instead, the acclaimed pugilist and boxing salon proprietor offered a hand and helped Tregaron to his feet. Tregaron had long since stopped minding MacDougal's being a full head shorter than he, but was forever the one looking down at him as he sat, reclined, or lay flat as a flounder on the floor. The man was built like a tree stump with arms. And he had fists like anvils.

"I have a question for you, MacDougal," he announced as the man followed him to a bench, one anvil hand hovering just in case he should totter or go down again. 'With no offense intended."

"I'll do my best to take none, m'lord."

"Good. Good. It's about you Scots."

"Aye?"

Tregaron sighed. "Is there an inherent ability to completely flatten men like me, or is it learned?"

"I suppose all the porridge and haggis help build strong . . .

Ah." MacDougal nodded. "You've found yourself a good Highland lassie, have you?"

Tregaron had no idea what he had found, but he was certain of the location. "Argyll, actually."

"God love you, m'lord. And help you."

"Thank you, MacDougal."

"Think nothing of it." The boxer watched in concern as Tregaron lowered himself onto the bench—wondering, probably, if he'd knocked something vital out the other side. "I'd say to hide the knives . . . and to spend as much time at home cuddling your lass in front of the fire as you possibly can. You'll be a lucky and happy man."

Tregaron grunted. "So you say."

"I do indeed. Now I've a question for you, m'lord, seeing as you're among England's foremost n' finest."

"Debatable, that," Tregaron murmured, "but ask away."

"What *is* all the rot about driving about, hmm?" MacDougal propped a foot on the bench and rested his arm across his knee, displaying a hand full of huge and knobby knuckles and not quite straight fingers. "Daft if you ask me, a fellow perching himself all the way up there on the box, then slapping his horses into running hell-for-leather. It's just asking to be tossed off and battered head to foot."

Tregaron gingerly felt his own sore ribs, then surveyed the other man's crooked nose and permanently quirked eyebrows. To each his own sport, he supposed. He shook his head. "I am afraid I am the wrong man to answer that one, my friend."

"You and every other fellow who walks in here. Haven't found one yet who can give much of an answer."

"It must be that you have a more sensible clientele." Either that or they'd all had their brains sufficiently rattled to be a far more hamheaded clientele. Tregaron wasn't at all confident of his own wisdom at present. "And for what it's worth, MacDougal . . ."

"Aye?"

"I have far more Welsh blood in my veins than English."

The boxer grinned, displaying a dimple and several missing teeth. "Do you now? Well, that's all right, then. All of my family since my great-great-grandda' from Mull has been born 'n' bred in Yorkshire, not Scotland."

A quarter hour later, steadier of leg and sense, Tregaron

quitted the salon and headed for his rooms. Gryffydd, whose presence was not welcome at MacDougal's due to his tendency to bite at the ankles of anyone sparring with his master, would be expecting a walk. Tregaron was anticipating a hot bath.

He did not see Vaer until the man was nearly on top of him. "Tregaron!" He flinched first at the volume of the greeting, then at the blast of whiskey fumes. Vaer had clearly just come from a long, liquid luncheon, probably at his club.

"Sly fox, you. Been waiting for you to call on the girl, but noooo." Vaer came to an unsteady halt inches from Tregaron's shirtfront. His nose was vividly red, his cravat askew, and there was a wine-colored trail of spots running down the lapel of his pink waistcoat. "S'pose you're waiting to talk pounds and pence."

"To be honest, sir—"

"Quite right. You're plump enough in the pockets. Land, then. I've a pretty ace . . . er . . . acre or two we can throw in the pot."

"Vaer." Tregaron glanced around, half looking for a convenient hedge into which he could deposit his would-be father-in-law, half to see how much attention they had drawn. Not so very much as yet. A curious passerby had stopped on the opposite side of the street; several shopkeepers were peering through their doors. "Perhaps we can summon you a—"

"Live goods, then. Not a man in England can resist a fine set o' legs and good teeth."

Tregaron could only assume the man was speaking of horses.

"Tregaron!"

There was no mistaking that voice, nor the red hair and face that went with it. The whole of the parts was now approaching at a rapid clip, having appeared as if from nowhere.

"Earith," Tregaron muttered.

"House in Ireland," came from Vaer. "Castle really. Forty-odd rooms. Just needs a bit of work to make the perfect love nest."

"What will it take to send your black soul back to Wales?" Earith demanded.

At present, a swift-moving conveyance and quick stop at the Albany to collect his dog would have sufficed. Tregaron did not say so, however. He resisted, too, the urge to remind the man of the time his son and heir, a milk-faced pup at the time, had taken to writing *billets doux* to the much older, undeniably gorgeous, endlessly feckless wife of a viscount who made even the Duke of Earith's temperament resemble that of a lamb. As it happened. Tregaron had been attending a ball at the viscountess's house on the very night Earith's son had decided to make himself comfortable in the lady's bedchamber—just as the viscount decided to check for such lovestruck intruders. For no reason he could fathom, Tregaron had hustled the young idiot out a connecting door and had faced the viscount himself. He'd nearly had a dawn encounter as a reward for his good deed. As it was, the pounding he had received from three of the viscount's behemoth grooms had been nearly as uncomfortable as a lead ball.

"Well?" Earith spat. "What will it take? Money? The business end of my gun?"

"He ain't going anywhere!" Vaer insisted. "We're discussing important matters of business here."

The duke ignored him. "You've been sniffing about my Chloe, and I won't have it, Tregaron. Do you hear me?"

"I expect half of London hears you, sir," Tregaron replied wearily. They had finally attracted a bit of an audience, the three of them. In fact, a sizeable crowd was gathering nearby. "Perhaps we could take this—"

"Don't you be thinking you can worm your way back into respectability by marrying my daughter. Girl might be a senseless little bit of fluff, but she's a Somersham and has her consequence. But not for the likes of you. I'll see you six feet under before you sully the family name!"

"Oh, cork it, Reggie. You've been trying to marry the girl off for a year," Vaer announced, then hiccuped. "By all means, m'boy, worm your way with my chit. 'Spectable as the Regent's wife and a damned sight easier on the eye."

"Best teach her to shoot like Manton," was the duke's dire pronouncement.

"Oh, balderdash," Vaer retorted. "Man like Tregaron only makes a mistake such as he did once. Elspeth'll be just fine."

Enough was enough. And Tregaron could not decide which was worse: Earith's grunting and growling when he was far more concerned for the family name than his offspring, or Vaer trying to sell his daughter like so much chattel in a street auction. Deplorable, but hardly surprising, if one thought about it. Belinda's father had been much the same, lamenting the introduction of so much hot Welsh blood into his own impeccable lines, desperate enough to marry his daughter to a title that he'd been ready to add the moon to the settlement.

"Gentlemen." Tregaron spoke just loudly enough to get their attention, forcefully enough that Earith closed his jaw with an audible click and Vaer took an unsteady step closer. "No more."

He looked directly at Earith, whose face was now a distinctive shade of purple. "The closest I have been to your daughter is across a crowded room or two. And while I have never once heard that Lady Chloe is senseless, I would suggest that she do something about the bouncing. It is rather disconcerting."

To Vaer, he announced, "I have no need of money. I have ample land in Wales, which happens to include a castle of sorts, to make any sort of nest I desire. I like a nice set of legs and good teeth as much as the next man, but presently have no need of cattle. And should I feel the desire to . . . worm, I will do so elsewhere. As much as I appreciate your very public displays of generosity, I am not so certain the lady in question would. There is nothing for me to take and, at present, I find I have naught to give.

"In short, gentlemen, at this very moment, marriage could not be further from my mind! As far as I am concerned, we may all merrily go our separate ways understanding each other perfectly. Hmm?"

Earith was glaring at him from beneath his beetle brows, hands clenching and unclenching at his side. Tregaron had always thought the man a boor, but never outright stupid. He would figure out that there was nothing more to be said soon enough. Vaer was staring at nothing in particular, one hand scratching at his rotund belly. Chances were, he would recall just enough when he'd sobered to pander his daughter elsewhere—or to come after Tregaron with a primed pistol. Odds were even.

"Now, sirs, if we are quite finished . . ." Without waiting for a response, Tregaron tipped his hat, swept his stick in a quick arc that was half an expression of nonchalance and half warning should anyone decide to get in his way, and strode away.

Vaer's garbled "French brandy? Just smuggled from Calais last week!" had him clenching his teeth in a silent curse, but he did not stop.

The sight of his cousin dead ahead did.

Charles Reynolds was there, too, with Lucius Gramble and Freddie Fortescue. All were splendidly attired, carefully coiffed, and as welcome a sight as a press gang.

"Damme if that wasn't a drama and a comedy in one, Tregaron," Gramble announced blithely. "You could have demanded threepence admission."

"Sixpence, even," from Reynolds.

"With you gentlemen in competition?" Tregaron gave a thin smile. "You hold the comedic genius quite captive. I would be out of business in minutes."

"Port?" Vaer called. "Claret?"

Tregaron sighed.

Edgar, especially resplendent in a canary yellow waistcoat and emerald coat, yawned. "Still don't know why you came back to Town if you ain't looking to leg-shackle yourself. No one wants you here."

Tregaron supposed Edgar could truly believe he had not come looking for a wife. The fellow had always been one of the dimmer candles in the family sconce. Then, too, Edgar had been counting on inheriting the marquessate for years now. Perhaps he had not been the very first in line to see the current marquess strung up for murder; he probably would have been perfectly content to know his cousin was rotting away alone in his Welsh castle . . .

"Best take yourself back to the outlands. Molder there in peace."

"Ah, Cousin." Tregaron shook his head and announced with a sarcasm that was forever lost on Edgar, "I can never guess what thoughts are coursing through the uncluttered corridors of your mind."

Edgar took that with a gratified smile. He was never stupider than when it came to knowing he had been insulted. But then, Tregaron derived no pleasure from baiting the brainless, so he chose his moments.

Again he tipped his hat; again he started on his way. Gramble did not quite smack him in the shin with a gold-tipped stick, but came close. Tregaron could have shoved the thing out of the way or stepped over it, but decided he might as well give these people, whose opinion really meant nothing at all, their chance to take a shot at him.

"There is some Marlowe play or another opening in Covent Garden Friday," Gramble said with nearly convincing affability. "Will you be attending? Terribly old hat, of course, but always entertaining. And I do believe a comedy, no less."

Tregaron was rather fond of Marlowe, as it happened. He thought very little of Lucius Gramble. "*She Stoops to Conquer*, isn't it?"

"Quite right."

"No, perhaps not right at all. That is Goldsmith. How careless of me. No, I do believe it is *School for Scandal.*"

Gramble nodded.

"Or is that Sheridan?" Tregaron shrugged. "You see, I have no taste for comedy. Ah, well. I hope you find it vastly edifying, sir." Once more, he tried to leave.

"Oh, I won't be there," Gramble called after him. "The Jermyn house party is this weekend. I assumed, of course, that you would not have been invited—Do pardon me. That you would not be attending."

"And you were so thoughtful as to look out for me in the absence of that choice entertainment." Tregaron maintained his cool smile, hard as it was. No, he had not been invited to that renowned event. Not in eight years—since he had . . . Belinda had . . . How typical of this meritless creature to raise that specter. "You are a generous soul, Gramble. I daresay you could advisee me in any number of matters."

The man's small eyes glittered. Disappointed at the lack of response, no doubt. "Your servant, sir. Should you ever wish to discuss the matter of women . . ."

Tregaron felt himself stiffen.

"Curious creatures, are they not?" Gramble continued. "Seldom what they seem on viewing. And of course there are always the addled papas to add to the mix. Or uncles, of course."

"Of course." Tregaron had had more than enough. Had he wanted a full afternoon of headaches, he could have stayed at MacDougal's. "Uncles. Good-bye, Gramble. Edgar." Best bored-to-the-teeth expression in place, he toed Gramble's stick out of the way.

The truth of the matter was that he had just amended his plans slightly. Instead of heading toward Piccadilly, he turned north. With the departure of the drunken Vaer and apoplectic Earith, the street had cleared of most of its gawkers. Tregaron actually managed to get a few yards along his way before a lithe figure levered itself away from a hat shop window.

"Hurrying home, Tregaron?" Fremont asked with nearly convincing affability. "And how is the house coming along? I have thought several times to drop in and have a look. I am acquainted with your architects, you know."

"I am aware you have previously met Miss Buchanan." Curiosity warred with distaste and gained a narrow advantage. "It was through her uncles, was it?"

"Not at all." Fremont studied the cuff of his coat with apparent interest. "Are you pleased with their work?"

"I am. I don't suppose you are looking for me to recommend them, since you have known them longer than I."

The other man gave a sharp smile. He owned little property that he could not carry on his person. "A recommendation? Perish the thought. No, no. I am merely making a friendly inquiry into *your* opinion of the Buchanans."

Friendly as a serpent, Tregaron thought. And he was beginning to get the feeling that, short of throttling it out of the man, he wasn't going to get any more answers about Cate than she herself had given.

"I will certainly discuss my experience with my architects with any who should ask."

"Yes, well, I am sure that would be quite a fascinating conversation. So many nuances." Fremont acknowledged someone behind Tregaron's back with a short wave. "Just take care you receive only what you expect."

"What an appalling thought, the contrary," was Tregaron's dry reply. "I have been fortunate in my life to have very few persons cross me. I believe they deem it unwise."

"Yes, I would imagine that is true. But the world *is* full of such unscrupulous sorts these days." With that, Fremont flicked his fingers at his hat brim. "Good day, sir."

He collected his unpleasant little band and the lot of them strolled away toward Bond Street. Tregaron, with the disconcerting feeling that he had quite missed something in that exchange, went the opposite way. He was going to visit his house and make certain it had not tumbled down around someone's ears. He would chat with the Misters Buchanan who, odd though they might have been, had yet to displease him. Then he was going back to his rooms. Gryffydd's walk would have to wait. The master required a stiff drink.

As it happened, the drink would come even sooner than planned. The architects were nowhere to be found.

"Will they be back this afternoon?" he demanded of the ever surly MacGoun.

"I've no idea, m'lord."

"Have they been here today?"

"To be sure. One of the Buchanans has a head-to-head with me each day."

Tregaron tapped his stick against the opposite palm as he glanced around the bedchamber. He'd had to walk all the way up as MacGoun had clearly not been about to come down. He didn't think he had ever been inside this particular room before. It was one Belinda had always kept ready for guests—who never seemed to arrive while he was in residence. He had come to ignore the chamber, just as he had so much else about his wife.

There were no holes in the walls, but all of the glass had been removed from the windows, letting in a brisk afternoon breeze and, unless Tregaron was very much mistaken in the scattering of small feathers on the floor and stuck to the foreman's rough trousers, a bird or two as well.

He must have been scowling, for MacGoun scowled right back and explained, "We'll have a good tarp over the windows tonight and new glass in tomorrow. Miss Cate . . ." He grunted and fell silent.

"Miss Cate did what? I hardly think she broke all three windows. One, perhaps, with that grand wingspan of hers, but certainly not three."

"She didn't break anything," MacGoun snapped. Then,

more calmly, " 'Twas Miss Cate who noticed the caulking was rotted away. One more good storm and you'd have had shattered glass on the floor and a pond under the bed."

Tregaron suddenly felt more defeated than he had sitting on the boxing salon floor. Sighing, he ran a hand through his hair and scratched at the back of his head. "You know, MacGoun," he said wearily, "I have had the damnedest day. I am beginning to wonder if perhaps I ought not go back to bed and start it all over again."

To his great astonishment, the glowering foreman dropped a heavy hand onto his shoulder and gave it a brief squeeze. "Try whiskey, lad. And lots of it." Then, with one of his familiar sharp grunts that could mean anything at all, he spun on his heel and clomped out of the room.

Chapter 11

Cate was beginning to see the end. There came a point in every job when all the details suddenly came together, when she could see less to do than what had already been done. She was there.

True, some of the floors still needed finishing; a few walls and ceilings still required plaster details and paint or paper. The new grates needed to be installed in the fireplaces. The masons had only just begun filling the chinks in the exterior stonework. Uncle Ambrose was painting his bacchanal with all the speed of molasses. But Cate's work was nearly done.

It was so tempting, to wander through rooms smelling of paint and varnish, to imagine small details she would never get to see there. The south wall of the drawing room had the perfect spaces for a little pair of marble-topped commodes; the hearth wanted nothing but an embroidered cheval firescreen in autumnal colors. The dining room, with its rich, leaf-patterned topaz paper, needed a Chinese vase or two on the mantel. And the north-facing sitting room of the master bedchamber suite positively cried out for a brocade chaise with a mohair throw and plump silk pillows for reading.

Cate would come, perhaps once, when the upholsterers were completing their tasks. But she had already seen Henry Gordon's—no, she corrected herself with a smile—Henri desJardin's designs, had in fact worked with him to create a palette of subtle autumn colors and lush, heaven-to-the-touch fabrics to complement the paints and wallpapers. MacQuarrie's chandeliers would be ready for mounting the instant the last drop of paint had dried. Rugs, both new and carried from the attics for cleaning, were rolled and waiting to grace the glossy floors. A devout disciple of Capability Brown had already dug up half the rear garden.

He swore he would put something back in well before the end of the Season.

It had always been a good house, one full of promise. Now it was on the verge of being a truly wonderful place.

Gordie appeared in the dining room doorway. "Sorry to disturb you, miss, but we've just gotten the bricks from Sussex."

"Well, thank heaven, and it's dashed well about time," Cate muttered as she followed him out the door. "Are they the correct ones?"

"Salt-glazed black, miss. Fine enough for the facade of the Prince's next folly."

Cate smiled as she descended the stairs. Fine enough for the front of the next Carlton House or Brighton Pavilion indeed, but these bricks were destined for the kitchen and to line the fireplaces of Tregaron House. It was an extravagance, to be sure, but what a delight it would be, flames and heat reflecting off the glossy black.

MacGoun was muttering over the loaded hods when Cate and Gordie reached the ground floor. "Bloody piracy," he grumbled, the bill clutched in his thorny fist.

It was an argument they'd had before, and one Cate was in no mood for now. "Are they all here? I need them installed before Jamie moves the grates in."

"Aye, aye. They're all here. But look at this, Miss Cate." MacGoun waved the bill in her face. "Just you look at the *tax*."

She didn't need to look. If she did, she knew she would wince, and MacGoun needed no further fuel for his ire. "Would you rather have to learn French, Mac?"

"As if Boney has a chance," he shot back. "Our lads would shove him right back into the sea should he even get a toe on British soil."

"Yes, well, someone has to pay those lads and purchase their various shoving and shooting implements. So our bricks have this tax and we pay it. Or rather, Lord Tregaron pays it."

The foreman had never quite been satisfied with that explanation in the past. He wasn't now. "Bloody piracy, I say," he muttered, then stomped off to find a few strong backs to lift the hods.

Cate needed to find Jamie. Bricks and grates would have

to go into the selected fireplaces before the final touches were put on the floors. There was wallpapering to be supervised, paint to be approved, an endless array of small tasks. Well begun, half done, she reminded herself, and headed again for the stairs.

A gentle baritone flowed from the ballroom, rich and melodious and perfectly suited for the stage. It was singing of the massacre at Culloden field. At that moment, the bulk of the Clan Fraser was meeting a gruesome death, in explicit detail.

Cate stuck her head in the doorway. Uncle Ambrose was atop his miniature painter's scaffold, cheerfully detailing a centaur's head as an unfortunate Fraser lost his to a Borderer's sword. "Looks marvelous!" she called.

Ambrose stopped singing and grinned at her over his shoulder. He was wearing enough paint from head to toe to resemble a casualty of war himself. "Not bad. Not bad at all if I do say so myself. Recognize him?" He extended his brush toward a massive, cheerful Dionysus, arms spread benevolently to his guests, cup running over.

"I do, and a handsome fellow he is there as well as in life."

As Ambrose's face graced the god of wine and revelry, other familiar visages looked out from the picture. There was Angus as goat-bodied Pan, a representation he would not appreciate and which was, Cate assumed, retribution for his having sculpted Ambrose as the lumbering Goliath in a massive marble garden statue the year before. It was a good-natured artistic wrestling match, one that Cate expected would go on for a great many years to come.

She found Lucy's fair face shining out as beautiful Nyaiad, a bacchanalian nymph. She located herself, flatteringly lithe and lovely, armored as an attendant to Artemis. "Thank you, O Dionysus," she murmured, blowing her uncle a kiss.

Wellington the Centaur was there, looming over a roast boar that bore a distinct resemblance to the Bonaparte. Among the satyrs, the horned and hairy, oafish and lascivious creatures who served Dionysus, Cate saw a subtle Prince of Wales, a not so subtle Duke of Argyll, and the last three men who had commissioned garden follies from the Buchanans.

The face most notably absent was that of the man paying for this pictorial extravaganza. By all rights, Tregaron should have been the center of the piece, but he was so far from the jovial, gregarious Dionysus that Cate understood her uncle's decision there—his own narcissism notwithstanding. And he couldn't very well have put his employer's face on a satyr.

"Are you not including the marquess?"

Ambrose, back to singing and dabbing at the wall, pointed briefly to the top corner of the picture. It was an area sketched in but yet to be painted, and Cate had to stand on her toes to see.

"Zeus?" she asked, studying the strong, somber profile observing the party from a cloudy clime.

"Do you approve, Catey lass? I'm rather proud of it, myself."

"It's perfect."

And it was. Only, something niggled at Cate as she stood beneath the image. It was proud, aristocratic, grand, and . . . Alone, she realized suddenly. Lonely. While other denizens of Olympus made merry below, this figure remained apart, watching.

The last of the ballad's noble Scotsmen fell. Ambrose ended the song with a bellowed flourish, then made a last dramatic sweep of his paintbrush. "That's it, then. I'm calling it a day."

Cate pulled her mother's little gold watch from her pocket. Half-three. "Already?" she asked, more in irony than in expectation of an answer.

Irony, as always, was quite lost on Ambrose. "I'm to meet Angus at the p—at the museum."

"And what museum would that be?"

"Just a little one, lass. Just a little one, but filled to the brim with inspiration."

He clambered down from his scaffold, absently wiping his brush on the smock that didn't quite cover his sleeves. Cate knew he would take the time to care fully for his supplies, far less for himself. But the denizens of whatever tavern he and Angus were to frequent were unlikely to object to a bit of paint.

"You don't mind if I go, Catey. Do you?"

As if it mattered. Cate leaned up and gingerly kissed her

uncle's paint-smeared, sandpapery cheek. "Off with you. Everything here is well under control."

She heard him leave some ten minutes later, the door thumping shut behind him. From the master bedchamber window, Cate watched him disappear down the street. His step was light, his hat at a cocky angle. She opened the window to hear him whistling.

He never said so, but Cate knew he wanted to be away from other people's houses and tucked up inside his own studio, where he was lord and master. With luck and a bit of increased effort, he would finish the mural soon and wouldn't need to come by the site at all. Cate imagined he would be a happy man on that day.

A brisk breeze brushed by her shoulder. Behind her, there was a loud clatter and muffled curse. She turned to see a young bricklayer hopping on one foot while glaring at a toppled pile of glazed bricks. "Sorry, miss," he offered for the curse, blushing slightly.

Cate waved off the apology, then one of the feathers that forever seemed to be decorating the floors. "Well?"

"We can have them all in by Wednesday. Grates can go in the next Monday."

"Good. They're lovely, aren't they? The grates."

The young man scratched his head. "Can't say as I would ever have thought of them that way, but if you say so, miss."

So far, only the man who sold the iron Rumford grates had shared Cate's enthusiasm. Well, she would be vindicated when the things started turning up in every house in Mayfair and further afield. "Never mind. Have the rest of the bricks been put in the right rooms?"

"All but the closed room downstairs. Jamie said to check with you first."

"Ah, yes, the library."

Cate had not set foot in the library since that very first day when Tregaron had been so very rude and arrogant. Nor, to her knowledge, had anyone else. And she fully intended to obey his mighty lordship's decree that nothing be altered. Nothing, that was, except the fireplace. He could rot away, alone in there with his books, if that's what he wanted. In fact, Cate supposed she would be helping. Once the new grate was in, he would never be either frozen or smoked out of his cave. He could stay there forever.

The outside of the library door had been refinished many days back with the rest of the doors on its hall. There was no reason its newly glossy surface should look any darker than the rest, nor that the quirked beads carved into the frame above it should resemble teeth. They did. Scolding herself for fancy, Cate strode briskly down the hallway.

She could not, however, push her way so casually into the room. She took a breath, grasped the handle and, when the door resisted, used her shoulder. The door gave with a sound that was half grunt, half sigh. It would seem the workmen hadn't wanted to disturb what lay beyond, either, and had closed off the room before the varnish was dry.

Cate stood on the threshold for a full minute. Her eyes adjusted slowly to the gloom inside. The heavy drapes were closed. Not that there was much light to let in. London's skies had been sullen all day, grey and heavy, threatening rain that had yet to come.

Needing whatever light she could muster, Cate wove her way around the shrouded furniture and cluttered floor. Her booted foot struck a hard, round object that rolled off the musty-smelling rug and onto the wood floor with a clatter. When she nearly stumbled over an ornate floor pedestal a moment later, Cate decided the ball had been a globe. Before she reached the window, she had avoided, kicked, or nearly tripped over countless books, the individual parts of a writing set, a cut glass decanter, and a squishily soft object that her first horrified thought told her had once been a living thing until she realized it was a wad of loose stuffing that had come from a nearby broken and gutted footstool.

She had not noticed the full pattern of destruction on her first visit to this room, but now it appeared that some sort of small war had been fought within these walls. Once she got the heavy curtains open and had recovered from a vigorous sneezing fit brought on by a fall of dust, she took a good look around. The shattered remains of a second decanter were scattered dully in the fireplace, too dusty to glint as broken glass should. The sphere she had kicked, which did indeed turn out to be a carefully carved and painted globe, rested now between the cobwebby rails of a bookshelf ladder. The globe's shell, its interior painted to depict the heavens, lay in two pieces beneath the massive desk.

The dropcloth had come half off that piece of furniture. Or, perhaps, had never been fully in place. There was certainly the feeling of sudden and complete abandonment in the dusty air. Cate took a peek beneath the canvas. She saw an elaborately gold-embossed leather blotter, a tarnished letter opener that was clearly the work of a master silversmith, an overturned but intact crystal glass whose glory still shone through despite what had probably been years in its present spot, and the majestic lines of the desk itself.

Turning, Cate identified the painting over the mantel with complete certainty as a Gainsborough. If she was not mistaken, the square tapestry on the opposite wall was Flemish and quite probably dated from three hundred years before. The statue of Mars resting on its side on the mantel looked Roman and about a millennium old. Years of living among artists had given Cate a fairly accurate eye for such things. She wasn't quite sure what to make of the pair of rough-hewn wooden spoons next to Mars, but could only assume they were aged and valuable, too. This was a room full of very precious objects, one that, anywhere else, would have been the pride and haven of its owner.

Then, of course, there was the one full wall of floor-to-ceiling bookshelves, and the second with its shelves flanking the fireplace, mantel, and Gainsborough. There were plenty of empty spaces, some large, their former occupants clearly scattered over the floor. Everywhere else, rich leather bindings stood against one another. Dust had dulled many of the tomes, but could not obliterate their fineness.

Tilting her head back, Cate let her eyes drift up to the twenty-odd-foot ceilings. On the upper shelves were entire sets of books in perfect, matching, heavily gold-embossed bindings. Curious, she climbed up a half-dozen rungs and lifted one book from its shelf. More cobwebs pulled free and drifted the fifteen feet to the floor. The book was from a set of Carpenter's *Life of Spenser in Twelve Volumes*. The pages were uncut. As were those in the nearby set of *Norse Fishing Ballads*. And, above, the complete Aristophanes oeuvre, translated into French. Upper shelf after shelf held books that had probably never been opened, let alone read.

Shaking her head at the caprices of the wealthy, Cate climbed back to the floor. She would have very much liked to have spent more time perusing the shelves, but she was in the room for one purpose only—to measure the fireplace. After that, she would close the door behind her and not look back.

She did take a last look at the shelves however. A thick little book caught her eye. A Kearsely's *Peerage*. There had been one on her mother's shelf years and years back, unread, as was the Julian's *Baronetage* that had listed both Mary Buchanan's father, Sir James Hamilton, and Mary herself beneath his meager sentences.

Smiling to herself, humming quietly, Cate set her measuring tape down on the desk and pulled the peerage from the shelf. She had no intention of allowing Tregaron liberties of any sort with her person now, but she was not going to pass up the opportunity to learn the forename he'd been so unwilling to share.

She checked the publication date. 1804. A mere few years before Tregaron had left Society. She flipped quickly to the alphabetical General Index near the front. M. *Marlborough, Duke.* She flipped through several more pages. *St. Helier, Earl.* She turned the page. *Townshend, Marquess. Traquair, Earl. Tregaron, Marquess.* Page . . .

She nearly leapt from her skin when the book was jerked from her hands.

Her first thought was that no man Tregaron's size should be able to move so silently. Her second was that the silence was probably about to be shattered. She bit her lip and waited for the explosion.

It did not come. Tregaron, face hard and impassive, closed the peerage with a snap and set it on the desk. Then he leaned one hip against the shrouded surface, crossed his arms over his chest, and regarded Cate inscrutably. She opened her mouth to speak, but managed nothing more than a muted and embarrassing squeak.

"And a good afternoon to you, too," he said blandly.

"I . . . ah . . ."

"You know, Cate, I am beginning to wonder whether

this is my house or yours. You seem to be much more in residence here than I."

His eyes, Cate noticed, were mahogany in the limited light. They were also fringed by lashes so thick and dark that a pang of envy came right behind the frisson of warm awareness. She wondered how she had missed that stirring little feature. Then she wondered if she had perhaps taken leave of her senses. Eyelashes were hardly the important matter at hand. Or rather they should not be.

She took advantage of the fact that Gryffydd was at her ankle, demanding a pat, to drop her own gaze. "I am here to visit . . . to help . . ."

"Yes, yes," Tregaron said impatiently. "Your uncles. For God's sake, Cate, stop looking at me as if I'm going to send you headfirst out the window. I don't care if you do take up residence here. You can't very well hang about Binney Street all day every day. What I want to know right now is why you felt compelled to ignore the only specific instructions I ever gave, and come in here." He gestured to the discarded peerage. "And prying as well? You seem to have an inordinate interest in my private matters."

He could see that stung. Had Cate possessed visible hackles, they would have risen before his eyes. She stiffened, unruly head to sturdy toe. "That is not fair."

"Isn't it? Come now, Cate. Tell me you were not digging through this silly lump of moldy paper in search of my name."

"I . . . I was n . . . Well, bother!" she snapped. "Yes. Yes, I was. I do not like being deceived. Or at least, I do not like that you see fit to use my Christian name—when I have never given you leave to do so—without even sharing yours."

Oh, she was splendid when she was on her high horse, Tregaron mused. A bronze Hera, all spark and flame. He suppressed a smile. "Shall I return to always calling you Miss Buchanan?"

"No," was her instant retort. "I mean . . . Well, no. I do not really mind. I simply do not care to be on such unequal footing."

Truly splendid. "You do not believe we are unequal?"

Her firm Scottish chin went up another notch. "Of course," she said icily. "How could I possibly believe otherwise? You are the high and mighty Lord Tregaron. A marquess. A nabob. A man. I am—"

"About to back into the ladder," he informed her. She stopped her stiff withdrawal and stood rigid as a statue. "Oh, Cate. I do not doubt for an instant that you are my equal. In fact, I would imagine that in a great many ways, you are my superior. I do, however, reserve the right to keep certain matters to myself, at least in my own home. If you are so intent on learning the minute and not particularly interesting details of my life, do so elsewhere. In the meantime, I will give you a list of any number of names, some of which I will actually answer to, just for your selection.

"Now," he continued, gratified to see a fine line of discomfiture between her gingery brows, "unless you can convince me that you have an inarguably good reason for being in this room, I suggest we leave it."

He did not *want* to be in here. Not with so many possessions he had enjoyed, so many books he had looked forward to reading, leaving the pages uncut until such time as he could sit down and delight in the complete process. He did not think he *should* be alone in here with his memories. Or with Cate.

Her mouth opened and closed once. Finally, she announced, "I came to measure the fireplace. For my uncles."

"Did you?" He glanced without much interest at the cold maw of the hearth. "Why?"

"To be certain the bricks and grate will fit."

"Correct me if I am mistaken, but are there not already bricks and a grate there?"

She fidgeted for a moment, something he had never seen her do before, glancing at the floor as she prodded the moth-eaten carpet with a toe. "Do you really wish to discuss such matters, my lord? With me?"

"Why not? Illuminate me, Cate. Otherwise, in my newly fascinated state, I shall be forced to seek out your uncles who, I suppose I should inform you, are nowhere to be found."

"There is no need to be snide," she chided. "I daresay my uncles have just stepped out to confer with . . . some supplier."

"Fine. So tell me about my fireplace."

"We . . . er . . . the men will be installing a new Rumford grate, with a special flue to keep the smoke out of the room and glazed brick behind to reflect the heat into it. It is, I believe, a rather novel innovation, but then, I know little of such things. I am only here to—"

"Measure the fireplace."

"Well, yes."

Tregaron shook his head wryly. "Fine. We will measure the fireplace."

She scooped up the measuring tape from the desk and was at the hearth before he could intervene. She did not bend to her task immediately, however, but grasped the tipped statue on the mantel and reverently returned it to its rightful position. It was a futile act, Tregaron thought, considering the state of the rest of the room, but a touching one.

Then she ran a fingertip over one of the wooden spoons. "Are these from the Orient?"

"No."

"The Indies?"

"No. They are Welsh."

"Ah. Celtic. Were they found in a burial mound, perhaps? Used in ancient pagan rituals?"

He did not especially want to discuss the spoons, but could not muster the requisite churlishness to refuse. Beyond that, he could only imagine what Cate was envisioning as the pair's pagan use, and he found himself amused. "I suppose that would depend on your concept of ancient and pagan. That pair were wedding gifts, carved well into the Christian age."

He saw her flush. "I am sorry. I did mean to bring up your . . . er . . ."

"They were given to my grandmother on her wedding day by one of my grandfather's tenants, the man who carved them. They are called love spoons and are as deep a part of Wales as—"

"Dragons," she whispered.

"Coal and ale," he said tartly. He watched as she lifted one spoon. It went nearly from her fingertips to her elbow, the bowl as long as her palm and the handle decorated with three carved chain links and a Celtic cross. The carving was rough, almost primitive, but proud. "The cross symbolizes marriage," he murmured, repeating almost by rote the words his grandmother had said over and again when she'd passed on the spoons. "The links are the number of children to be born to the marriage."

"Were there three?"

"Yes." Only one of whom, his father, had grown to adulthood.

"And this?" Cate held up the second spoon. It bore a pair of intertwined hearts and an anchor. "Lovers and a sea voyage?"

"Love," he agreed tersely, "and steadfastness."

"And did they . . ."

"They had both."

They had indeed, his grandparents. Love and faithfulness and more joy in each other than almost seemed fair.

"It seems to me that your Welsh love spoons are rather pagan, to be sure, and those who carve them rather wonderful prognosticators."

"They fail as often as they work, like all predictions," he retorted, hearing the bitterness in his own voice. "Toss enough possibilities into the pot and something is bound to come true. These were only so much rubbish when it came to my marriage." He broke off, appalled with his loose tongue, then nearly jumped when one of Cate's hands came to rest, light and fleetingly, on his arm.

"These weren't carved for you, were they?" she demanded softly. "Your chain and anchor haven't been cast yet."

Rattled suddenly, unsteady, he tugged the measuring tape from her hands and moved to crouch on the hearth. "Tell me which dimensions you require."

After a long silence she did, then jotted the numbers he gave her in a little pocket notebook. It was not particularly easy work, nor comfortable; he had to contort himself in several odd ways. And all for a grate which, he was sure, would send as much heat up the flue and as much smoke out of it as any. But there was something restful, something companionable about doing this ridiculous little task with Cate jotting away nearby, and somehow the room did not unsettle him so much as it had since his return, so he gritted his teeth and rotated his shoulder to reach the last spot.

Gryffydd chose that moment to come have a look. The

little animal shoved his nose under his master's armp[illegible]
wriggled forward to get two paws on the old grate and a good half of himself into the fireplace.

"Gryffydd . . ."

"Oh, my lord, do not . . .!"

But it was too late. His elbow jogged something, his fist jiggled something else, and eight years worth of debris came tumbling onto the hearth. Soot, dirt, leaves, and small objects Tregaron did not care to identify flowed over his arm, his feet, and his dog. The resulting cloud was enough to obscure his view of the room for a few long seconds.

When it settled, Gryffydd promptly scuttled under the desk, where he crouched, sneezing and pawing at his blackened face. Tregaron spat grit from his mouth, blinked more from his eyes, and rose slowly to his feet. "I trust," he muttered, pausing to brush a sooty feather from the tip of his nose with his one clean hand, "you can manage without that last measurement."

Cate was doing her very best not to laugh. So far she was succeeding, but now, as Tregaron stalked regally away from the hearth, she was losing the battle. Half of him, the half that had been facing away from the fireplace, was very nearly tidy. The other half looked as if it had been dipped in a dustbin. The soot did not show so much as the dust did on his navy coat, but it generously dusted his skin, shirt, and waistcoat. There were more feathers scattered from shoulder to knee, and the twiggy remnants of a nest caught in the fine fabric of his coat and breeches.

"I think," she managed, swallowing hard, "I will be fine with what we have."

It was ultimately the sight of the dog emerging from beneath the desk that snapped her control. There was a distinct line around the middle of the animal's stocky body. The rear half was its usual mustard color, tidy and twitching with its usual good humor. The front half was soot black, relieved only by Gryffydd's grinning mouth and the very narrow rim of white in his eyes.

Unable to help herself, Cate laughed. And kept laughing until she was nearly doubled over, groping in her pockets for a handkerchief. When the cleaner of Tregaron's hands appeared in her line of vision, proffering his own handkerchief, she nearly fell over. "No, no thank you," she gasped, waving him off. "You have slightly more need of it than I."

She heard him grunt. When she was at last able to take several steadying breaths and straighten up, she found that he had indeed availed himself of the expensive silk square. His face was relatively clean with the exception of a few lingering bits of debris at his hairline; both hands were only slightly grimy. He was presently trying to remove some of the dirt from the dog's face. Gryffydd was having none of it and soon cheerfully wriggled free to climb under the desk again.

Determinedly, Cate kept a straight face and suggested, "Perhaps you ought to go home and see to . . . ah . . . a bath for Gryffydd." In truth, she would be sad to see an end to the companionable time, but all good things, she knew, tended to end abruptly.

Tregaron grunted again, then stalked to the door, which Cate had not noticed him shut earlier. He paused there, hand on the knob, and appeared to be engaged in some significant inner contemplation. He rattled the knob several times, but seemed in no hurry to actually leave the room.

Cate waited as long as seemed polite, then queried, "My lord?"

"Yes, Cate?"

"Were you not departing?"

He shot her a caustic look over his defiled shoulder. "Trust me, my dear, nothing would please me more just now."

"Well?" Cate demanded, hands on her hips.

"I cannot open the door."

Chapter 12

"What do you mean you cannot open the door?" Cate demanded. "Of all the ridiculous things to say. Of course you can open the door."

Tregaron glanced back again, brows raised in challenge. "Care to have a go?"

She did, of course. And got less of a result than he had. She could not even find a knob to rattle.

"I don't suppose," he said dryly after she'd spent a good minute searching the door, the floor, and even, for some reason, her pocket, "this is what you are looking for."

She turned slowly. He had his hand outstretched, the doorknob resting in his open palm. "Oh, for pity's sake," she snapped and, snatching it from him, prepared to make her escape.

It did not take her long to realize there was another problem. The square spindle that connected the knob on one side of the door to the knob on the other was, in fact, on the other side. Meaning that while Cate held a perfectly good doorknob, she did not possess the piece necessary to engage the inner latch-bolt mechanism.

She dropped to her knees, hoping to see under the door. This detail, however, was like so many in the house—beautifully attended. The door fit snugly in its frame, not enough space at the bottom to admit so much as a mouse. Cate remained where she was, crouched on the floor, useless knob clutched in her fist.

"I would guess that I am getting a much better view than you are."

Realizing she was, in fact, giving him altogether too much of a view of her elevated posterior, Cate hurriedly rose to a point where she could sit back on her heels and glare at him.

"The door was already sticking earlier. You must have loosened the spindle when you closed it," she announced grimly.

"I suppose I could have, although I am but guessing what a spindle is." Tregaron had gone back to leaning on the desk, the picture of bored elegance, if one ignored the soot and twigs. "Only I did not close the door."

"You must have. You have forgotten."

"Trust me, my dear. As delightful as I find your company, I am not so covetous of it that I would have the blatantly poor judgment to closet us alone in my library."

For some reason, Cate did not particularly care for that response. She was not, however, going to take the time to figure out just what it was that bothered her. Pressing her eye to the hole where the spindle would go, she peered into the hall. Rotate as she would, she could see no farther than four or five feet in either direction. She certainly did not see any fallen door pieces.

"Mac?" she called. Then, louder, "Gordie?" And finally, *"Anyone?"*

There was no response save some distant pounding.

"I did not see anyone on this floor as I came in," Tregaron informed her.

"No. They are all upstairs or down in the kitchens. Or . . ." Inspired, Cate sprang to her feet and ran to the nearest window. It looked out onto the garden—the empty garden. Apparently the visionary Mr. Patton and his men had finished their digging for the day and, with nothing yet to place in the trenches they made, had gone home.

"I suppose we could go out the window," she said dubiously, gazing at the stone patio several floors below. "We could tie the dropcloths together."

"We will do no such thing."

"It might work. Come have a look."

"No."

"But I really do think it might work. Why . . . ?"

He scowled. Not quite the fearsome scowl of all those weeks past, perhaps. Cate was becoming used to his expressions, she supposed. Used to him. "Because," he said sharply, "I am not about to let you go swinging out a second-story window, and hell will freeze over before I do so myself."

"Well." Cate debated arguing, but thought better of it. As it happened, she had no great desire to go swinging from any window. She returned to the door. "Help!" she called through the hall. "Anyone!"

"Cate." Tregaron was behind her suddenly, one hand on each elbow, hauling her to her feet. "You will shout yourself hoarse. Now"—he pulled the doorknob from her hand and gave her a gentle shove toward the covered divan—"sit down for a moment. Let me see what I can do."

Cate was ready again to object, this time simply in response to his officiousness. But she found herself carefully lowering herself onto the dusty dropcloth instead, propping elbows on knees, chin on fists, and watching.

Tregaron knelt in front of the door, then folded himself smaller when he was still too tall to see through the hole. A moment later he was sliding a long finger into the works, trying to engage the latch mechanism. He kept at it for several minutes. Cate waited for the click that would indicate success. It didn't come. A quiet if audible string of rather impressive curses did.

"It's no good," he announced finally. "We need the piece, whatever you called it, from the other side." He sat back on his heels, brow furrowed. Then, rising, he went to dig beneath the desk's drapery. Cate watched as he opened one drawer after another. He was clearly in search of something specific, just as clearly unsure of where it was. Or, perhaps, if it was there at all after so many years.

When he gave a satisfied smile and came up with a handful of quills, Cate could not imagine what was in his mind. Writing a note and shoving it through the door was all well and good, should someone happen along the hallway. In which case, shouting or banging away at the wood would serve as much purpose as a little letter requesting that the passerby release them. Beyond that, Cate expected there would be something of a problem in finding usable ink in the long-abandoned desk.

Tregaron chose the longest quill and rolled it carefully between his fingers as if testing its strength. Then, to Cate's surprise, rather than seeking out other writing necessities, he pulled his grubby handkerchief from his pocket. Nor did it make much sense when he attached the thing to the quill point and carried it back to the door. It wasn't until he stuck the creation, handkerchief first, through the knob-hole, that she understood.

"I take it we surrender."

He surveyed his handiwork as best he could. It would do. "I've done enough battle against immutable objects in my life to know when surrender is the best option."

"Clever," was her response, nodding to the visible, feather-end of his makeshift flag.

"Only if someone sees it."

Satisfied that he had done what he could for the time being, Tregaron walked away from the door. Deciding that he might as well sit down, he joined Cate on the shrouded leather divan. It creaked. She moved to the far end. Doing his best to ignore the sting of that, he stretched his legs out in front of him, and crossed his ankles. If no one came along in the next half hour or so, he would try something else. For now, there was nothing to do but wait.

"God," he growled to himself, "I hate this bloody house."

"You shouldn't." Cate was staring at him intently from her comically safe four feet away. "It's a wonderful house."

He grunted.

"And," she continued, "it will be what you want it to from now on."

"What on earth is that supposed to mean?" She flushed. Novel, he thought, his Amazon blushing.

"I mean that the house is merely stone and paint, wood and glass, some furniture. Whatever you place on the walls and tables. If there is more here . . . poor . . . associations, it is up to you to banish them."

"As easy as that, hmm?"

He had not meant to be sarcastic, not really. But her naive assurance pricked at him. She could guess, perhaps, about what had happened within the house's walls, but couldn't know. She was an outsider and, her spirit and intelligence aside, was clearly inexperienced in the ways of the world. She wouldn't understand the love that had been made in these rooms, the battles that had been waged, the histories decided. He himself wasn't aware of all of them throughout the house's history. He had more than enough to choose from among those in which he had participated.

"Not necessarily easy," Cate was saying now. "I never said easy. It requires some effort, and perhaps some help."

In that instant, Tregaron could think of a hundred ways she could help banish some of the ghosts and cobwebs. Taking a broom to this very floor would be a decent start.

That, he thought, that glibness, was beneath even him. It was the first train of thought, of the ways she could ease his aches, that had been poking at him in so many different ways lately. The thoughts were there even when Cate was not present, surprisingly strong when she was. Cate, with her unpredictable tongue and predictably inelegant appearance. Not at all what he was looking for.

As if that ever mattered when bloody inconvenient lust was concerned.

"Are you offering to help?" he demanded.

She stared back at him. One of her hands, he noted, was worrying at a worn spot in the apron she was wearing over yet another deplorable dress. "I have always endeavored to be as much use as possible to my family's business."

Tregaron did not think her uncles would care to know just what sort of business he had in mind. He might have laughed, only he laughed rarely and this was fast becoming a very serious situation.

"Well?" he pressed. "Are you offering me your succor, Cate?

Cate's fingers drifted over her knee to unravel more of the apron's frayed hem. Her eyes, however, were fixed on his, sharp and fiercely blue. "Will I regret it?"

She saw she had surprised him. Insofar as her whirling thoughts would allow, she had meant to. She was not quite so naive, she decided, as he thought.

"Will you regret it?" He appeared to ponder that for a moment. "I don't know. Are you the sort to regret your decisions?"

"Only the poor ones," she shot back, and lifted her chin.

He understood.

"Ah, Cate. Do you have any idea what you've begun?"

In a single motion, smooth as water, he slipped from his seat and came to kneel before her on the thick rug.

Everything was there in that face: a warning and a summons, weariness and vigor, a wickedness—and a tenderness so potent it made Cate shiver. Most of all, there was a desire in his eyes, for her, that could not be mistaken, even by the most suspicious heart.

He reached for her.

Cate considered herself well read. While she would never have admitted it to her family, the earthy, passionate poems of John Donne were among her favorites. And she was not wholly without experience. Perhaps her brief and ill-advised interludes with Lord Fremont had ended unpleasantly—and, in retrospect, not precisely overwhelmed her while they were happening—but they had been illuminating.

Nothing in her life could ever have prepared her for the Marquess of Tregaron.

He moved slowly enough so that she could have easily evaded his touch. Instead, she watched, wide-eyed, as, one at a time, he undid the little buttons at one wrist. Then the other. While the voice of decorum in her head screamed that she was being *disrobed* by a man, the rest of her sat utterly still while he loosened her sleeves. Gently and still so slowly, he pushed each sleeve up, past her elbow. And then he grasped her by the arms.

She shivered as his hands tightened. Then she actually gasped aloud when his thumbs slid into the hollows where her arms bent. Soft as a whisper, he moved his thumbs back and forth over the suddenly sensitive spots. Had she been standing, Cate knew her knees would have failed her. She had the distinct feeling that her bones were melting, one after the other. And he was just touching her inner arms.

She lifted slightly hazy eyes, looked into his face. His features were hard, unreadable, but his eyes were warm. And drawing. "Come to me, fiery Cate," he commanded, and pulled.

In a breath, she was on her knees on the floor, facing him. Only then did his hands leave her arms. He cupped her jaw in his palms, his thumbs tracing her lips this time, first the upper, then the lower, gently urging them apart. Cate very nearly went into an ungainly heap. She swayed backward, and was held upright only by the hard frame of the divan.

And Tregaron stayed right with her. His hands slid into

her hair, scattering what pins had made it through the day, releasing the springy mass to tickle at her cheeks and tumble over her shoulders. He threaded his fingers deeper until they met and cradled the back of her head. Cate's eyes began to drift shut.

"Not yet," she heard him say gruffly. "Look at me."

She did. She watched as his face came closer to hers. A thick lock of night-black hair, always so controlled, had slipped forward to fall in an unruly arc over his forehead. One brow lifted, slowly.

"Well, Miss Buchanan?"

It took Cate a moment, but she realized he was waiting, asking her permission to go on. She nodded shakily, thinking she had never wanted anything quite so desperately in her life. He smiled—a slow, wicked smile that she felt all the way to her toes.

"Now," he said. "Now you can close your eyes."

And he kissed her.

Perhaps it was that he tasted and smelled of woodsmoke. Or that they were so close together that she could feel the radiating warmth of him. Or perhaps it was just the kiss. Whatever the reason, Cate was certain she was on the verge of bursting into flame. His lips were hard as they slanted over hers, yet amazingly yielding. And thorough—so very, very deliberate and thorough.

Cate couldn't summon up so much as a sliver of memory from her short embraces with Fremont. She summarily dumped twenty-odd years of faery tale notions. This was what she had been waiting for.

When he broke the kiss, gently holding her face away from his, she sighed with the loss. "So?" he asked. "What have you to say for yourself, my dear?"

Cate sighed again. "Is it a regret if I am sorry that I had no idea what I've missed?"

He chuckled, low in his throat, as he shoved several books and an empty inkwell out of the way behind him with one hand. The other he wrapped firmly around her waist. When he lay back, stretching his full length over the carpet, he took her with him. She was leaning against him now, one hip pressed against his, one hand on his chest, her hair a tangle aura around her pale face as he looked up at her.

It was all too scandalous to be contemplated, and too wonderful to be refused.

"Someday," he murmured, tracing a fingertip along her jaw, "painters will return to depicting the mythological and legendary. Hippolyta, Guinevere, Saint Joan. And when they do, Catherine Buchanan, you will be their muse."

Had he known how easy it was to make her blush with the right words, he would have taken to doing so much earlier. The pink started at her throat and rose all the way to those marvelous cheekbones, softening her face, giving it a glow.

"Don't flatter me," she said.

"Whyever not?"

"Because it is all flummery, and I do not need it."

Tregaron disagreed. Oh, he imagined Cate believed her own words, but how wrong they were. Every woman needed to be flattered. Not for vanity's sake, like members of his own sex, but for the acknowledgment that members of his sex, a dismally dim-witted lot among whom he fully and unhesitatingly placed himself, noticed her.

Cate Buchanan, he decided, had not been flattered nearly enough in her life. He supposed he could change that easily enough. Just not right then.

"Let us get back to matters at hand," he suggested, running one hand up her back until it rested between her shoulder blades. "Kiss me, Cate."

Her mouth curved. "A thieving bard and a rake."

He found himself smiling back. "No man with a Cate in his arms could help but steal that one line. And I am a dismally poor example of a rake."

"I don't believe that for an instant," she whispered, single-handedly turning the term *rake* into the highest of praise.

"Only because you have so little with which to compare me, my dear."

As quickly as it had appeared, her smile vanished. Suddenly, he was holding a very solemn, noticeably hard-faced woman. "I find that contrary to what I once believed, I have *nothing* with which to compare. But you . . ." She glanced down as if studying their intertwined arms and the meager distance between her breast and his. "Oh. Oh, dear."

"Cate . . ." He held on, but she still managed to pull away until she was sitting upright by his side.

"Did you love her very much?"

"Who?" he demanded, knowing damn well of whom she spoke.

"Your wife."

"Good God, Cate. This is hardly an appropriate time to bring up Belinda."

"I disagree," was the sad reply. "I think it a perfectly appropriate time. She puts me in my place, you know."

He hauled himself up onto his elbows and stared at her, completely bewildered. "And what is that supposed to mean? She is dead. She does nothing."

"Nothing?" Short of calling him a liar, Cate's shrug couldn't have said it more clearly. "Yes, she is dead, and she was beautiful and vivacious, mistress of all this"—she waved an arm at the walls—"and perfectly suited to a title and this wretched Town."

"Cate, I have no idea what on earth you're trying to say, but it is not adding to the moment."

"Yes, I know. Stupid of me, isn't it? Here I am in a perfectly wonderful, wholly improper position, and I cannot seem to keep myself from spoiling it." She tugged one sleeve back down and toyed with a button. "Did you love her very much?"

"Not at all, according to so many of my peers," he replied caustically. "The others claim I loved her to the point of madness."

"Oh, hang your peers," she retorted, startling him. "I want to know why she haunted you right out of your home for so many years and why I feel so haunted now when all I did was engage in a bit of a roll on your filthy library floor!"

That one struck him, much like a fist in the sternum. True or not . . . true, perhaps, but . . . "Is that what we were doing?"

"Isn't it?" she shot back. "I was not thinking to demand a declaration. You were certainly not going to give one. No man would feel compelled to offer for a long-in-the-tooth spinster whom he merely kissed once."

"Good God, Cate. Where did all this come from?"

She waved off the question with a sharp jerk of her wrist.

"Forgive me, my lord. I am overset. I lead a simple life, you see, and could not help but be tipped off balance by the circumstances—"

"Rot."

"I beg your pardon?"

"What rot!" he repeated, irked himself now. "You are one of the least henwitted young women I know and quite probably the very least to be rattled completely out of countenance. Rot, I say.

"So you want to discuss love and marriage, do you? Fine. Marriage is purgatory, Cate. Promised Heaven when the truth of it is that no matter how hard you work and how good you are, you are always just trying to get past one prior sin after another. And you never know if there is a reward awaiting you just around the corner or merely more of the same. It is virtually endless, rarely virtuous, and endlessly demanding."

"I did not—"

"Yes. I loved my wife. In the beginning. And I hated her in the end. Just another Society marriage. The question, I suppose, is where I was more stupid—beginning or end."

There was a heavy silence. "For what it is worth," she said shakily, "I do not believe you had anything to do with your wife's death."

Exhausted, frustrated, Tregaron dropped back to lie flat on the rug, arms splayed, eyes on the dirty ceiling. "For what it's worth, and I say this with all due respect, Miss Buchanan, you are a fool."

Her response, whatever it might have been was interrupted by a soft tap at the door. Someone cleared his throat. "Er . . . my lord? Miss Cate?"

Tregaron lifted his head in time to see the quill disappear out the latch hole. The knock came again. "Yes, damnit!"

"We are here, Gordie," Cate called, rising from the floor.

"Ah, well, er . . . good . . . ah . . . I have the knob here. Shall I use it, or would you prefer . . . ?"

"Open the bloody door!" Tregaron bellowed, pushing himself to his feet.

He saw Cate frantically scrabbling among the folds of the divan cover. She poked several pins into her hair as she found them. She looked so distressed that he was of half a mind to tell her that it hardly mattered; post *roll*, as she'd chosen to call it, the fiery mass looked no different than usual.

He retreated to the desk, and she took a shaky seat on the divan, just as the door clicked and swung open. A comically concerned face peered in. "Done, my lord," the workman said unnecessarily.

"Thank you . . . er . . . Gordie," Tregaron muttered. "We appear to have been on the wrong side of a bit of bad luck."

"Aye." The other man's eyes scanned the jumbled room. "Miss Cate?"

"Oh, I'm fine, Gordie." Anyone who didn't know her might miss the slight tremor to her voice. "We have not been trapped long."

"Where the hell were you?" Tregaron demanded, offering Cate a hand up from the divan. Not surprisingly, she declined.

"We're all working upstairs today, my lord. I came down when I heard—"

"After you." Tregaron rested a hand lightly on Cate's back to hurry her along. He would not have touched her, but she was moving with all the speed of molasses. He felt the familiar flare of heat where his hand rested. He felt, too, her flinch. "Gordie, go fetch Miss Buchanan's uncle. Either one."

'They are not here," Cate said dully. "They are at the museum."

"My lord, I think perhaps you ought to—"

"A *museum*? Oh, for God's sake, They are supposed to be here, seeing to their damned work."

"My lord—"

"What *is* it, man?"

The Scot ran one hand through his wiry hair and cleared his throat. "You have guests, my lord."

He stepped aside then. Tregaron looked down the corridor. There, not six feet away, stood a familiar pair. "We were passing by, Tregaron," the elder announced grandly, "and decided we simply had to see what old stains you had painted over."

"Lady Reynolds, Miss Reynolds," he greeted the pair with a flourishing bow. "If I had but known you were arriving . . ." He might have locked himself in the library *and* dismantled the doorknob.

He did not know Caroline Reynolds at all, other than observing that she always seemed to be chattering away at the entertainments they'd both attended, but he knew her unpleasant brother. The fellow was a member of Fremont's set. Her mother, to add to the dismal situation, was well known to possess a mouth that moved far faster than her brain. Gossip was not merely a pastime, but a longstanding, ardent occupation.

All in all, she was just the sort of person—they were just the sort of pair—he did not want to be facing just then. But just as leopards did not change their spots, he doubted fate would ever see fit to look upon him differently.

Fate was certainly being predictable today. "There is a message for you in the foyer, Tregaron," Lady Reynolds informed him. She was doing her best to look into the library. Tregaron pulled the door shut smartly behind him. "I did not mean to intrude on your privacy, of course, but it is rather difficult to miss."

Caroline was staring intently at Cate. Cate was staring at her own sturdily shod feet. Tregaron decided it was time to end the encounter, no introductions made.

"Ladies, if you would forgive my appalling rudeness . . ." He did not care one way or another. After being regarded as a monster, impoliteness would be a mere nick in his repute. "I fear I am very much pressed for time. Miss Buchanan."

Cate needed no urging. She slipped around the unwelcome little party and nearly ran down the corridor. By the time Tregaron caught up with her, she was fumbling with the front door. He placed one palm against the portal, keeping it tightly shut.

"My lord, I did not . . . I cannot . . ." She was not staring at her feet any longer, but still did not lift her gaze above his watch chain. "I do not know what to say about . . . what happened."

"No? Fine. Perhaps you can shed some light upon that instead." He pointed.

On the south wall, just above the spot where once had stood a hideously ugly table originally from Versailles, a wedding gift from Belinda's family, was the message Lady Reynolds had mentioned. Fashioned of foot-high letters, it appeared to have been written with coal.

"*Impostor begone!*"

Chapter 13

If there had ever been an instance of going from pan to fire, Cate was living it now. She'd climbed from the hackney Tregaron had all but shoved her into, wearily let herself in her own front door, and been deposited firmly in a sort of Cruikshankian hell.

"Catey," Lucy called from the sitting room, "is that you?"

Cate, wearily stripping off her worn gloves and felt hat, looked in. Lucy was seated prettily in the room's best chair, flowers decorating the tables all around her. Becky the maid was in her Aunt Rebecca garb—an old mourning dress of Lucy's—and was stuck in the far corner, facing the glowing hearth, draped and shrouded in several shawls and at least one lap robe. Cate did not think they were paying the poor girl sufficiently for this.

Four gentlemen had risen from their own seats. Cate did not know Evan Althorpe well, but was pleased to see him nonetheless. She did not know Lord Newling at all, but was perfectly willing to bid him welcome. She could even have tolerated Edgar St. Clair-Wright's presence. He was, after all, too stupid to do any real harm on his own. But Cate had never met him when he was not dancing attendance on Fremont, and this was to be no exception.

"Now our happy little party is complete," Fremont said smoothly. "Miss Lucy said you might not be home for some time, Miss Buchanan, and we were most dejected."

"Were you?" Cate would have liked nothing better than to crawl upstairs and lock herself in her bedchamber for the next sennight or so. But Althorpe was graciously urging her into his seat, and Cate did not know how she could refuse. At least it was across the room from Fremont.

"Thank you," she said to Althorpe, having already expended her words for the other.

"And where have you been this fine afternoon?" Fremont asked. He had never been one to be easily ignored. "There is a most becoming blush to your cheeks."

Cate imagined she still looked rather like a boiled lobster. Humiliation and anger had a way of doing that to her appearance. Given the choice, she would have opted for fragile pallor, but such was not her lot.

"I have had a brisk walk," she lied. Then she lied again. "It is a marvelous day."

The weather might be fine indeed, but the day thus far had been blessed awful.

"Tell me you were not in Oxford Street, Catey," Lucy chided. "You know I am in need of countless things, and it would not be fair at all for you to visit the shops without my list."

"Oh, I daresay, Miss Buchanan was not shopping at all," Fremont announced before Cate could respond. "In fact, I am quite certain of it."

He was the very picture of *ton* elegance, lounging as he was, one arm propped on the back of his chair, legs stretched over the worn carpet. With his rakishly tousled blond hair and enigmatic smile, he was a sight indeed. Even the battered old parlor chair looked opulent beneath him. Cate deliberately turned away and thought she heard him chuckle as she did.

"And how, sir," Lucy demanded, "can you be certain of my sister's activities?"

Fremont did not answer for a long moment. Unable to resist, Cate tossed him a quick glance. He was staring straight at her, looking, she couldn't help but think, like a blond tomcat with something rodential in its sights.

Finally he spoke. "She has nothing intriguing for us to examine." Another pause. "No parcels, you see."

The entire party turned to Cate then, as if expecting her to produce said parcels, or at least to say something of interest to be pondered. *I have just come from a perfectly incendiary embrace with the Marquess of Tregaron*, she could have told them. *In comparison, Lord Fremont's kisses were no more than the mouth gapings of an oversized fish.*

That would certainly give the company something to discuss. Of course, she would have to omit the final scenario.

He does not truly want me any more than you did, Lord Fremont. And it hurts a thousand times more fiercely to know it.

She was ultimately saved from having to say anything at all by the appearance of Cook. The eternally red-faced woman stomped in with fresh tea and biscuits, looking none too pleased to have been given Becky's tasks atop her own. The tray hit the table in front of Lucy with a distinct clack and rattle of china.

"Ere's yer tea, miss," she muttered. "I were going to give ye scones like ye asked, but 'aven't time to make a batch if ye want supper on the table tonight."

Lucy, completely unperturbed, set in to pour. "No scones, gentlemen," she informed her guests cheerfully. "I don't think you'll mind overmuch."

Of course they would not mind. Lord Newling looked ready to chew on coal should Lucy serve it to him with a smile and a large enough cup of tea.

As Cook stomped back out again, there was a knock at the door. Cate saw Becky half rise from her seat in the corner before sinking back into the pile of wrapping. No doubt she did the same each time someone arrived.

No one else seemed to have noticed. Nor did anyone seem terribly curious as to who was at the door. For her part, Cate wanted to know who was going to *answer* the door and decided she herself could do so and then keep right on going down Binney Street. Then she heard Cook's Yorkshire voice, muted, and an equally quiet, much deeper one—male, smooth, cultured.

Cate's heart, taking no cue whatsoever from her sensible brain, did a joyous little leap. He had come. Tregaron had come to apologize and bear her off . . . somewhere.

"If you would excuse me," she murmured to no one in particular, and slipped into the hall. She paused halfway down the narrow steps to the foyer. Her heart thumped again at the sight of a well-formed back, of night-black hair and dark blue coat.

It dropped with a sorry thump when the man turned.

"Miss Buchanan!"

Julius Rome looked perfectly delighted to see her. Cate

managed a welcoming smile as she descended to the bottom step. It was not his fault, after all, that he was not Tregaron. And he was such an agreeable fellow that, had he been able to transform himself into another man, he would almost surely try to do so, just to be amiable.

"Good afternoon, Mr. Rome. How lovely to see you. Do come in."

"With pleasure." He handed his hat and stick to Cook with such a charming smile that the woman actually dropped into a lopsided curtsy.

"You have come to see Lucy." Cate turned to lead the way back up to the sitting room.

"Not at all. I was hoping to see you."

"Really?"

He loped up the first several stairs to stand just below her. "To be sure. I fancy us to be friends of a sort, and I have seen so little of you about Town that I decided I must come see what has kept you in such thrall here."

Charmed, Cate gestured wryly at the house's narrow stairs and dull paint. "Enthralling it is not, sir, but you brighten its modest walls."

"Truly?" He looked pleasantly flattered. "Well, then, I am delighted to serve."

Just then a thump and ripple of laughter came from above.

"Sounds lively enough to me," Julius commented. Cate sighed.

"My sister has guests."

With a single, lithe leap, Julius was past her and standing on the step above. Then, almost comically, he leaned down, tilted up her chin with a forefinger, and gave her face a good once-over. "That," he said after a moment, "is a frown not to be ignored."

"Oh, nonsense."

"Who has come to call?" he demanded shrewdly.

"Lord Althorpe."

"A delightful fellow, though rather hard on one's pocketbook, so there must be more. Who else?"

"Lord Newling," Cate replied.

"Ah. Witless creature. And . . . ?"

"Mr. St. Clair-Wright."

"Ahhh."

"And Lord Fremont."

"I see. Right, then." Julius nodded decisively. "You'd best come along with me." With that, he plunked two hands on her shoulders, turned her about, and urged her gently but persistently back the way they'd just come. "We'll go to Gunther's for a bit of refreshment. I have it on *very* good authority that a shipment of ice has only just arrived from the Greenlands, and we can expect to find fruit ices of several different flavors."

"On *very* good authority?" Cate could not resist repeating. She should have minded, she knew, both this man's ease with her person and ease of uninvited command. Instead, she felt as if she were being affectionately bullied by an old and dear friend. And she could use an old and dear friend. She had far too few.

"Very good," was Julius's reply as he rushed her down the last steps. "Gunther is fond of taking out advertisements in the *Times*, hawking his wares. I daresay he would list every cake and tart if there were but room."

Gunther's—bastion of Mayfair's elite, haven of those dubious adults with sweet cravings and more money than sense.

"I don't know . . ." Cate protested. "I cannot . . ."

"Of course you can."

With yet another brilliant smile, Julius reclaimed his possessions from Cook, who had not moved. She promptly curtsied again and looked ready to stand just where she was indefinitely, should the delightful Mr. Rome have need of anything else.

Cate glanced around the foyer with a frown. Her hat and spencer were upstairs in the sitting room, precisely where she had left them. All that was downstairs was a particularly frothy millinery confection belonging to Lucy and a matching canary yellow wrap. Now she truly could not go. If she were forced to return to the sitting room, it would be too hard to explain skipping out again.

Julius was already tugging Lucy's shawl from its peg. Before Cate could object, he settled the thing around her shoulders with a flourish, then handed her the hat. "Hurry up, now," he said with a wink, "or all the ice will have melted."

Why not? She could do with something sweet and frivolous. Ignoring the certainty that she would only look ridiculous, Cate donned the elaborate composition of pale straw, Prussian net, and endless silk flowers, tied the ribbons jauntily beneath her chin, and led the way out the door.

It was not such a long walk to Berkeley Square. Cate swiftly dismissed Julius's suggestion of a hack. She welcomed the fresh air and had no intention of returning home before she absolutely had to.

They crossed busy Oxford Street. Cate would not feel guilty for either setting foot on that thoroughfare without her sister's endless shopping list or for commandeering Lucy's garb. As she and Julius turned onto Bond Street, she spied countless hats very similar to the one she wore—large, elaborate, and excessively frivolous. She blended right in.

She also felt very much the fraud, melding into a place where she clearly did not belong. The impostor.

Impostors begone. Cate's stomach clenched, much as it had when she'd first read the words, just as it had during the dozens of times she had recalled them since.

Someone knew she did not belong, that she was not who she claimed to be. And she didn't belong here in London, with its rules and hierarchies and refusal to see a man—or woman—for who he was. Oh, she would miss the little slices of life she tasted when she could: the theater where there was as much to be seen in watching the audience as the stage; Vauxhall with its countless entertainments and soft wash of starry gaslights; Mayfair—beloved, hated Mayfair, brimming with mostly unimpressive people and grand, glorious houses.

She would miss a small handful of people and one small dog. But what she would miss was far less important than what her entire family would lose should they not complete their work and depart before their secret was exposed. They'd had such great plans for Buchanan and Buchanan here. Cate would have continued as she was; the uncles would act as figureheads and each successive job would have given them more freedom to do their art.

Well, they would have the Marquess of Tregaron's town house on their *curriculum vitae.* And there was plenty of work to be had in Manchester, York, Edinburgh . . .

It all sounded so convincing. Why, then, Cate wondered, did it feel like a ticket to Paradise lost?

"A winter scarf would suit me just perfectly."

She blinked and turned back to her all-but-forgotten companion. "I beg your pardon?"

Julius grinned. "You were woolgathering with such intensity that I figured there must be enough to knit me a muffler."

"Oh. Oh, I am so sorry. I did not mean—"

He patted her hand where it rested on his arm. "I sport with you, Miss Buchanan, the poor behavior of a vain man who is being ignored by a lovely lady. Beyond that, we have nearly arrived."

Charmed again by this splendid young man, she allowed him to usher her into the famed Gunther's. A bell tinkled merrily over the door as they entered. Cate caught herself gaping slightly at the vast, crowded spectacle inside. Table after glossy table, display after glass display of the confectioner's famous wares. Cate was promptly overwhelmed. "I believe I have a stomachache already," she murmured.

Julius laughed. "Not yet. You are not allowed to feel indisposed until you have consumed several ices, a fruit tart, and a selection of cream cakes."

Cate had no idea how he managed it, but Julius somehow secured them a place next to a window. The table was tiny and sticky, the seat uncomfortable, but marvelous nonetheless. The very air was delicious, smelling of warm sugar and fruit—pear and lemon, strawberry and red currant.

"Ices first," Julius decreed, "then cake," and rattled off a child's dream list at a harried-looking serving clerk.

In minutes, Cate had a spoonful of lemon ice in one hand, cassis in the other. Julius was cheerfully digging his way through pear and something a dramatic shade of blue. "Now this," he declared, waving one long-handled spoon with adolescent glee, "this is where I belong!"

Impostors . . . Who wanted them exposed and gone so badly? Cate knew there were options aplenty. A disgruntled workman, perhaps, although she did not know of anyone whom Mac had dismissed, nor of anyone expressing discontentment with the arrangements. But there was always at least one on a site. Someone who had known the Buchanans before, perhaps. In truth, it would not be all that difficult to learn the secret if one were often in Cate's company and looking closely. Fremont could know. How easily he could know. Even Gramble . . .

"Winter stockings," came from across the table. Cate opened her mouth to apologize again, but Julius waved her off. "Don't be silly. I would allow you to gather enough wool for a blanket if it did not seem to be making you unhappy."

When she nearly dropped her spoon, he reassured her, "Don't worry. I won't press. If you want to speak of it . . ." He spread his hands, and waggled his fingers toward himself. "If not, so be it."

"You are too kind," Cate managed through a tight throat. She meant the words for perhaps the first time in the countless times she had spoken them.

"Rubbish. I am an insatiable nosy beastie who just happens to have a bit of patience." He winked, then peered intently out the window. "Well, well. Looks dashed miserable, doesn't he?"

Cate could not have prepared herself for the painful jolt she got at the sight of Tregaron striding along the far side of the square. She could not see his features clearly, but there was no way to miss the stone-stiff set of his shoulders, the way his stick cracked hard against the street with each step. Even Gryffydd, right at his heels, seemed tense, his bat ears back and foxy smile absent.

"Perhaps I ought to go fetch him. Feed him something appallingly sweet—"

"No!" Cate reached out, and placed a stilling hand over Julius's before she could stop herself. "He is on his way to conduct business, I daresay, and would not care to be waylaid."

Julius raised a brow, looked at her altogether too closely for a moment, then shrugged. "Off to see his grandmother, more likely. She lives just around the corner. Only member of his family with whom he spends time since . . ."

Cate pounced, before she could lose her courage. "What do you believe of his wife's . . . of the story? What do you know of it?"

"Not a thing, I'm afraid. I have only old gossip to go on. But it never looked good for old Tregaron, not as the tale is told."

He spooned up the last of his blue ice, expression thoughtful. "What do I believe? I suppose it had to have been a terrible accident. He would never have pushed her, I'm certain of it. But if *she* pushed too far, went too far in her behavior, he would have spoken his mind, no doubt. An argument on the balcony, too many passions and a few bad steps . . ."

"You like him."

"Certainly I do."

"Why?" Cate demanded, feeling a tug behind her ribs as man and dog vanished from her sight. "He is so very austere, forbidding."

"He is, yes, and he quite terrified me when I was a boy. I'd never met anyone quite so hard. And, my dear, had you ever met my brother before Sibyl worked her magic on him, you will know that I am more than familiar with the grim, rigid sort."

"Why, then . . . ?"

"Why did I take a liking to Tregaron? Because he was kind to me in his austere way on those occasions when our paths crossed. Our familiars were close. He and Tarquin were in the same house at school, years ahead of me. In fact, Tregaron was but a term from leaving for Oxford when I arrived, but he always knew my name. Sent me a canary and a box of sweetmeats when Tarquin mentioned I was laid up with a broken leg. Thumped one huge fellow another time for stealing my cap."

"It awes me sometimes," Cate said thoughtfully, "what sort of loyalty an act or two of careless kindness to a child can engender."

Julius's smile was as wry as it was warm. "Children have more discretion than we give them credit for, I believe. But that isn't the point." He gazed across the square in the direction Tregaron had taken. "He always showed the same careless kindness to absolutely everyone."

"I refuse to take you anywhere in your condition, Colwin."

Tregaron nearly smiled. For being so averse to so many entertainments, his grandmother possessed a rather crowded social calendar lately. He thought he had a very good idea why. The more events to which she dragged him, the more likely she thought he'd be to develop a *tendre* for some pretty young thing. Or at least take enough of a fancy to said thing to marry her and beget an heir.

She would also know that he had less than no interest in tripping merrily through the Marriage Mart. If his "condition," whatever that was, precluded his appearing in polite company, he would be in no hurry to make repairs. He'd already had one extra bath that day.

"Honestly, boy, you look like the business end of an ill-used mop."

"When, madam, did you last come into contact with any mop, used or otherwise?"

His grandmother smacked a palm smartly against the arm of her chair. "Don't you get cheeky with me, you infant! I can still reach your mouth with a piece of soap, you know." Then, far more gently, "Tell me you are not ill."

"I am not ill."

The dowager marchioness nodded, and her grandson read relief in her eyes. "You still look horrendous."

"I am not ill, Grandmother."

"I am most glad to hear. More glad than you might think."

He raised a brow. "More glad?"

"You must be in love."

"What?" Tregaron felt his jaw dropping.

Vitality renewed, Lady Tregaron gave the maid's bell a hearty ring. Gryffydd, knowing that bells in this household always preceded food, took his place beside her chair. Both appeared much more invigorated than they had seemed mere moments before.

"I trust you have a basis for that statement," Tregaron muttered. "Otherwise, it is much like striking a man with an iron skillet with no warning."

"What sort of warning do you require, my dear? Or is it my reasoning that you require?"

"Grandmother—"

"Oh, do not try to growl and spit fire at me, Colwin. You are not a dragon, despite what your imbecilic—"

"Grandmother."

She completely ignored him, instead ordering refreshment from the familiar maid who had appeared in the doorway. Then she announced, "It is all very simple, really. Men have precisely four reasons for looking as wholly shattered as you do today. The first is a dire illness. We have disposed of that possibility.

"Second," she continued, ticking the numbers off on lavishly beringed fingers, "is a substantial loss on the 'Change. You have too much sense and far too much money for that to be the case. The third is the death of a hound or horse." She scratched absently behind Gryffydd's ears, sending the animal into a delightful heap at her feet. "The beast is still here, so it cannot be that."

"And the fourth, I assume," was his dry rejoinder, "you believe to be love. As opposed to, let's say, the demise of an adored elder relative."

"Love," the adored elder relative insisted firmly. "And I tell you, Colwin, you were not half so afflicted with Belinda."

He did not possess the requisite energy to argue over any of it. Once his grandmother got an idea in her regal jaws, she clung to it with the tenacity of a bulldog.

"I don't especially want to talk about Belinda."

"I don't blame you in the least. That was a terrible mistake on your part."

"Grandmother."

"Well, it was, Colwin. The pair of you were a disaster from the onset. It's no wonder you ended up—"

"Tipping her off a balcony?" he demanded wearily.

"My darling boy, had I been there, I would have done it for you."

Yes, he rather thought she would have.

"And there would have been nothing accidental about it," she added.

He believed that, too. "It amazes me that, with my past and your opinion of it, you are in such a rush to see me married again."

"As I said, you made a mistake, one you'd not make again. You've grown so far past being dazzled by gaiety and a beautiful face. And I am not in a rush to see—" His raised brow had her shrugging. "Fine. You go right ahead and look at me that way. Daggers to my heart, I tell you. All I wish is for you to be happy.

"You do not fool me in the least, you know. Some men are simply meant to be married, and you are one of them. This facade you have of the eternally content solitary creature is as easy to see through as glass. You are a fraud, Colwin, and I am most disappointed in you."

A fraud. *Impostor begone.*

He had not lingered to reread the words. One quick look had been enough. He had hurried out of the house, hurried Cate out ahead of him. Shoved her into a hack and sent her home while his body was still humming with the memory of hers against it and the smell of her still filling his head.

Ah, Cate. Peppery, vibrant, glorious Cate. Who was not afraid to challenge him, mock him. Kiss him with all the fire of a passionate spirit.

He had handled it all badly. He had handled Cate with unforgivable callousness, pushing her away and punishing her for acting reasonably, for asking perfectly reasonable questions. Then he had shoved her into a hack and sent her home.

Even before he'd realized how much he wanted this woman, weeks and weeks before, he'd handled himself badly. He'd thought he could return to Town, move among those who judged him, without being stung or thwarted by their contempt, and carry off some replacement for Belinda to his Welsh lair. Now he was being called on his deception and his arrogance.

He didn't belong in London, among persons he considered peers only in that they shared a level of birth. He was not one of them at all. And someone felt strongly enough on the matter to—twice now—tell the Welsh impostor exactly how he felt.

"Really, Colwin, it cannot be so bad as all that."

"Hmm?"

"You appear to be contemplating something truly horrid. What nonsense. Simply go sweep the girl off her feet, or whatever it is young men do these days."

Tregaron had no idea what young men did these days. More than a decade past, when he'd been dazzled by Belinda, all he'd really had to do was play the gallant for a fortnight, then have a long, involved talk with her greedy father about money.

He sighed. "Has it not occurred to you, Grandmother, that there are a great many ladies in the world who would be averse to being approached in any manner by me?"

"Fiddlesticks. You are, after all, you."

"Precisely my point."

"Oh, Colwin, really. You are a splendid catch."

"You, madam, are partial."

She gave an indelicate snort. "My partiality hasn't anything to do with it. I saw the way she was looking at you at the Tarrant fete. If she had been adverse to anything about you then, I am the Virgin Queen of England."

"I haven't the slightest idea of whom you speak."

"I am quite willing to believe you are a little mad, Colwin, but I refuse to believe there is anything at all wrong with your memory. And while I cannot say I am wholly pleased with you wedding a girl with red hair, I do not disapprove."

"Grandmother, I do not—"

"Oh, do stop denying it, boy. You are becoming tedious. Just admit how right I am about the Hepburn girl."

"Buchanan."

Lady Tregaron smiled smugly. "How right I am this time—as usual. Admit it. You will feel ever so much better. Ah, here is our tea!"

Tregaron nearly smiled. His grandmother was right this time, as usual. Of course he was in love with Cate. Perverse fate would have it no other way.

Chapter 14

"Shameful!" Lady Leverham declared, rapping a plump fist against the interior panel of her town coach. "Outrageous! Honestly, could you not have shown a tad more discretion than to flaunt your utter disregard for propriety in front of the Reynolds creature and her flighty daughter? Who, I feel compelled to inform you, wasted not an instant in spreading the tale to as many people as possible. Oh, to think of the gossip that I have *not* yet heard!"

This had been going on for a good several minutes. The air in the closed carriage was warm, and the lady was wilting visibly. The feather decorating her rather Byzantine-looking hat was drooping to starboard; her extensive wrap was lying in a gauzy puddle on the seat beside her.

"I really do not like doing this," she continued. "Scolding. It does so knock the stuffing out of one. But I would be remiss as a friend and neighbor to all Buchanans indeed if I did not say something. Now, what have you to say for yourself?"

Tregaron smiled thinly at the lady and scowled at her monkey, who was perched on the opposite seat. The little beast had been eyeing his gold watch fob with interest for quite some time, looking ready to spring. "What do you wish me to say, madam?"

"Why, that it is not true, of course!" she shot back with alacrity.

"I am afraid I cannot do that."

"I did not think you could, but you asked for my wish, and so I gave it to you."

He nodded, and reminded himself to whom he was speaking. "Upon my honor, madam, I intended no blight to fall upon your fair friend."

"Hmph," was the response, but Tregaron thought he detected a very faint smidge of approval in the syllable.

He searched for any further medieval-sounding phrases that might aid his cause, but came up only with "forsooth," and he could not see how that would help anyone or anything. He needed a pot of strong coffee, an hour with the *Times*, and a further half hour or so free of chattering human contact. He was not accustomed to being summoned from his apartments in the middle of breakfast, and was suffering for it. Lady Leverham had been firmly parked in her firmly parked carriage, and had sent in the message that she would stay right where she was until he appeared.

He'd appeared as soon as he could get appropriately dressed, of course.

It was too early in the day to be facing the severe and strident complaints of an irate matron. It was far too early to hear that the unfortunate events of the day before were being bandied about Town. He wondered if Cate knew.

"I will consider what I can do this morning, madam. I am afraid it is a difficult situation—"

"It is a dismal situation! Catherine hasn't the standing in Society, and you certainly do not have the repute necessary to stamp out the gossip. I will do what I can, but heaven only knows what will happen to Lucy regardless."

"Lucy?" He'd thought they were speaking of Cate.

"Lucy. Catherine is a delightful girl, and I am very fond of her, but she doesn't give a fig about her reputation. She has no expectations to marry, has never possessed any, and so does not pay adequate attention to the subtle precepts of feminine delicacy. Her sister, on the other hand, wishes to make a match, and a splendid one at that. This will not help."

No, he didn't suppose it would, but he was not concerned with Lucy. The Lucys of the world always landed on their feet and shone on. He had a very good idea that matters were not so simple for Cate. He certainly did not believe she had never hoped to marry. Perhaps she still did. Any gossip spread about by Reynolds *et fille* would have a much more adverse effect on her than on her sister, no matter what Lucy's expectations.

"I will most certainly pay a visit to Miss Buchanan," he

offered, uncertain what purpose that would serve, but hoping it would be the start to something. "This morning."

Lady Leverham humphed again.

"If you have any better suggestions, madam . . ."

"Go home, Tregaron."

"I beg your pardon?" he demanded stiffly. He was getting heartily tired of people suggesting he decamp for Wales. He would be delighted to return to Wales. He simply was not going to be bullied into doing so.

"Go to your home, sir! Now. Catherine is there."

"Ah." Light dawned. It appeared he would be paying his second visit in as many days to Hanover Square. "Thank you, madam. I will do so."

Matron and monkey withdrew into the squabs. It was clear the interview was over. Weary, feeling as if he had just been introduced to a cadet branch of the Inquisition and not fared well, Tregaron opened the carriage door and climbed to the street.

"Good d—" he began.

"Well, go on, sir. And this time, once you arrive, stay in plain sight!" Lady Leverham snapped. Then she called "Drive on!" to her coachman, barely giving Tregaron time to close the door and step back before they rolled away.

"You look all done in, guv."

He turned to find the familiar little sweep not five feet away. "Good morning, Harris. You look as if you have been busy." The boy was dirty as ever and liberally dusted with feathers. "Have you eaten today?"

"I 'ave, guv. 'Ad me porridge at dawn. I'm just in between jobs now, 'aving meself a bit of a rest. 'Til 'e scuttles me off, anyways."

From the corner of his eye, Tregaron could see the porter lurking in the Albany's doorway. "If he bothers you," he informed the boy, jerking a thumb at the door, "tell me and I'll see to it."

Harris grinned. "Thanks, to be sure, but I can see to meself, I can."

"Yes, I quite believe you can."

"But you now . . ." Harris stuck one of the small, pointed rods he carried down the back of his grubby shirt and scratched his back with it. "You look like you could use some 'elp. A mort is it? Some rum dodsey?"

"Where *do* you pick up these expressions? They are rather alarming."

"Mort, article, baggage. All the same to me. And that wasn't an answer, guv."

"I owe you no answers." Tregaron reached into his waistcoat pocket for a coin. It vanished quickly into the boy's fist. "And I suppose I really must be on my way."

"They like flowers. And little sparkly things."

"I take it you are speaking of morts."

"What else?" The boy rolled his eyes. "For such a toff, you can be dim as dusk, guv."

"Yes, I expect I can. Any further advice?"

"Aye. Promise 'em the sky. The whole ruddy sky. You'd do well to 'eed me words there."

"And you'd do well to limit your counsel to matters about which you have some knowledge." Tregaron shook his head with a smile. "Heaven help me when I start taking direction on such things from an infant."

"I'm older than you think, guv. But you go right ahead and court your lady your way." Harris jerked his head toward the Albany. "I 'ear these ain't bad digs a't'all for a bachelor. You'll be fair comfortable 'ere in your flannel waistcoat days." With that, the sweep tipped his ragged hat, flashed his gap-toothed grin again, and flitted off down Sackville Street, tool pouch bouncing against his back.

Tregaron found that he was still smiling as he headed back to his rooms. He did not think Cate was the sort to demand flowers or sparkly objects. But there was a sort of grandeur in young Harris's third suggestion. Promising the sky, indeed. Clever little bounder, especially so considering he spent his days going up and down chimneys.

Still, Tregaron had always found that real help had a way of coming from the strangest quarters.

Cate had spent days in odder places than the one she presently occupied. As it happened, she had been chased into this spot by her sister and Lady Leverham, and planned to stay just where she was until doomsday if necessary.

Where she was happened to be at the very top of the library ladder. While Lucy had relentlessly chased her through the house, demanding explanations and offering unwelcome sympathy, the girl had drawn the line at the library. She had entered initially on Cate's heels, but had scuttled out when MacGoun, bless him, had stuck his head in and asked Cate if she'd seen any more rats beneath the dust cloths. Mac was almost as eager to have Lucy, with her chattering and emoting, and distracting of the crew, out of the house as Cate.

So now Cate was up the ladder, removing books one at a time and loading them into a basket in which she lowered them to the floor with a sturdy cord. She then followed them down, dusted them off, and packed them into waiting boxes. When the shelves had been refinished, the books would be returned to them. It was all slow work, its tedium thus far unrelieved. The highest shelf appeared to be all massive sets of medical and astronomical tomes—in German. Cate did not read German, so she could only grab one book after the next, not read a word of them, and think.

She did her very best not to think of Tregaron, but was failing miserably on all counts.

Among the last words he had spoken to her, the very *few* words he had spoken between hustling her out of the house and into a hackney had been the terse command to inform her uncles that they could do what they liked with the library. Or nothing at all.

Cate had no idea what changed his mind. Two sets of unpleasant memories now, perhaps, to be obliterated. If he did not care to be reminded that he had shared a few very heated minutes on the rug with his employees' niece, it would be easy enough to replace the rug. Whatever the reason, and Cate was not so much of a martyr as to spend time torturing herself with the possibilities, she was taking him at his word and planning what changes the room would see.

In truth, there were not many. As with the rest of the house, the original design was good. Some of the furniture, most notably the cracked or gutted chairs and divan, would go. Other pieces, like the magnificent desk, would be returned to their proper glory and left in the room. The stained, moth-eaten rug was suited for nothing but the dustbin. The irreparably broken books and shattered glassware would join it. The floors and bookshelves only needed refinishing, the hearth new stone and the Rumford grate.

It was not easy to be in the room, not when Cate kept

recalling the feel of Tregaron's hands on her, the very slight sandpaper scrape of his jaw. Everywhere she looked, something gnawed at her memory. The rug, of course. The wooden Welsh spoons. Even the German books in her hands. They were elegant, austere, marred, and completely, utterly indecipherable. Just like the man who owned them.

Unable to help herself, she clasped the volume she held to her chest, which had felt so very, very hollow since the hackney had driven her away the day before.

"What in God's name are you doing up there?"

The harsh voice so startled Cate that she nearly went tumbling off the ladder. She did drop the book, which hit the floor eighteen or so feet below with a solid thump, breaking apart, and only just missing Tregaron's head.

"Get down from there!" he snapped.

Cate gaped at him. "What are you doing here?"

"I seem to forever be asking you the same. Come down from that ladder and we will discuss it. Cate," he added, voice lowering dangerously when she did not move. "Now."

She felt herself flushing with indignation. How dare he stalk in and play Lord of the Manor? It hardly mattered that it was, in fact, his manor. She was having none of his arrogance.

"No," she snapped back. "I am quite comfortable where I am."

"You are twenty feet in the air, on a narrow ladder!"

"So I am."

"How comfortable could that possibly— Oh, to hell with that. I will ask you one more time," he ground out between clenched teeth. "Come down from there."

"That was not a request. It was a command."

"Cate . . ."

"I do not like commands, my lord. And I do not wish to speak with you. Good day." With that, she turned back to the shelves, removed another book from the set, and opened it, all the while trying not to feel half so foolish as she knew she looked.

"Damnit, Cate." The ladder shook slightly as Tregaron grasped the rails. Cate glanced down, and was amazed to see him put his foot on the lowest rung. He climbed another, then stopped. "Oh, for God's sake," he muttered, stepping back to the floor. "This is ridiculous!"

He looked so fierce, almost past gentility, as he stood glaring up at her. The hands gripping the ladder were large, powerful-looking, and Cate had the feeling that he could tear the massive thing from its runners and send it—and her—flying with a mere flick of his wrists. For a long moment, she was convinced he was going to do just that.

Then he gave a snarl and let go of the rails. "Suit yourself. Stay up there." He stalked to the hearth, where he stopped to lean stiffly against the mantel. "There is talk . . . about us."

"I know." No wonder he was so furious, she thought. To have his name murmured about Town again, paired with hers. Better than being labeled a murderer, certainly, but the tale could do no good to his quest for a second Society bride.

Lady Leverham had confirmed all of Cate's suspicions on that matter—in between wringing her plump hands and scolding. There was no doubt in that lady's mind that the marquess had returned to London to find himself a new wife. Cate had no doubts, either. What neither knew was how far the tale had gone. Not that it mattered, really. With Tregaron as a player in the piece, it would certainly reach most of the *ton* by nightfall.

Should Fremont decide to add to the gossip by telling of their dismal little connection, Cate's humiliation would be complete. More important, she told herself, Lucy would be tainted, as would Buchanan and Buchanan. Cate was far from stupid. She knew how little it took, how absurd the reasons could be for Society, even in the most distant climes, to turn its back on people like her and her family.

"It is likely we will be going home to Scotland as soon as possible," she said, only half intending to speak aloud. "Until such a time, I do not need to appear in public."

"So you intend to seclude yourself more than you have already during your time here."

"I don't see an alternative. Nor do I particularly want one."

He had picked up one of the wooden spoons from the mantel now, and was slapping it against the palm of his hand. Cate flinched at each audible smack. He did not even appear to be feeling a sting. "I have an alternative for you."

"But I have just said I do not want—"

"Yes, yes. I heard you. Very resigned and noble. But hear me out." He stilled the spoon and began to trace the links and Celtic cross that decorated the handle. "I feel responsible for the situation."

"Don't," Cate said shortly. "I am a grown woman. I was not coerced." Seduced, perhaps, she thought, but oh so eagerly and willingly. "I am more than ready to face the consequences of my actions."

"Very mature of you," he muttered. "Now do be quiet and let me finish. As I said, I feel responsible for the situation in which not only you find yourself, but also the other members of your family. I would not see your sister or your uncles' business suffer for my . . . lapse in good judgment."

Cate had never thought of herself as a lapse in good judgment, appropriate as the phrase might be. The kiss she had shared with Tregaron had not been sensible, no, but it had been wonderful, and it hurt to have it dismissed so cavalierly by the only other person who could have known how wonderful it had been.

"I have no idea what, precisely, is being said," he went on, "but I can guess. It matters little to me; I am accustomed to the lash of flapping tongues. You, however . . ."

"I will survive."

"No doubt. I expect you would survive a direct hit with an arrow. However, I see a very simple way out of this twist. You must marry me."

Cate felt her jaw dropping.

He continued, "You, of course, would be removed from censure the moment our, er, connection is legitimized. Once you are Lady Tregaron, nothing from your past would signify at all. You have no desire, I am sure, to move in the so-called first circles. Furthermore, as Lucy would then be my sister-in-law, I would be pleased to settle upon her a sufficient dowry for her to wed whomever she chooses. And I have more than enough property to keep your uncles occupied for years to come." He set the love spoon back on the mantel with a decisive click. "What do you say?"

Words completely evaded Cate for a long moment. Then, "Have you gone completely daft?" she demanded.

"Daft?" He gazed up at her, a confused frown on his face. *"Daft?"*

"Daft! Beyond being insulting to an extreme, that . . . that *proposal*, if it can be called such, is the most ridiculous thing I have ever heard! My goodness, you might just as well be suggesting we dip into a cup of hemlock. It would be every bit as dramatic and every bit as unnecessary!"

"Now, Cate."

"Don't you, 'Now, Cate' me!" she nearly shouted. "I might have allowed you certain liberties, Lord Tregaron. I might even have led you to believe that I would allow more. But I never once gave you leave to treat me like a dimwitted serf in Your Majesty's imaginary demesne. And I *never* gave you leave to use my name!;" She raised the book she was holding into the air, ready to send it flying down for emphasis.

"Catey!"

Both she and Tregaron spun to face the door. There, filling the doorway, was Uncle Ambrose. Just visible over his shoulder was a tuft of Uncle Angus's wild hair.

"What in God's name has gotten into you?" Ambrose demanded.

"Be a good lass and put the book down," Angus suggested, wriggling around his brother's vast bulk to enter the room, "before you brain somebody with it."

Mortified, Cate set the book back on the shelf.

"Sirs, if you would—" Tregaron began.

"As for you, you arrogant pup"—Ambrose shook a large finger in the marquess's direction—I'm just sporting enough to give you a running start before I come after you for upsetting m'niece."

"Now, now, Ambrose," Angus murmured. "We have no idea yet what happened here."

"He insulted me unforgivably," Cate informed them.

"I made her an offer of marriage!" was Tregaron's hot retort.

Angus rubbed uncomfortably at the crown of his head. "Well," he said, "I suppose to some, there might be an insult there . . ."

"Ach, Angus, you daft haddie." Ambrose rolled his eyes.

"Still your tongue, man." Then, to Tregaron, "Was it serious—the proposal?"

Slightly red of face, the younger man replied, "It was."

Cate snorted. Uncle Ambrose shot her a look from beneath his formidable brows before rounding on Tregaron again. "Was the insult serious, too?"

"The proposal *was* the insult!" Cate snapped.

Ambrose regarded her for a long moment. "Have you been doing something you oughtn't, Catey, lass?"

It was her turn to roll her eyes. "That," she replied, "would require a dictionary and a list." At her uncle's grunt, she lowered her gaze and muttered, "If you're asking if Lord Tregaron's offer was motivated by necessity, the answer is no."

"Well. Grand." Ambrose rubbed at his jaw, which was faintly pink. "Good. Now, are you certain about refusing, Catey?"

"Quite."

"He's got a decent house here."

"I can live without the house," she said tartly.

"He's rich as Croesus."

"Uncle Ambrose!"

Her uncle shrugged. "Just stating facts. Of course you don't have to have him if you really don't want him. It's just that since these matters always seem to come down to money in the end, I thought why not get right to the heart of the matter?"

Cate resisted the urge to smack him with the book, then the urge to smack her own head against something hard.

"You know, Ambrose," his brother announced, " 'tis times like this that show why you never married. You've no notion of the romantic sensibilities."

"Oh, aye?" Ambrose crossed his arms over his barrel chest. "And what's your excuse?"

"Gentlemen," Tregaron tried.

"My continued bachelorhood certainly has nothing to do with a lack of romantic sensibilities," Angus retorted, chin elevated. "I am an aesthete—a connoisseur of life's delicacies. You, on the other hand, would not know a sensibility of any sort were it to fall onto your thick skull."

"Gentlemen, please." Tregaron thumped a clenched fist against the mantel. "I cannot see that this discussion is apropos to the situation at hand. I am certain you are both well justified in your single state—"

"And you're one to be commenting," Ambrose spun on him. "You've just had a proposal tossed back at you like spit in the wind."

Cate saw Tregaron's already rigid jaw tighten. "Consider it withdrawn!" he ground out. "God send me Robert Adam next time I look to renovate my home."

"He's dead, m'lord," Angus informed him.

"I *know* he's dead!" Tregaron bellowed and, thrusting both hands into his hair, stomped from the room.

"Well, that's that, I suppose," Angus offered when the door thudded loudly behind him.

"Aye. You'll be hearing no more of this marriage nonsense," was Ambrose's addition. "Happy now, lass?"

"To be sure," Cate replied with a sigh. "Overjoyed." There was no sense in trying to explain to them—or herself—that how she really felt was a bit ill. "Was there something you needed me for?" she asked wearily, thinking a change of subject would be wise.

'Nay, nay." Ambrose shook his massive head. "We'd come to tell you we've had another commission, just this morning. And since you're so close to being done here, we thought we'd ask when you'd be ready to start the next."

"Another commission." Cate was not as thrilled as she thought she would be, somehow, but considering the current state of affairs, it was no wonder. This little boon might be whisked away from them at any moment.

"Aye, and we're expecting another after," Angus informed her cheerfully.

"In London?"

"Ach, nay." Angus shrugged. "First one's near York. Fellow was here in Town on business, saw this place, and wrote us when he'd reached home again. Wife wants their digs redone top to bottom. The other, if we get it, is Dumfries. Cousin or some such of Lord Leverham."

"York," Cate murmured. Dumfries. Far from the gossip, certainly. But so far from so much else as well.

"I'll miss the museums something fierce, I will," Ambrose was saying.

"And the churches," was Angus's glum addition.

Cate slowly descended the ladder. She wandered past her

uncles, to the front of the house, where she stood in the open window. A brisk breeze fluttered her sleeve then fell still. Below, Mayfair coursed with its daily activity. Somewhere in its streets, a man was walking away. Cate looked both ways, but he was gone. She'd missed him, obviously.

Tregaron marched away from his house, his pulse pounding angrily with his stride. How dare she? he fumed. How dare she throw back his offer of marriage as if it were an invitation to walk on broken glass? For all her appeal, Cate was not likely to receive many more such proposals in her life. She was too forward, too sharp, too bloody *tall* for the men she would meet. Tregaron could not think of a single fellow who would want to be tied to her quick tongue, agile mind, and long . . . supple form . . . for life.

He did. He wanted Miss Catherine Buchanan rather desperately. He wanted every little quirk and corner of her. And she had just made it abundantly clear that she would not have him if he were presented to her dipped in gold.

A bit of soot fell onto his sleeve from the air. He brushed it off with a growl. No, he bloody well didn't think flowers would have helped. He would only have looked silly, standing so far beneath Cate, posy in hand. Nor would a small sparkly object have been any better. He could only imagine Ambrose Buchanan's reaction should he have seen Tregaron trying to present Cate with a diamond brooch. He would have thumped first and asked his questions later.

As for offering to give her the sky, well, he could have tried that one. Matters could not have turned out any worse than they actually had. Perhaps that was the way to woo women after all—flowers, gems, promises a man could not possibly think to keep.

He needed a brandy. So what if it were not yet noon.

At Bond Street, he automatically turned south toward St. James's. He was halfway to Piccadilly before he recalled that his club had very politely invited him to resign his membership eight years earlier. And he had done so without a fight. At that point, he hadn't planned on coming back to London. Now he had a choice. He could wander around looking for a place to drown himself in a bottle, or he could get on with his day, with his life.

He went in search of a pub.

"Didn't listen to me, did you, guv?"

Tregaron slowed as young Harris suddenly fell into step beside him, cherubic face filthy and creased into a smug smile.

"What makes you say that?"

"You look like a thunder cloud. 'Ave you a shilling to spare?"

"Why?" Tregaron demanded, even as he reached into his pocket.

"Just trying to ask politely," was the response. "Me mam always tells me to ask politely. I'll give you another bit of advice for it, though."

"Take the coin and welcome if you'll keep the advice to yourself."

The shilling vanished into the boy's pocket. "Will you be going back to wherever you came from, then?"

Oh, the thought was tempting. "Wales. I might."

"Don't suppose you'd have need of a valet there." Harris pronounced it "vale–it," and Tregaron nearly smiled.

"I don't, as it happens, but I'm sure my estate manager could find something healthy for you to do—when you weren't in school."

"School?" the boy's eyes widened in comical horror. "You'd make me go to school?"

"I suppose you believe you have nothing left to learn about life, puppy."

The little fellow puffed out his narrow chest. "I've learned plenty in all me years 'ere."

"Ah, and there have been so many." Tregaron tapped the boy's cap brim. "Don't tell me you enjoy what you do."

Harris pondered this question for a minute, then shrugged. "Never asked for me work, that's for certain. But it's me lot in life. Just thought I'd ask about the valet bit."

"Politely, too. Well, you know where to find me should you decide to accept my aid."

"The shilling's more 'n enough, guv. Now, I keep trying to 'elp *you* . . ."

"Oh, I appreciate the thought, Harris, but I daresay I'll go on much as I have, on my own."

The sweep grunted. "Dim as dusk, I say."

Tregaron pondered his dimness. No, he decided firmly, he was not stupid. Not in the least. He merely went through life acting as he saw fit to keep from being banged about too much. Of course, fate seemed to take perverse pleasure in tipping everything off-balance occasionally.

"Ah, Harris. Isn't life a poke in the posterior with a sharp stick?"

"I don't know that I have ever looked at it precisely that way, old trout, but if you say so."

Tregaron turned to find Julius Rome at his side. There was no sign of the boy. "Where did he go?"

"Who?"

"The sweep. We were discussing Life."

Rome's dark brows rose, but all he said was, "I did not see a sweep, but they are such flitting little shadows." Then, after a moment, "I might be a bit out of line here, but you look like hell."

"Do I? Fancy that."

"Trouble, thy name is Buchanan. Am I right?"

"You are out of line," Tregaron muttered, but without much rancor.

"Frequently. I say, would you care for some snuff?"

Tregaron rarely touched the stuff, but now seemed as good a time as any to indulge. "I wouldn't mind." He waited for the younger man to pull out a box.

"Oh, I haven't any with me. But I was just on my way to Friburg and Treyer's. Care to come along?"

"I was on my way into a large bottle of brandy," Tregaron countered. "Care to come along?"

To his credit, Rome did not look at his watch, although his hand strayed toward his waistcoat pocket. "As it happens, I haven't eaten. Why don't you join me at my club for a bit of breakfast."

'I am something of a *persona non grata* in St. James's, you know."

"Are you? Hardly a tragedy. Half of the members at White's on any given day are quite dead. No one notices because the line between rigor mortis and deadly dullness is rather fine in the Tory ranks."

Tregaron felt a smile tugging at the corner of his mouth. "Still—"

"Waiters," Rome announced, as if that solved everything. "Food like ambrosia from the heavens."

"I have little experience with the heavens."

"Yes, well, the rest of the place is rather less divine. This way, my friend."

Tregaron allowed himself to be led down Piccadilly.

"Now," Rome said as they went, "I thought you might be interested in a very interesting bit of gossip I heard recently . . ."

Chapter 15

Tregaron quit his rooms after dark that evening. He'd chosen the finest—or at least the most ridiculously expensive—items from among his mostly unworn Schwarz and Noble wardrobe. With old shoes. The shoes were perfectly acceptable-looking, buffed to as much of a shine as one could coax from ten-year-old leather, the silver buckles polished to brilliance. He possessed newer pairs to choose from, certainly fancier pairs. He wanted to be dressed for the occasion; he had no idea how far he was going to have to wander to get to the occasion. Comfort was crucial.

He had barely stepped out of the Albany's grand front circle when a small figure launched itself directly into his path. Thinking it was Harris, Tregaron instinctively reached for a coin, ready to hand it over with a brusque apology for being in too much of a hurry to chat. But the face below the too-large cap was unfamiliar.

"Be ye Lord Treedragon?"

"Probably," Tregaron replied, one eye scanning the street for an empty hackney.

"Eh?"

"Tregaron. Yes."

"Then this is for you." The boy handed over a folded, creased, and slightly grimy paper. Then waited expectantly.

Tregaron gave him the shilling. "Who—" he demanded, but as soon as the coin was in hand, the boy scuttled off into the shadows.

Less curious than harried, Tregaron scanned the missive as he flagged down a hack. After giving his destination and climbing inside, he read it again. He'd seen it correctly the first time.

You have been warned.

"Well, bloody hell," he muttered. He didn't have time

for this little game. He had life matters to attend, and when a man had life matters to attend, he wanted to attend them immediately, effectively, and without distraction.

There was a bit of a traffic snarl at Oxford Street, courtesy of one rustic wagon and one flashy phaeton that were both halted right in the middle of the road. From what Tregaron could tell, when impatience had him leaning out the window, a coalman was giving a loud piece of his mind and looking ready to employ his fists on a younger man who was futilely trying to capture his loose, starched-into-rigidity collar with one hand and keep the padding from escaping his torn coat shoulder with the other. Irate drivers yelled from their vehicles; the pedestrian crowd seemed to be having a jolly time just watching the spectacle.

Tregaron thumped a fist against the window frame. Had he wanted to visit a circus, he would bloody well have gone to Astley's.

"Drive on!" he commanded the driver. "No, wait."

Grumbling to himself, he climbed from the hack and pushed his way into the crowd. He reached the center just in time to see the coalman twine one very large fist in the younger man's wilted cravat and lift him until he was standing only on the very tips of his toes.

"Gentlemen." Tregaron nodded pleasantly to the grim-faced coalman. "Sir. Reynolds."

Charles Reynolds's face paled slightly, quite a feat considering that he was being throttled. "Tregaron," he croaked.

"You seem to be in a bit of a fix. Whatever did you do?"

"Ain't done nothing," was the strangled reply. "This oaf—" Reynolds, never an attractive specimen, grew positively bug-eyed when his foe tightened his grip and gave him a good shake.

"It would appear your worthy opponent disagrees," Tregaron offered. He turned to the other man. "Is there damage, sir?"

The coalman, sensing an unexpected bit of support, jerked his free thumb toward his rough wagon. "Came around the bend like a blind stirk. Made me wrench a wheel, he did, and m'beast lost a shoe. That"—now he gestured with his massive jaw at the ridiculously sprung phaeton—"ought to be tipped into the Thames!"

Tregaron nodded. "I quite agree."

"With this little rat tied to it!"

"I can quite see your point. How much?"

The man didn't even pretend to misunderstand. "A guinea'd do it."

"A guinea?" Reynolds sputtered. "For that piece of worm-eaten—" He squeaked as he found himself being lifted quite off his feet.

"Tsk, tsk. I should be more polite if I were you," Tregaron advised. "After all, you're the blind stirk in the scenario." He leaned in and quietly said, "Pay the man." At Reynolds's muffled croak, he turned back to the coalman. "Perhaps you ought to put him down so he can see to matters."

Reynolds would have gone all the way down onto his well-rounded posterior had Tregaron not managed to grasp the back of his coat collar. "Can't pay," he gasped.

"Whyever not."

"I haven't got a guinea."

"Oh, good Lord." Tregaron rolled his eyes. The coalman took a menacing step forward. They were not all that far from the Thames, really—less than a mile. "I really don't know why I should care . . ."

Tregaron released Reynolds, who managed to stay on his feet even if he did list somewhat to starboard. Then, reaching yet again into his pocket, he located the required coin. "For you, sir," he said, handing it to the coalman, who was soon stomping off to his battered wagon.

Perceiving that there would be no further entertainment, the crowd dissipated. Tregaron turned back to Reynolds, who was actually trying to restore some order to his appearance—a vain and utterly futile act.

"Go home," Tregaron muttered.

Reynolds, when he finally looked up, had the surprising grace to look ever so slightly abashed. "I must thank—"

"Don't. Just go home." When the man made his shaky way toward the phaeton's step, Tregaron snapped, "At a walk!"

He left Reynolds to negotiate his way up into the silly vehicle. He was very nearly back to his own back when he had a thought. Spinning on his heel, he returned to the phaeton's side. "As it happens, I have use for you. I want you to deliver two messages. The first, and I trust"—he made very certain Reynolds was going to be cooperative—"you will phrase it more gently than I am about to, is to your dear mama and involves the not small matter of her flapping tongue . . ."

Minutes later, he was back on his way. It took little time to reach Binney Street. He was out and heading up the steps to the Buchanan house before the carriage had rolled to a complete stop. He pounded on the door, then again, harder, when there was no quick answer. It seemed an eternity before a little maid finally appeared. He walked right past her, into the foyer.

"Sir!" she protested, but without much force. He was twice her size.

"Don't worry," he tossed grimly over his shoulder as he took the stairs two at a time. "I won't steal anything."

He threw open the doors to one parlor, the dining room, and the back hallway—all small, a bit shabby, and quite empty—before happening on a snug little chamber where he found the Buchanan brothers comfortably settled at a wobbly table, port bottle and backgammon board between them.

"My lord." The larger brother rose unsteadily to his feet, bumping the table in the process and sending bottle and board sliding to the rear.

"Lord Tregaron." The smaller used the table to help himself up, sending bottle and board right back to their original positions.

The two men were clearly one good sheet to the wind if not more. "Gentlemen," Tregaron said, "please, sit." He did not want to take any chances with either of them going face first onto the hard floor. "I am here to see Catherine."

Both brothers returned to their seats, the larger with a tremor that Tregaron felt across the room. "A good lass, our Catey," Ambrose said jovially. "Did you come to have another go at her, then?"

"'Ambrose!" the other scolded. "Forgive my brother, m'lord. He is sadly lacking in refinement at times. Drink?" He gestured to the bottle. Tregaron declined. "So, have you come to have another go at Cate?"

"A good question, that, Angus." Ambrose reached across the table to give his brother an approving thump on the shoulder. Angus would have gone right over backward had not the room been small enough that his seat was placed helpfully close to a solid if threadbare wing chair.

"Well?" Ambrose demanded of their guest. "You'd best get on with it, then. Catey's making noises about packing us all up and heading north. Made Lucy cry, that did. Or was that you, Angus, lad?"

" 'Tis the churches," came the mournful reply, accompanied by a damp sniff. "Can I help it if I'd miss them something fierce?"

"Nay, nay. You cannae. And the museums . . ."

Tregaron's patience, already worn thin by the events of the past several days, was near snapping. "Gentlemen, is Catherine here?"

Angus lifted bleary eyes. "Catherine here? Why, I don't know. Ambrose?"

"I'm here."

"Ambrose is here," Angus informed Tregaron.

"Yes, so I see. Thank you. And Catherine . . . ?"

"Catherine," Ambrose repeated softly, thoughtfully. Then, with a bellow that might well have reached Scotland, *"Becky!"*

"Becky." Angus brightened. "Becky's here, m'lord."

And the little maid did appear eventually. "I tried to stop him, I did," she began protesting before she was fully in the room, "but he's so *big*."

"Is Catherine here?" Ambrose asked, still shouting. He clearly wasn't angry, just making certain he was heard.

"No, sir," was the maid's reply.

Angus gave a decisive nod and thumped the table with his fist, sending the bottle a few inches to his left. "There you have it, m'lord. Catherine's not here. Thank you, Becky. You may go."

Tregaron counted three. "Becky." She froze in the doorway. "Do you by chance know where Miss Buchanan is this evening? And"—he anticipated her response— "should the answer be yes, please be so kind as to add where she might be found."

"Yes, m'lord." And after a pause, "Lady Leverham's, my lord."

"Thank you, Becky." Feeling somewhat revived, and more than ready to be gone, Tregaron bowed briefly to his nominal hosts. "Gentlemen." Then he all but sprinted for the door.

Cate glanced around the crowded room for an escape. The gilt-painted double doors of the ballroom beckoned warmly, but there were a good two dozen warriors, armed to the teeth, between her and that exit.

A few were garbed in leather, some in chain mail, and several were sporting complete sets of armor. They carried lances, maces, broadswords, crossbows, and, in one case, a longbow that seemed twice the height of its diminutive bearer. Cate did not think any of these men were actually dangerous, but she still didn't fancy weaving her way between the various blades and spikes.

Their companions did not seem to mind. If the gentlemen were shiningly impressive, the ladies were blinding. Silks, satins, velvets, all in brilliant colors, tangled with sable and ermine, gold and jewels. There were conical hats aplenty, some seemingly horned headpieces, and an endless supply of floaty scarves.

It was the monthly meeting of the Mayfair Medieval Society.

Diminutive Lord Leverham, looking uncomfortable but graciously resigned, was swathed head-to-toe in shiny mail. By his side, his wife positively glowed in cascading red velvet and towering hat. She was holding court among her guests, not all of whom were costumed, like a plump Eleanor of Aquitaine.

The speaker, a dusty old don long retired from his active duties at the university, had spent a long hour lecturing on bardic tradition. Now, his listeners, eager and bored-to-snoring alike, were gathered in the ballroom, devouring the authentic if odd-looking victuals and chattering about bards, Crusades, and the fact that King John had not been a good king.

Cate was ready to leave. Sighing to herself, she seemed to have been ready to leave—her house, the Hanover Square house, various parties, London—ever since arriving from Scotland. It wasn't the way she would have chosen to live, always halfway out some door, but that's the way it was. She would leave now, but she knew Lady Leverham had informed her firm and formidable butler that, should

Miss Buchanan try to wander off alone into Mayfair, the staff was authorized to sit on her until the lady herself could be summoned.

Beyond that, Lucy was having a marvelous time. Perhaps the gentlemen surrounding her were slightly fewer than usual, but that was only to be expected considering the occasion. Still, garbed in a lush, yellow silk dress commissioned by their hostess just for the occasion, hair caught up in a gold net, draped in a selection of Lady Leverham's jewels, Lucy was quite the princess, and she had her share of eager swains paying court to her. When Cate last walked by, she had been holding forth to Lord Newling and comrades on Gothic architecture. And, being Lucy, she had known just enough of the right words to outshine the wrong ones and to sound perfectly knowledgeable indeed.

She was enjoying herself, Lady Leverham was in heaven, and Cate had no desire to be sat upon. So she decided to escape to another part of the house. Some fresh air would be welcome.

Keeping to the wall, she slipped to the rear of the ballroom and out the small door there. In moments, she was in the cool hollow of the Leverhams' equivalent to a marble garden folly. In deference to his wife's passions, Lord Leverham had built a turret onto the back of the house, complete with rough stones and crenellated roof. The only floor, made of wide wood planking, was at the very top, level, with the house's third floor. There was a large, glassless window and a plain bench for the lady's meditations. Authenticity, apparently, had been more important than comfort. The chamber, such as it was, was reached by stone steps that spiraled with the tower's walls, their only concession to modernity the sturdy iron banister that was set against the stones, leaving the outside of the steps open all the way to the floor.

It was cold, rough, and slightly damp, but Cate had to admit that there was an aura of peace and isolation about the place. The view, too, out over the house's lovely knot garden and the neighboring gardens, was lovely—at least during the day. At night it was dark and tranquil. Cate chose to sit on the window ledge rather than the bench. She breathed in the night air, tried to clear her mind of its countless concerns.

"The lady in her ivory tower, inviolate in its shadowed bower."

She felt her jaw stiffen. "I do not much care for poetry."

"Liar. You love Donne." Lord Fremont climbed the last several steps until he stood on the wooden floor. "Really, Cate. Did you think I would forget?"

"I suspect you are rather selective in what you remember," she retorted. "Why are you here?"

"Because you are, of course." He wandered over to stand beside her, looked down, and whistled. "You've certainly chosen a lofty clime, but then, you've become something of a lofty creature since last we met." He came closer until his knees were almost brushing hers and she was forced to crane her neck to see into his face. It wasn't quite so angelic in the single torchiere Lady Leverham kept lit in the tower. "How fortunate that I know you are not nearly so indifferent inside as you seem."

Was there no end to this man's arrogance? Cate wondered. Probably not. Fremont had always made Narcissus seem selfless.

"Were the messages to Lord Tregaron not enough?" she asked him wearily.

"Messages? Did he repeat our conversations to you? How curious." Fremont's satisfied smile widened. "How very droll. I do wonder what he thought to gain from it. It's not as if he could ever get the upper hand on me."

Cate stared at him closely, but saw only vain amusement. So it hadn't been Fremont after all.

"What is it you want from me?" she asked at last.

"What if it is simply you that I want?"

She snorted. "You never wanted me. You wanted my cow-eyed devotion."

Tell me you adore me, Catherine, he'd coaxed her under the Scottish moon. *Just let me hear the words.*

This was after a sennight of pursuit, of recited poetry and stolen flowers from his hostess's garden, of stolen kisses. When he'd requested the words, Cate had dutifully spoken them. And again, louder, at his command. For the benefit, as it turned out, of his cronies who were hiding in the shrubbery that grew around Lady Maybole's gazebo.

He'd grinned, patted her on the head, and said, *Good girl.*

"You had it briefly," she said now, "and will not have it again, so why don't you be a *good boy* and go away."

His mouth thinned for a moment before relaxing into its familiar smirk. "You don't mean that."

"I d—"

"You don't," he repeated and bent toward her.

Cate gasped as, instinctively moving away from him, she suddenly found herself leaning backward, partway out the window. Her fingers scrabbled for good purchase on the rough sill. "Back away, sir," she commanded, her voice reasonably steady.

"Certainly," was his response. "All you have to do is pay me with a kiss."

"Why?"

"Why? Good heavens, what a silly question. Because it is what the moment demands." He moved closer.

Cate was leaning farther out the window now and darted a quick and unwise glance at the gardens far below. She did not believe for an instant that Fremont would let her fall, or even wobble much, but she also knew he was perverse enough to let her hover there for far longer that would be comfortable.

If she did it, if she kissed him, he would win. He would best her again. If she didn't . . .

One second he was there, looming above her. The next he was doing an almost graceful pirouette across the chamber. He fetched up hard against the far wall, then slid gracefully indeed into a heap on the floor.

"When a lady requests that you back away," came a familiar growl, "you listen, you miserable toad."

Almost immediately, Cate found herself being hauled from her precarious seat by a pair of very strong, very welcome hands. The night breeze whistled by her, fluttering the gauzy wrap Lady Leverham had insisted she wear over her perfectly substantial grey cotton dress. Then she was being pressed to an even more substantial chest. "I will not ask why you are here. I am getting used to finding you in unexpected places."

Cate's heart was going like thunder as she stared up into Tregaron's beautiful, shadowed face. What she saw in his eyes was enough to keep her heart pounding for years to come. "What took you so long?" she demanded.

They were both distracted by a grunt from across the chamber. Fremont was hauling himself slowly to his feet. His elegant cravat was crooked and unraveling; there was a sizeable tear in his coat, displaying some white shirt and even more thick batting.

"I will give you the benefit of the doubt and assume Reynolds did not find you," Tregaron snapped.

Fremont glared for a moment, took a half step forward, hands fisted. Whatever he saw then must have changed his mind. He came to an unsteady halt and shook his head.

"If you move quickly," Tregaron continued, "you might be able to reach him before he meets with his mother."

"What do I care for his mother?" Fremont hissed.

"Oh, you will care, very much, when she starts spreading the remarkable tale her son will be telling her soon. It involves a certain penniless baron and a predilection for certain costume dramas."

Fremont snarled as he all but launched himself down the stairs. In a minute, his footsteps could no longer be heard.

"What on earth did that mean?" Cate asked.

Tregaron shook his head. "I have done my gossiping for the day."

Cate didn't press the matter. In truth, she didn't really want to know. Instead, she asked, "How did you find me—us—here?"

"I followed him following you out of the ballroom just as I arrived," was the brusque answer. "Forgive me for not arriving sooner. Lady Leverham insisted on giving me those."

Tregaron pointed to the floor by the stairs. Cate couldn't help but laugh. There, in a tangle, rested a mace, a dagger, and a small crossbow. "I am impressed that you even got them up the stairs."

"Your lack of faith in my strength wounds me." He paused then, glancing over her shoulder and through the open window. "Oh, hell."

Suddenly, he was leaning all of his considerable weight on her. Cate, glancing at him in alarm, saw he looked very grey of face. Wasting no time, she guided him as best she could to the bench. He sat down with a thump, pulling her with him.

"My lord?" She chafed his wrists, alarmed by the sheen

of sweat that glossed his pale brow. "My l . . . Colwin? I will fetch help."

His hand wrapped around her wrist, holding her still. "No. I will be fine. I am fine."

"You are shaking like a leaf!"

"Thank you, my dear, for continuing to flatter me with comments on my fortitude."

"I am going for assistance. You are ill."

His sigh was far stronger than his grip had been moments earlier. "What I am," he muttered, "is bloody well terrified of heights."

"What was that?"

"You heard me." Some of the pallor had left his face, and his scowl was nearly enough to scare the devil. It made Cate want to go climbing into his lap. "I cannot even sit in the front of a theater box."

"Or come anywhere near the edge of a balcony."

"Or come anywhere near the edge of a balcony."

Cate shook her head at the utter folly of man's pride. "Why did you not tell people, after . . . Why did you not explain that you could not possibly have harmed your wife?"

"Because," came the quiet answer, "it did not matter in the end. So Belinda took a drunken tumble that night—the how did not matter. I made her miserable; she took her wine and her laudanum and her lovers. I might as well have pushed her off a balcony. Or she me."

"You don't mean that . . ." Cate let it go. Instead, she said softly, "You know I will probably push you to the point of apoplexy on occasion."

"Undoubtedly."

"And beyond, I expect."

"I am certain of it. And I will revel in the experience."

"I'm so glad." Sighing in contentment, Cate rubbed her jaw against the impossibly soft wool of his coat. "Did you only just realize you needed me?"

He grunted. "Hardly. It struck me like a barb to the back ages ago. There was no way, no matter how much I writhed and struggled, that I was going to pull it free."

Cate rolled her eyes. "So romantic."

His arm tightened around her. "Teach me. Tell me with

pretty words how you were smacked into knowing you adored me."

"Mmm. Well. It was more of a slow creep, actually. Like a rash, or a mold, taking over a little bit more of my heart every day."

"So romantic. Kiss me, Cate."

So she did, and found herself surprised when the bench did not begin to smolder beneath them.

"My lord?" A faint voice drifted up from the stairwell. "Lord Tregaron?"

He gave an inward groan. He wanted to go on kissing Cate Buchanan indefinitely. Then he wanted to promise her flowers and sparkly things and the sky. Then he thought he would kiss her some more. He did not want to deal with Lady Leverham and her ridiculously dressed guests. But he supposed he would have to. And he would have to be polite. They were, after all, Cate's friends.

He pulled back and, steeling himself against her soft protest, asked, "Has it been awful? The gossip about us?"

She blinked slightly unfocused eyes. "Gossip? Oh, good heavens. I'd forgotten. There was no gossip, not really although now . . ."

"What do you mean, no gossip?"

"Well, there was talk, certainly, but it hardly countenanced."

He appeared baffled. "Lady Leverham—"

"Lady Leverham," Cate said tartly, "is terribly sweet and a bit of a peagoose. She failed to notice that in all the nonsense being said about you, no one actually mentioned *me*." She grinned. "I am an utter Nobody, it seems. Lady Reynolds does not know my name and couldn't be bothered to come up with a better description than 'tall and blowsy.' "

"Oh, Cate."

"It doesn't matter. As long as you speak kindly of me."

Oh, and he would. Every hour of every day. "If you only knew—"

"Lord Tregaron?"

"Our peagoose of a hostess requires my presence," he muttered.

One of her hands fisted tightly in his coat—a precaution that Tregaron found as charming as it was sensible, considering his affliction and the long descent to the turret floor—Cate followed him down the stairs. As expected, Lady Leverham was waiting at the bottom.

"You have dropped your defenses, young man," she snapped. "I shall have to send someone up to fetch them."

"My apologies, madam," he replied, fighting a smile. "I have brought the fair maiden from the tower, however."

"So you have," the lady conceded. "That will do. Now come along, both of you. We are lining up for the gavotte."

"Shall we dance?" Tregaron murmured into Cate's ear.

"Not unless they play a waltz."

"Splendid woman!" He resisted the urge to waltz her right out the door and back into his bachelor rooms. "I'll take you home."

"Oh, no!" she protested. "I did not mean—"

"I need to speak with your uncles, Cate."

She blushed fetchingly. "Oh. Well, then."

From the corner of his eye as they went, Tregaron got a brief glimpse of a small figure with a bow and arrow. He shook his head at the lengths to which Society went to cast their own little nights of comedy. No doubt Lady Leverham had commandeered a tiger or two to play at being pages to her knightly guests. At least she had not weighed down the unfortunate fellows with chain mail.

Others were not so lucky. He and Cate were nearly out of the ballroom when Lord Leverham caught up, clinking and puffing. "This arrived for you, sir, not five minutes ago," he panted, handing out a folded paper.

Tregaron thanked him and took it. "Well," he announced after reading the single line, "they were bound to abandon subtlety sooner or later."

"What?" Cate demanded as he hustled her down the stairs and into the foyer. "What is it?"

He sent one of the Leverhams' footmen off to find a hack. "Do you often pry into private business, my dear?" he asked blandly. Cate promptly looked at her feet.

"No, I . . . Well. I think perhaps there is something I ought to tell you."

"Yes?"

"Well, you see, I . . . we . . . Oh, bother! You might be so very angry when you hear. You see, I . . ."

"Is this perhaps what you are trying to say?"

He gently waved the message in front of her. She snatched it from his hand and read aloud. "*Angus and Ambrose Buchanan did none of the designs for your house.* Oh, dear."

"Don't worry, darling." Tregaron lifted one of her hands and patted it. "I have known for quite a long time that *you* are Buchanan and Buchanan. Ah, here is our transport."

"How?" she asked as he lifted her into the carriage. "How?" He gave the direction to the driver. *"How?"*

"Ah, Catherine"—he climbed in and settled himself beside her—"How dense do you think I am?"

"I do not . . ."

"Good," he muttered. "That's settled."

With that, he hauled her off the seat and across his thighs. When a man had the urge to kiss the great love of his life breathless, he wanted to kiss her immediately, effectively, and without distraction.

It was a slightly disheveled Cate and deliciously uncomfortable Tregaron who entered the Binney Street house sometime later. He waited only until they'd both regained a modicum of composure before marching her into the chamber where he had found her uncles earlier.

Both Angus and Ambrose were still there, but they'd moved. Each was ensconced in a wing chair, vaguely if blissfully staring into the almost nonexistent fire. At Cate's entrance, they did their best to get promptly to their feet. It took a few moments and some fascinating acts of balance.

Tregaron waited until they were reasonably upright. "Gentlemen, I am going to marry your niece," he said firmly. "And you are going to stop sending me absurd little messages. From now on, if you have something to say to me, for God's sake, *say it*!"

Epilogue

Cate watched from the front window as the very last of the workmen trotted down the stairs to the street. "That's it, then. Done."

Tregaron came to stand just behind her and she leaned back, reveling in the strength of his arms as they encircled her waist. "Thank God," he muttered. "I was becoming convinced we would never see the last of them."

She patted his hand where it rested at her hip. "As was I. But you do have a beautiful house, Lord Tregaron."

"Mmm. All due to you, Lady Tregaron. Now, when can we depart for Wales?"

Cate laughed. It was a daily question. And now that the last bit of paint was on the walls, the last piece of brocade tacked to its chair, and the trenches in the garden filled with trees and shrubs that looked exactly like those Mr. Paxton had uprooted, Cate had an answer.

"We should not need to be in Sussex above two months. Your grandmother and I are already finalizing what designs we can before I actually see her house."

"God help me. Two months among the Granvilles. Two months under my grandmother's roof."

"You will have a marvelous time. And Gryffydd will get quite fat, I'm sure."

Hearing his name, the little dog trotted from the sunny spot below the other widow, happily rolled over onto his back at Cate's feet, and presented her with his already round belly for scratching.

"Two months," Tregaron repeated glumly. "Then we will go to Wales."

"Absolutely. I do not need to travel to York till spring. And I have informed the Leverhams that I cannot even think about their son's new house near Tarbet until next autumn. Lady Leverham and Lucy are designing new Gothic decor together, and both uncles are commissioned to help. Plus, they will all pitch in on my other projects."

"Whatever pleases them most," was her husband's grim response.

"They are pleased," she said gently, seriously. "The uncles are free from their obligations and are so proud to see me recognized for my designs. Yes, yes, I know you are still annoyed with their methods, but they did not know how else to . . . retire, and to make my skills known. Perhaps their lapse into intrigue was a bit much, but they're ever so pleased with themselves. And Lucy only talks about her plans for next Season when Lady Leverham prods her into it. I believe she has quite lost interest in the Social whirl."

"Only until Althorpe returns from Bath. If he ever returns."

"His aunt died," Cate scolded. "It's only right he sees to settling her estate."

"His estate now. Should he formally succumb to your sister's charms, he will be able to keep her quite nicely in her flounces and furbelows." Tregaron's arms tightened. "I, on the other hand, seem quite determined to keep you out of such things."

Cate shivered deliciously. "You simply hate my wardrobe."

He did not bother to deny her assertion. "It improves with each visit to the modiste."

There, wrapped in his arms while sunlight streamed through the windows and Mayfair—hated, beloved Mayfair—bustled below. A boy stood on the edge of Hanover Square, too far away to see clearly, but his cheerful whistling could be heard. It was a Burns tune, about love and red, red roses.

Behind Cate, her husband placed a whispering kiss on the nape of her neck. Suddenly, the force of her love for this man struck her like a hot spark in her breast. Turning in his arms, she demanded, "Do you have any idea how much I adore you?"

Grinning, he eyed the brocade chaise behind them. With its mohair throw, plump silk pillows, and choice spot between the fireplace and window, it was the ideal for reading. And not a bad option for other activities. "Why don't you show me?"

Silently applauding her marvelous vision that had become reality in the chaise, the Realm's newest arbiter of architectural elegance set to her current project with skill and enthusiasm.

From Debrett's Peerage, 13th Edition, 1820

DRACO LLYWELYN ST. CLAIR-WRIGHT, Marquess of TREGARON, Viscount Colwin; succeeded his father, May 1792; born Sept. 27, 1780; married, first, November 1806, Belinda, only daughter of Benjamin Wycombe, esq. of Lancashire, who died 1809. His lordship married, secondly, July 12, 1817, Catherine, daughter of Alpin Buchanan of Scotland, by whom he has issue: John, Viscount Colwin, born January 1, 1819 . . .